EXECUTIVE
ORDER

Other Titles by Max Allan Collins

EXECUTIVE ORDER

MAX ALLAN COLLINS

WITH MATTHEW V. CLEMENS

🕊 THOMAS & MERCER

Text copyright © 2017 by Max Allan Collins

Published by Thomas & Mercer, Seattle

www.apub.com

Amazon, the Amazon logo, and Thomas & Mercer are trademarks of Amazon.com, Inc., or its affiliates.

ISBN-13: 9781477819432
ISBN-10: 1477819436

Cover design by Ray Lundgren

Printed in the United States of America

FOR ALAN TURKUS
who elected to publish

"In the scheme of our national government, the presidency is preeminently the people's office."

Grover Cleveland, twenty-second and twenty-fourth President of the United States of America. Served 1885–1889 and 1893–1897. The only president to be elected to two nonconsecutive terms.

ONE

From a hilltop in Azbekistan, through night-vision binoculars, Jake McMann looked down on the Kerch Strait Bridge, wondering if he was about to make history.

That such a detached thought would float through his mind wasn't unusual—keeping a distance, being outside yourself, was part of any field agent's makeup. Still, McMann considered himself a genuine student of history—with a Ball State University degree to back it up. And the professional path he'd taken indicated how seriously he took such things.

His short brown hair riffled by the evening breeze, his muscular frame draped in black fatigues, the CIA operative grinned at himself—*me making history. Jesus.*

But wasn't he on the front line of a predicted, even inevitable conflict? Why shouldn't he be seized with the sense that, on this night, he would have the chance to make an entry on the pages of history?

Or anyway a footnote.

Never one to question orders—in or out of uniform, McMann was a soldier—he nonetheless couldn't help wondering what the hell he and his team were doing in this tiny Crimean Peninsula excuse for a country. All he knew was that they were here to reconnoiter from this position, and wait.

Azbekistan had been just one victim of Russia's annexing of most of the peninsula back in 2014. The Russians had built the bridge below, from the Taman Peninsula in Krasnodar Krai to Kerch on the Crimean; they'd opened it in 2020, one year behind schedule, back when they still controlled the little country.

Five years later, with mounting threats from the United Nations and determined fighting by Azbekistani rebels, the Russians retreated to their side of the bridge. Now, barely six years later, they threatened to return and overrun Azbekistan yet again. McMann's four-person team had been sent here to assess the country's defenses. But why bother? The Russian invasion seemed inevitable, as did the fall of Azbekistan (again).

The strait wasn't that wide here, less than three miles, and McMann thought he heard some kind of noise echoing off the water; but with the swirling wind, he couldn't pick it out.

Turning, he looked down the hill to the south. He saw nothing, at first. Pulling on his night-vision goggles, he spotted two men climbing the slope to join him.

The taller, almost spindly one—Willie Meeks, McMann's part-ner—was an African American agent from Villa Rica, Georgia, a sleepy suburb of Atlanta. McMann and Willie were called Ebony and Ivory by their peers back at Langley, but McMann supposed that was better than Salt & Pepper, which similar duos had been christened back in the Agency's glory days in the 1960s and '70s—back when black agents in the CIA were more rare than female ones, and there weren't ten of those.

Next to Meeks, Vitor Gorianov—one of the two analysts they'd been sent here to protect—was an American of Crimean descent, and also their translator. Craggy, and burlier than Meeks, Gorianov also knew his way around an AK-47, which was a nice bonus in circumstances like these.

As the men neared, also attired in black, night-clinging fatigues, McMann eased the goggles back up to his forehead.

"Where's Liz?" Gorianov asked, in a near whisper, knowing voices really carried out here at night.

The fourth member of the team, Liz Gillis—the other analyst, blonde, blue-eyed, boyishly attractive—was not yet thirty, but knew her shit.

"She went for a walk," McMann said, also sotto voce.

"A walk?" Meeks asked, almost too loud. He caught himself. "You let that fresh-faced analyst go off on her own, in the wild?"

McMann met his partner's eyes. "She can take care of herself, Willie."

"In what could be a fuckin' war zone any time now? Jake, get serious—she's just a goddamn analyst."

From behind Meeks and Gorianov, a confident female voice came, softly: "A goddamn analyst who's got the drop on you three."

They all wheeled toward her. Her blonde hair tucked under a black watch cap, Gillis stood there grinning. She was tall, almost willowy, yet the AK-47 looked perfectly at home in her delicate hands, its snout lowered but ready.

Gorianov, his words clipped, asked, "What the hell were you doing out there?"

"My job," Liz snapped.

"Keep your voices down!" Meeks said, too loud.

McMann held up a hand and said, "Okay, everybody—unbunch your panties. Chill already."

He waited while they all took a breath.

The entire team was tense, including McMann, and why not? The Russians seemed poised to invade, and Azbekistan appeared almost ready and willing for them to do so.

Which was damn dumb: the Azbekistani army was not exactly intimidating, despite fancy new uniforms. As rebels, citizens fighting for their homeland, they had been tenacious pit bulls; as an organized, under-equipped army standing up against an overwhelming enemy, they were more like lapdogs.

But at least they would look sharp as they got slaughtered.

McMann asked, "What did you find, Liz?"

"The Azbekistanis are sound asleep. Except for the ones just napping."

"Vitor?" McMann asked.

"Same thing to the south. Maybe they think they can dream the Russians away."

"Where's the closest Azbekistani force?"

Meeks said, "Other than that glorified bridge tollbooth? A two-jeep patrol about a click away."

As they headed back toward their vehicle, a thought kept gnawing at the front of McMann's mind: *Why are we here?* Everybody in the CIA, not excluding the agent at the desk in the lobby at Langley, knew this invasion was coming, and that the Azbekistanis were about to get rolled over. His four-person team could hardly prevent that inevitability.

So why the hell were they here?

They were still nearly a thousand yards to the trees where their car, a Skoda Citigo, was hidden, just off a back road, when the wind shifted and McMann suddenly heard distant thunder—*or was it?*

The sounds were low-pitched, but as the wind brought them to him, he knew—*no, not thunder.* Spinning, he pulled down his night-vision goggles and trotted over to where he could look back down toward the bridge.

Tanks.

A whole damn column of them, already better than halfway across.

"Damn!" McMann blurted. "It's on—the Russians are on the move! Right the hell now!"

All four of them sprinted toward the car. McMann ran hard, but some detached part of his mind recalled the Nazis storming across the border of Poland in 1939. Just up ahead were the two jeeps that Gorianov and Meeks had spotted earlier, lumbering toward them. For a second, McMann wondered if his little team would end up pinned down between the two sides.

But the Russians were still a few clicks away, and the four of them would be long gone by the time the tanks rumbled through. That thought gave him some relief.

Some.

Running just behind him, like a relay man about to pass a baton, Meeks yelled, "You *hear* that?"

Until now—lost in his immediate thoughts of escape and his reflective flashes about the history they were in the middle of—McMann hadn't; but now he did—a low-pitched rumble, different from the tanks. But he didn't turn and he didn't slow as he sprinted through darkness across uneven ground, only then the noise was right above him, and he risked a glance skyward.

On this moonless night, the planes were not visible, though he could make out parachutes dropping out of nowhere. Not only would he and his team fail to get away in time, they would soon have Russian paratroopers landing all around them.

Ready to fight.

"*Faster!*" McMann shouted.

Somehow they all picked up the pace, though McMann had a grim feeling they wouldn't even make it to the car, let alone get away.

The Azbekistani jeeps were closing, but not as fast as Russian invaders were materializing from the sky. His team sprinted even harder—they had orders not to engage the Russians unless fired upon.

McMann unsnapped his holster and drew his Glock.

To his right, the first Russian thudded to ground. The paratrooper was a good distance away, judging by the sound, and they were now only two hundred yards from their car. Two football fields, two lousy football fields between them and the chance to get away before the Russians and Azbekistanis opened fire on each other.

Sweat burning his eyes, his lungs burning too, McMann kept running, kept urging his team on. Young slender Liz was leading the way, Meeks keeping up with McMann, though Gorianov was slowly falling back.

"*Vitor,*" McMann yelled, "*pick up the pace!*"

Somehow Gorianov found an extra gear. Again, for a moment, McMann thought they had a chance, right up to where the Russian soldier landed hard in front of him. Meeks circled around the guy, but McMann had no choice but to hit the brakes. Gorianov nearly ran up his back, but dodged left in time.

That left McMann face-to-face with the Russian as the paratrooper came up, AK-47 at the ready, pointed right at McMann.

The CIA agent shot the man in the head.

It was all reflexes and his action meant that if they weren't in a shitload of trouble before, they sure as hell were now.

When McMann fired, the other three on his team opened up, too. This was a target-rich environment, getting richer by the second. Looking up, all McMann could see were shadows, but he knew each one was a Russian paratrooper . . .

. . . *and there were shadows everywhere.*

He holstered his pistol, then leaned down, picked up the fallen paratrooper's AK-47, and started shooting, doing a slow, deadly pirouette.

Not only were they suddenly in a firefight on the ground, but paratroopers who hadn't even landed yet rained fire down on them. Gorianov took a hit, went to a knee, wincing, but kept firing. The next second, he was up and moving again, though not nearly as fast.

The Azbekistani jeeps were on them, headlights lancing through the inky night, and men riding opened fire, raking the field with machine gun rounds even as they rolled forward.

Because we don't have enough *trouble*, McMann thought, emptying the magazine of the AK-47.

Dropping the depleted weapon, he got out his pistol again. Their progress had slowed to a walk now as they moved toward the car, firing at Russians all around. McMann looked over at Meeks and saw a shiny black spot on his partner's leg, leaving him barely able to limp along now, much less run.

They kept fighting, did their best to keep moving. Gorianov got hit again, this time in the chest. They all wore body armor, but having been hit like that more than once himself, McMann knew it hurt like a son of a bitch and knocked the wind out of you as surely as a fist to the belly. Suddenly Gorianov was on his back, arms and legs flailing.

With his free hand, McMann went to Gorianov and grabbed a fistful of the man's fatigues and pulled him up to a sitting position. He was about to help the analyst to his feet when a Russian bullet exploded Gorianov's skull, the lifeless, near headless body sagging back to the ground.

Spattered with gore, McMann swung and fired at the paratrooper, killing him as dead as Gorianov.

But their pistols were no match for AK-47s, and they were outmanned a hundred to one, not to mention the Azbekistani jeeps firing indiscriminately into the night, unaware that Americans were on their soil.

Meeks took two hits, one in the body armor, one not, spun, dropped, fought his way to his hands and knees, then Gillis and McMann each caught him under an arm and dragged him toward the car.

"Jesus, are we screwed," Meeks burbled. Hurt bad.

"And it's all your fault," McMann said, a standard line between them when the shit was coming down.

Meeks tried to laugh, but summoned only a choke, then he stumbled and Gillis lost her grip. McMann waved for her to keep going, and get to the car. If she could, maybe they could still make it out of here alive, that back road so close, so very close . . .

McMann felt a sudden searing pain in his leg, and dropped to the ground, looking down to see a nasty wound in his thigh, shiny with bubbly blood. Turning to Meeks, he said, "Come on, Willie, quit loafing—time to go."

"Cut a guy some slack," Meeks said, and smiled, and died.

McMann dragged himself to his feet, no time for sorrow, just as an Azbekistani machine gun tore into Gillis and shook her like a rag doll, less than fifty feet from the Citigo. Her slender, bullet-riddled form dropped in an awkward pile.

Shit.

His leg burned, shock setting in, sweat pouring out everywhere as he limped toward the car, both sides of the battle seeming to turn their gunfire toward him, tracers streaming like fiery ribbons.

He was hit once, twice, three times, two in the body armor, another time not, stumbled, fell, rose, like a nearly knocked-out fighter who should have stayed down for the count. Bullets buffeted him now, the car barely ten feet away. Machine-gun fire from one of the jeeps raked the vehicle's hood, turning the engine into something worthless, no doubt.

Still, McMann limped on, fell to his knees, got hit in the left glute. *Which one of these sons of bitches had actually shot him in the ass? If that wasn't covered by the Geneva Convention* (some detached part of his mind said), *it sure as hell should . . .*

Crawling, he got to the car, touched a tire, the feel of the rubber tread oddly comforting. He moved forward, the Russians coming right up on him now, the firing coming to a merciful stop. He reached up, his hand bloody, his arm barely working, and he touched the door handle.

Then in a crystalized instant he realized why he and his team were there. It all fell into place—*they had been* sent *here to die, so that* . . .

Cold steel against his temple cut his thought short—a muzzle. He tried to turn but couldn't see who held the gun. Did it matter? McMann heard just the start of the shot that killed him.

And felt no pain at all.

He was history.

"Do you want to know who you are? Don't ask. Act!
Action will delineate and define you."

Thomas Jefferson, third President of the United States of America, founding father and principal author of the Declaration of Independence. Served 1801–1809.

TWO

Nothing hit FBI Special Agent Patti Rogers in the pit of her stomach quite like getting summoned upstairs to see Assistant Director Margery Fisk. Somehow, no matter how benign the circumstances, it always reminded her of being called to the principal's office.

She felt that way right now, as she rode the elevator up to Fisk's floor. But if Joe Reeder—her task force's consultant, and her good friend—had been with her, this trip wouldn't have been unnerving at all. Or at least much less so.

She and Joe would be having dinner tonight. Since they had first been thrown together on the Supreme Court task force two years ago, the pair had become tight, and they had usually dined out every couple of weeks or so. In the last year, however, her social life had taken a decided upturn, so she and Reeder—there had never been anything romantic between them—were seeing less of each other.

When Rogers was shown into the Assistant Director's office, Margery Fisk sat behind a desk the size of Rogers' parking-garage space. The AD's short, rigidly coiffed dark hair almost touched the collar of her impeccable, expensive business suit, a gray tweed offset nicely by a black silk blouse. Rogers, at five six, with her medium build and shortish brown hair, could not fill out a business suit the way Fisk could. Nor could she afford as smart a one.

As good as Fisk looked, the woman was even better at her job, a role model for, and occasional mentor to, Rogers, who saw in Fisk everything the young FBI agent aspired to become.

Right now Fisk's unsmiling countenance betrayed not a trace of why Rogers had been called up here.

"Have a seat, Patti," the AD said, without rising or even looking at Rogers, attention on her monitor, the dominant item on her almost too-neat desk.

Rogers sat, and waited, figuring there was nothing good coming.

Finally, without looking at her, Fisk said, "How do you like having Agent Altuve back on your team?"

"He's a real boon to us. Nobody is better than Miggie when it comes to tech."

Computer expert Miguel Altuve had been assigned to the Supreme Court task force Rogers and Reeder headed up two years ago. Miggie's work on that case had earned him his own small but elite computer crime unit, which he'd been temporarily pulled off last year when Rogers (again with Reeder consulting) needed help in thwarting an attempted government overthrow.

"I'd like to say the change was made," Fisk said, "for all the right reasons. But I assume you know how and why the reassignment went down."

Rogers nodded—she didn't need to say, *Budget cuts*, the reason for Miggie's unit getting swallowed up by another one. And that quickly, Rogers understood why she'd been summoned.

"Things aren't easing up either," Fisk said unhappily. "We're having to cut two more units, and yours could wind up on the chopping block, too."

"I guess that's always a possibility, ma'am," Rogers said, unsure of what else to say.

"You're not going to make a case for your team?"

"When that becomes necessary," Rogers said, just a little tightly, "our record will be our best defense."

Fisk nodded. "One might say that the Special Situations Task Force has virtually snatched this nation from the brink of disaster. Twice."

But what have you done for me lately? Rogers thought, trying not to move a muscle.

"But lately," Fisk said, "you've not been producing much."

Working to keep defensiveness out of her voice, Rogers said, "We have closed over a half dozen cases since the Capitol matter."

Again Fisk nodded. "You have. A kidnapping, two bank robberies, and a few other more minor matters . . . but nothing that gets us the media attention we need. Not like the two big cases, the second of which frankly remains necessarily unpublicized."

Rogers sat forward. "They're threatening to close us down because we aren't providing enough publicity? Since when is law enforcement driven by how much press it generates?"

"Well, Agent Rogers, we're in the J. Edgar Hoover Building. Doesn't that say it all?"

Fisk did have a point.

The AD continued: "Your task force receives, agent-by-agent per capita, more funding than any other three units combined."

"Well, our agents are at standard pay grade, and so far when Joe Reeder has consulted, he's done so pro bono."

"But your investigations generate considerable expense at a time when President Harrison is cutting the budget of every agency in DC. The only way I can keep arguing against the deep cuts other agencies are taking is to generate publicity, to close high-profile cases, the kind that make the public sit up, take notice, and write to their congressmen to keep the FBI fully funded."

Rogers could not conceal her frustration. "You're saying that if I want to keep my team together, I need to find a high-profile crime . . .

and that we need to be the ones to bring it to a successful conclusion. How is that supposed to work? We don't generate the crimes. And you assign the cases."

Fisk took in a breath and let it out. "Patti, I like you and I admire you—you've done amazing things in your surprisingly short career. The Director himself has expressed how impressed he was with the Supreme Court and Capitol investigations . . ."

The former attracting considerable media attention, the latter a state secret.

". . . but the fact remains: you are the least senior team leader we have. Right now you face the imminent possibility of being reassigned to another leader's unit."

"Director Fisk, how am I supposed to—"

"Agent Rogers," Fisk interrupted, the "Patti" familiarity gone, "I'm not suggesting you do anything. If the right case comes along, I'll send it your way. If you can again attach Joe Reeder as your consultant, that would be a big PR plus. But you needed to know where you stand."

Rogers realized the nod that followed was the end of the meeting, and she quietly exited the AD's inner sanctum.

Not what Rogers wanted to hear, but not completely unexpected either. She'd figured that budget cuts would become an issue at some point—the United States had nearly defaulted, just six months before—but had hoped her work with Reeder would keep her and her team afloat a while. Now her hopes rested on some minor case evolving into something major, or Fisk coming through for her with a barn burner.

Maybe Joe would have a thought.

Bob & Edith's, a diner on Columbia Pike not far from Rogers' condo, drew an eclectic crowd that, depending on the time of day or night, ran the gamut from families with kids to whores with habits. Even when the clientele overlapped, there was never any trouble—whatever people brought in the door, they left in the parking lot. The place was an island of biscuits-and-gravy-induced peace, a Switzerland of comfort food. The only change in about the last fifty years had been the addition of flat-screens riding high in the corners, 24/7: CNN, Fox News, MSNBC, ESPN.

In a back booth, Joe Reeder, in a black polo and matching jeans, his ABC Security windbreaker flung on the seat next to him, waved Rogers over. His short, prematurely white hair, contrasting with the tan of a recent Florida vacation, made him easily the most striking man in the place, not excluding guys with mohawks, transvestites, and a couple of ripped bodybuilders.

She plopped down across from him.

"Another rough day at the office, huh?" he said, not really a question. His craggy good looks, as usual, gave nothing away, except perhaps tiny smile lines around the brown eyes in their white-eyebrowed settings.

She shuddered. "Brutal." Sometimes she hated that people-reading thing of his.

Reeder's expertise in the field of kinesics—the science of facial expressions and body language—dated back to his Secret Service years. It remained a major selling point for his firm ABC Security, which consulted with law enforcement agencies nationwide.

They took time to order coffee while they surveyed the menu.

Then he said, "It's the budget cuts, isn't it?"

She gaped at him. "How the hell . . . ?"

Her friend gave her half a smile. "Don't worry, I wasn't 'reading' you—it's not like these cuts haven't been in the news ad nauseam."

He nodded toward a screen where CNN was excerpting this morning's press conference with President Harrison explaining his latest efforts to balance the budget.

"It was only a matter of time till it was the FBI's turn," he said. "What's the skinny on your task force?"

She gave him the details of her meeting with Fisk, pausing briefly as the two friends ordered.

Reeder looked like he was about to advise her, then he stopped short, seeing somebody approaching. Without looking, she already knew who it was—Joe Reeder wasn't the only people reader at the table. Kevin Lockwood dropped into the booth next to her and squeezed her thigh under the table—he was working, so a kiss on the cheek was out of the question.

Kevin and Rogers had been seeing each other for the better part of a year now. They'd met when he was a material witness on the last case she and Joe had worked—boy-band handsome, Kevin wore his dark hair clipped short, his tortoiseshell glasses enlarging slightly his impossibly long-lashed brown eyes.

Those eyes had first drawn her to Kevin, even though at the time he wore eyeliner and mascara. Kevin sang at a club called Les Girls where he appeared under the nom de guerre Virginia Plain, though he took occasional shifts here at Bob & Edith's. Tonight he wore not a sparkly gown, but the customary waiter staff's white shirt, black bow tie, and black pants.

"Mr. Reeder," he said, nodding across the table.

"Mr. Lockwood," Reeder said with a wry smile. She'd noticed some time ago that he'd stopped asking Kevin to call him "Joe." Just didn't do any good.

"Working graveyard, huh?" she asked Kevin.

"Yeah, lucky me. Alexis called in sick, so Pinky called me and I said, 'Sure.' I hope you weren't thinking of doing something."

Pinky was the heavyset, henna-haired gal at the register.

"No," Rogers said, and raised her coffee cup toward Reeder. "I've already got a date."

"Tomorrow night, then. I'm not working either place. I'll take you somewhere nicer than this . . . meaning no offense, Mr. Reeder."

"None taken, Mr. Lockwood."

Kevin gave her a wink in lieu of a peck on the cheek, then rose and went off toward the kitchen window where somebody's food waited.

"Been almost a year, hasn't it?" Reeder asked.

She shrugged. "Who's counting?"

"Your folks back in Iowa are going to love him."

"Don't be mean."

"Hey, I like the guy. And I don't have to be much of a people reader to see that you do, too. In a different kind of way."

"So," Rogers said, uneasy talking about this part of her life, "you were going to say something? Right before Kevin showed up? Something that might help us keep Special Situations afloat, I hope."

"I don't know . . ."

"You don't know what you were going to say?"

He huffed a tiny laugh. "I don't know if it will keep Special Situations together."

She felt a tiny rush in her stomach. "You have something?"

"Maybe." He sipped coffee. "You ever have occasion to meet Amanda Yellich?"

Secretary of the Interior Yellich—a hard worker and valued ally of President Harrison—had died just under a week ago at her desk.

"Just once." Rogers shook her head, sighed. "Nice woman. So sad."

"Sad as hell," Reeder said. "Do you know how she died, exactly?"

Rogers shrugged. "Wasn't it a heart attack?"

Reeder leaned in. "Are you old enough to remember Mama Cass?"

"Who?"

He rolled his eyes, then said, "The Secretary died from eating a sandwich."

"A *sandwich*? What, did she choke?"

"Are you sure you don't remember Mama Cass? Food allergy—sesame."

FBI agent Rogers didn't love that the cause of death of such a high-ranking public official was unknown to her. "And you're privy to this how?"

"I know that she died at her desk over lunch because it was on the news. I know about the sandwich—and more importantly, the allergy—because . . . I knew Amanda."

"*Amanda?* You knew the Secretary of the Interior well enough to call her by her first name?"

With a little shrug, Reeder said, "Her marriage broke up about the same time mine did. We went to dinner a few times. Maybe more than a few times. But it was never anything really serious."

Rogers wasn't sure she bought that. "How well did you know her?"

"Well enough to know about her OCD."

Rogers cocked her head. "She had Obsessive Compulsive Disorder?"

"I don't know if it was ever officially diagnosed or anything," Reeder said, shrugging. "But I do know she ate at her desk every damn day. And that she had the same sandwich from the same *restaurant* every damn day. Hell, for all I know it was delivered by the same *delivery person* every damn day."

With some lightness in her tone, Rogers said, "Please stop saying 'every damn day.'" Because this clearly was something that was gnawing at her friend.

"OCD or not," Reeder said, "Amanda knew all about her allergy, going back to early childhood. She would have made sure the restaurant knew about it, too. It wouldn't take much sesame to kill her, a fact of which she was quite aware."

"*Kill* her? Really kill her?"

"Really kill her. Not a heart attack."

"Is this being covered up or . . . ?"

"No. There was a general assumption that she died at her desk of a probable coronary, which made the news initially. Follow-up reports mention the fatal reaction to sesame, but that was not page-one stuff. I mean, you didn't notice it."

"Who's investigating?"

Reeder shrugged. "Nobody that I know of. Death by misadventure, an accident. Might be that's all it is, but the Amanda I knew was pretty damn careful."

Rogers mulled a few moments, then asked, "You think Situations should look into her death?"

"Do you have any other pressing cases?"

"No," she admitted.

"Might be worth a look. Death of a cabinet member, if it's more than accidental or misadventure, could be just the kind of case that would satisfy your boss."

She smirked. "Or I could be accused of spending government funds just to satisfy your curiosity about the death of someone you knew intimately."

"Did I say I knew her intimately?"

"Did you have to?"

Their food arrived, fish and chips for her, a meat loaf plate for him. About to dig in, he said, "Well, if funding is your big concern, if it'll make you feel better—*I'll* buy dinner."

"Even though it's my turn?"

"Even though it's your turn," he said, lifting his fork of meat loaf in salute.

Truth be told, Reeder could have afforded to take her anywhere in town. His highly publicized success with her on the Supreme Court case had helped turn his already thriving ABC Security into a multinational corporation. But the political paparazzi had made dinner practically impossible at such favorite spots of theirs as the Verdict Chophouse, the Blue Duck Tavern, and Vidalia.

Reeder had first hit the headlines back in his Secret Service days, after stepping in front of a bullet meant for then President Gregory

Bennett. Prior to Reeder, Tim McCarthy—protecting President Ronald Reagan on March 30, 1981—had been the last Secret Service agent to take a bullet for a president.

Across the restaurant, a couple came in. The man wore a nothing suit, but the woman was wearing expensive jeans and a T-shirt.

"Them," Reeder said, as they sat quietly eating.

That was her cue for a game they'd been playing. In an effort to pick up her partner's people-reading skills, Rogers had coaxed him into coaching her as she studied kinesics and tried to improve her powers of observation.

She watched until the couple was seated in a booth in the back, near the kitchen. Even so, she still had a clear view of both.

"Well?" Reeder asked.

"Married couple. Rings on both. Hers is a huge fricking diamond, so they have some money."

"What about her body language?"

Rogers nodded at the prompt. "Defensive, arms crossed, brow furrowed."

"Right. She's pissed off. Any idea about what?"

She glanced at Reeder. "Oh, come on."

"It's there," he said.

She sneaked a look at the couple. The man was fiddling with his wedding ring, slipping it off, slipping it back on. "Ah . . . They're talking divorce."

"They are," Reeder agreed.

The woman smiled, but her eyes were teary and she used the napkin to blot them away. A waitress came and they ordered something without looking at the menu.

Kevin swung by and warmed their coffee. Smiles were exchanged. Then Kevin was gone, and Rogers asked Reeder, "How'd I do?"

"I'll tell you after you sum it up for me."

"They're a couple deciding whether or not to split. He's in favor, she's not."

"That's one option," Reeder said.

She glanced at them again, as discreetly as possible. "What am I not seeing?"

"His watch."

Another glance, though it didn't give her much. "What about his watch?"

"It's cheap—a Timex or something."

"So?"

"You said they've got money. His suit is inexpensive, off-the-rack. Shoes are worn. Yet she has a honking diamond ring, a professional manicure, and a hairdo that cost more than his suit."

"Then . . . they *don't* have money?" Rogers asked, unsure where this was going. "Or maybe they do but she spends it all?"

"They're married . . . just not to each other."

She goggled at him. "Where do you get that?"

"She has a lot of money, he has none."

"That still doesn't mean they're not husband and wife."

The waitress brought the couple coffee—probably all they ordered.

He shrugged. "Professional manicure, expensive hairdo. But she's not wearing makeup. He's wearing a worn, wrinkled suit. Been at work all day, right?"

"Okay . . ."

"Everything about her says 'perfect'—yet she left the house without makeup."

"Which means," Rogers said, "she left in a hurry."

"Yup," Reeder said.

Rogers sat forward, gesturing with an open hand. "He called her. Needed to talk to her and they met here because no one knows them. Just to be safe, they took a booth near the kitchen, away from the windows."

"Right. Mrs. America normally would never be caught dead in a place like this, but if she did, she sure as hell wouldn't sit near the kitchen."

"So I was way off about the divorce," Rogers said.

"Not entirely. Married man has finally told Mrs.-Somebody-Else he's going to leave his wife . . . so the star-crossed couple can finally be together."

Rogers shook a fist. "And she's pissed, because that isn't what she wants at all! She's got the money she wants in her current setup. *This* guy is strictly recreational."

Reeder nodded. "If he had any smarts he would go home to his wife."

"Does he? Will he?"

"Naw. When he slips the ring off? His eyes narrow for a split second, a micro-expression that says he's determined to act. He's made his decision."

She glanced at them again—discreetly—and this time she caught it. ". . . Poor SOB."

When she sent her eyes back to Reeder, his weren't on hers, rather on the TV in the opposite corner. She looked over her shoulder at what had caught her friend's attention. A red *Breaking News* banner flashed across the screen and quietly ominous words scrolled across: *Russia invades Azbekistan.*

"Well, hell," Reeder muttered.

One of the other customers said, "Hey, Pinky, turn up the sound, will ya?"

Behind the register, Pinky picked up the remote, pointed it, and did as she was asked.

A blonde newsreader was saying, ". . . *have overwhelmed the Azbekistani army. The United Nations is making vigorous protests, but at this point, the Russians remain in control of the beleaguered country. In a related story, unconfirmed by CNN, four American citizens are said to be missing from the Azbekistani capital of Troyanda."*

Reeder and Rogers traded a look.

The newsreader said, *"Further updates as this story develops."*

"CIA?" Rogers asked.

Shrugging, Reeder said, "I hope not. If the four are Company, and alive, we're going to want them back. If they're dead, then someone, probably the Russians, will be blamed . . . and the hawks will smell blood in the water."

She sighed. "Why does the world have to be such a shitty place?"

"World's fine. It's people that's the problem."

That made her laugh, but it caught in her throat. "You can be one cynical son of a bitch sometimes, Joe Reeder. Me, I prefer to cling to the hope that things can be better. Naive, I know."

He shook his head. "You're not naive, Patti. Don't sell yourself short. We've seen enough bad shit go down, both of us, that you have to cling to whatever hope you can. Be greedy about it. You've seen what happens when cynicism takes over."

She'd never heard this kind of thing from him before. *"You* have hope, Joe?"

He stared into his coffee for a moment, then brought his eyes up, locked on hers. "Don't tell anybody."

"Your secret's safe with me."

His grin was disarming and for once not at all guarded. "You know what John Philpot Curran said?"

"What, to Mama whozit?"

"Different eras—like us. John Philpot Curran, Irish judge and orator?"

She just stared at him.

"I'm paraphrasing," Reeder said, "but in essence, Curran said the price of liberty is eternal vigilance."

"I hear you," she said.

"Eternal vigilance is our job, and because I have a high opinion of you and me, I'm hopeful. We do our job, then maybe, end of the day, some liberty will be left."

"Pretty deep, Joe."

He shrugged. "I get reflective every time Russia invades someplace. Dessert?"

"My fellow Americans, ask not what your country can do for you, ask what you can do for your country."

John F. Kennedy, thirty-fifth President of the United States of America. Served 1961–1963. Assassinated on a presidential visit to Dallas, Texas, November 22, 1963. Section 45, Grid U-35, Arlington National Cemetery

THREE

Joe Reeder sat up in bed, pillows propped behind him, Nero Wolfe novel propped before him (*Might As Well Be Dead*), but he wasn't reading, despite Archie Goodwin's compelling narrative voice. Instead, Amanda Yellich dominated his thoughts—a petite redhead, as sunny and funny and fun as she was intellectually above him.

And she had liked Reeder a lot.

He had liked her, too. They had a number of nice nights together and a few afternoons, but after a promising easygoing start, she came to want more than he was prepared to give right now. Not that he'd broken it off—Amanda did that, when she realized Reeder was still in love with his ex-wife, Melanie.

Amanda hadn't been wrong about that, and he'd hurt her, if unintentionally. He still regretted that he couldn't give the woman what she needed emotionally, and the physical side, however rewarding, hadn't been enough. In recent weeks, though, there'd been many times he wondered if he should call Amanda and try again. He'd never quite done that. And now—now she was gone.

On the nightstand, his cell chirped. So few people had the number—and once he'd paid dearly for ignoring a call—that he'd made a point of answering, or at least checking out, every one. When it rang the second time, he eyeballed the caller ID—UNKNOWN.

With a sigh, he put Rex Stout down and picked up the phone. "Reeder."

A female voice on the other end said, "Please hold for the President of the United States."

There was a time when Reeder might have clicked off, chalking this up to a crank call. But in the past several years, the President was someone he'd actually spoken to on occasion—and one of those few people who had this number.

"Joe? Dev Harrison." The casualness of that liquid, self-assured voice coming over the line was at once disarming and intimidating.

President Devlin Harrison, the second African American leader to be elected in the country's history, was no crank-caller.

"Good evening, Mr. President."

"Apologies for the late hour, Joe."

"Not necessary, sir. I'm pretty much open for presidential calls any time."

A soft chuckle preceded a change in tone: "Obviously you've seen the news."

The President wasn't much for small talk. No president was.

"The Russian invasion, sir? Of course."

The surprise of receiving a phone call from the President was amplified by the apparent subject. The moment felt surreal.

The President's voice was deceptively casual. "What strikes you about our role in this incident?"

"The four missing US citizens."

Obviously.

"I'd like to talk to you about them, Joe. Tomorrow morning, my office . . ."

Right. That oval one.

". . . six a.m. Can you make that, Joe?"

"Of course, Mr. President."

"Our, uh, people weren't just regular citizens."

That was more than Reeder expected to hear over an open phone line. But he risked, "I didn't think so, sir. I can come now, sir, if . . . ?"

"No. I have things to do. Six a.m. Thanks, Joe."

A click in his ear signaled the end of the call. Good-byes were unnecessary.

He settled back in bed, trading the phone for the Nero Wolfe. So the President wanted to talk to him about missing citizens overseas, caught up in a Russian invasion, and who "weren't just regular citizens." CIA agents, clearly, as he'd assumed—not a big leap, as CNN and the other outlets had raised the same possibility, or anyway their talking heads had.

Reeder tried to get back to the book but instead fell asleep wondering how the hell he fit into this scenario. He dreamed a variation on the Situation Room scene in *Dr. Strangelove*, and woke up sweating, finding nothing funny about it at all.

The next morning, a few minutes before six a.m., Joe Reeder—wearing the dark gray Savile Row suit he saved for the special clients of ABC Security (and who was more special than his friend "Dev"?)—sat in a comfortable chair outside the Oval Office, warmed by the smile of the President's head secretary, Emily Curtis. The gray-haired woman, who might have been your maiden aunt, had been the gatekeeper for three presidents, and was as much a fixture here as the Marine guard at the West Wing entrance or the floating presence of Secret Service agents. She had, in fact, met Reeder during his own SS tenure here.

"The President should be with you shortly," she said, in her cheery yet businesslike way. "He's been up all night, so do take it easy on him."

"See what I can do," he said, and barely got it out before the Oval Office door opened and the President's chief of staff, Timothy Vinson, strode out, his mustache twitching like a caterpillar trying to crawl off his face, his stocky frame lumbering past Reeder without hello. The bureaucrat, in his fifties and balding, as cold as Emily Curtis was warm, seemed a man on a mission.

Vinson was already well down the corridor when half a dozen others, some in uniform, came out quickly, with President Harrison next, as if he'd shooed them out. Maybe he had.

Pausing to give Reeder a quick handshake and a tight smile, the President said, "Joe, good to see you. Walk with me, will you?"

"Yes, Mr. President," Reeder said, falling into step next to Harrison.

Typically, the tall, slender African American—whose physical resemblance to former President Obama had not hurt him with a majority of voters—was impeccably dressed in a charcoal suit with lighter gray pinstripes, his tie with muted red and blue stripes perfectly knotted. Yet somehow something seemed slightly off—maybe it was just the puffy dark circles hugging Harrison's eyes. The presidential gatekeeper had not been exaggerating: the man hadn't slept in some while.

On the march down the hall, Reeder found himself needing to slow, so as not to pull away from Harrison. He knew the President to be a fast mover, but today the man seemed a half-step behind. Exhaustion or worry? Could be either—could be both.

They reached the elevator near the offices of the Chief of Staff and Vice President. Vinson, already there, revealed his mission to be holding the elevator door for the President and his contingent. Reeder knew almost certainly where they were heading—the Situation Room.

With Russia invading Azbekistan, that destination would seem inevitable . . . if it weren't for Reeder's presence. Even when he'd been assigned to protect various presidents, he had not set foot within that space when it was actively in use. Reeder had been in there before, on security sweeps mostly, but never during an actual situation.

As the doors closed, Vinson—who obviously hadn't noticed Reeder on his way out of the Oval Office—asked the President, "What's *he* doing here?" The disdain in his voice—the nasty emphasis on "he"—undisguised.

Icily, Harrison said, "I invited him."

Vinson's mouth opened as if it had decided on its own to speak, but its owner fed it no words. The Chief of Staff's lips pressed back together and he swallowed, but his eyes remained narrowed on Reeder, with whom he'd had a run-in or two.

The rest of the ride passed in brief if uncomfortable silence. The doors slid open and the President was the first one out, Reeder falling in behind him, an old Secret Service habit. Vinson got held back by the other exiting staffers, and by the time the Chief of Staff caught up, the President and Reeder were approaching the two Marine guards stationed at the Situation Room entry.

Both Marines snapped to attention and saluted.

Harrison returned the salute, then one of the guards opened the door and held it for them.

They entered to find most of the seats at the vast conference table already filled. The faces had changed over the years, but the room itself stayed the same, a fairly nondescript, rather narrow conference room distinguished only by its many wall-mounted video screens. Certainly the art direction on *Strangelove* had been more impressive.

Seven chairs lined each side of the long dark oak table. They were now filled by the Joint Chiefs of Staff, the National Security Advisor, the Director of the CIA, and—at the far end on the right side (both literally and figuratively)—Senator Wilson Blount of Tennessee.

Everyone had risen, of course, upon the President's entry. In the chair immediately to the right of him was a slender bespectacled brunette, Vice President Erin Mitchell, a progressive added to the ticket to court the women's vote. Chairs for staffers and assistants lined the two long walls, each graced with a pair of monitors that were only slightly smaller than the one opposite the President's end of the table.

The President took his seat and then so did everyone else, including Reeder, who moved to one of the chairs along the wall. He could feel eyes on him. Some here may have wondered if he was back with the Secret Service. Even so, SS agents invariably waited outside.

Back in the day, even the powerful Senator Blount would have been on the outside. But in this era of increasingly tighter budgets, having in attendance the chairman of the Senate Appropriations Subcommittee on Defense only made sense . . . and Blount now held that chair.

Last year, the venerable Senator had been instrumental in pushing through a law lowering the minimum age for the presidency to thirty, an obvious attempt to clear a path for a new era of strong young conservatives. The President had supported that, as part of an effort to bridge the right and left, including a peace offering that saw the Senator's son Nicholas appointed to the cabinet as Secretary of Agriculture. The young Blount's predecessor had been assassinated last year in the plot to bring down the government, a coup that Reeder and Rogers had helped quash.

Admiral David Canby, the shaved-headed chairman of the Joint Chiefs—a politically savvy, by-the-book Navy man—trained his battleship-gray eyes on Reeder and said, "*He* doesn't have clearance to be here."

"He does now," Harrison said.

"By whose authority?" Canby asked. Demanded.

"Mine." The President's eyes were fixed on the admiral. For a long moment no one said a word, as everyone in the room decided not to further challenge Reeder's presence.

Vinson, seated at the President's left hand, gave Canby a patronizing thing that was technically a smile. He said, "Now that we've established that the President of the United States is in charge here, could we get down to business and find out what the hell happened to our people?"

Canby gave Vinson a quick glare, but he and everyone else here knew the power the Chief of Staff wielded in this administration. Reeder could see the admiral clenching and unclenching his fists, no doubt wishing he could deck the man. Harrison himself had probably considered doing that a time or two. But the truth was, Vinson made things happen.

The President indicated the screen that swallowed the wall opposite him. "What exactly are we looking at, Admiral?"

"You might say," Canby said somewhat wryly, "the crime scene."

The satellite view of scrubby, trampled ground included a handful of bodies, scattered carelessly; no massacre by any means. A few abandoned vehicles, jeeps possibly, some wrecked, and wisping smoke. The Azbekistani resistance, such as it was, had clearly been minimal.

President Harrison swung his attention to the Director of the CIA. With his wreath of white hair and wire-framed glasses, Richard Shaley—despite a grandfatherly look—was every inch the veteran spy, beginning as a field agent in the first Iraqi war. But it was his political skills that made him really dangerous—like J. Edgar Hoover before him, Shaley was said to hold the keys to every DC closet holding a skeleton, and that was a lot of bones.

"The CIA Director and I spoke last night," Harrison informed the group, "and I frankly was not pleased with what I heard. Director Shaley, have you had an opportunity to learn anything more about our dead people?"

Reeder stiffened—this was the first time anyone had said it out loud, and it was the President doing so: *our people are dead.*

Everyone at the table turned toward the CIA Director. The collective blankness of their expressions was like a witness considering the options at a suspect lineup. Shaley leaned forward, eyes meeting the President's. His shrug was a slow-motion affair. "What can I say? A mission went wrong, Mr. President."

"I was hoping for a little more," the President said.

"Well, it's a tragedy, of course."

Platitudes, Reeder thought. The President's reaction would not be pretty.

It wasn't.

His gaze unblinking and accusing, Harrison said to the CIA Director, "You were to find me answers, Dick. What are they? *Where* are they?"

"Mr. President . . ."

"Why were our people there in the first place, and against my direct orders, since we *knew* a Russian attack was imminent! Who in the hell signed off on sending them over there? Was it you, Dick?"

Shaley sat very still for a second. He spoke so softly that some at the table may not have heard, as if he wanted only the man who'd queried him to be privy.

"Mr. President," he said, "I was not the one to sign the order to send the team in there for what appears to have been a routine assessment of the situation."

"You made that clear in private. You were to fact-find. You've had several hours. Do you know who did?"

"Not for sure yet, Mr. President."

The President drew in a deep breath and said, "The media knows that four Americans have disappeared, and the commentators are speculating CIA, and even raising the possibility that our people are dead. But the CIA *itself* doesn't know who sent its own people into harm's way? Not acceptable."

Shaley appeared calm. Maybe he was, Reeder thought. You did not hold a position as powerful as Shaley's, for as long as he had, by getting rattled during questioning—even if the interrogator was the most powerful man in the free world. And even if those seated around him were among the most powerful figures in government.

All the Director said was, "We're looking into it, Mr. President."

"Look faster, look harder. I want an answer by the end of the day—understood?"

"Yes, sir."

Harrison nodded toward the looming screen. "Well, at least tell me this, Dick. Can we identify any of those bodies as ours?"

Shaley said, "No. But we believe the civilian vehicle barely visible at the edge of those trees . . . near where we have a glimpse of highway? . . . was theirs. There were several bodies nearby . . . specifically, four . . . that the Russians cleared out with their own minimal casualties. We believe those four to be ours, yes."

"Then the Russians killed our people?"

"Our best guess is yes, Mr. President."

Reeder had to give Shaley credit—he wasn't ducking responsibility.

The President's expression was placid but his eyes were hard as he again trained his gaze on the CIA CEO. "You're saying we don't know that either?"

"Not for certain, Mr. President. There were two factions firing on each other. It's an active war zone, after all."

Admiral Canby, leaning forward, said, "Mr. President—it's painfully clear the Russians killed our people. Director Shaley is correct in his assessment that this was a combat situation, but aside from friendly fire, there was no reason for the Azbekistanis to kill our people. They're our allies! No, this was an act of war, Mr. President, and should be treated as such."

Harrison regarded the chairman of the Joint Chiefs. "Then you would suggest we go to war, Admiral, before we have all the facts?"

"Sir, how many more facts do we need? Our people, almost certainly dead, were carted off a battlefield by members of an invading army."

The President's voice remained calm, resolute. "I want to know why our people were there when they shouldn't have been, who pulled the trigger on them, and who *sent* them into an active war zone. When I know those three things, then we'll act. Not before. In the meantime, we do not attack, we make no definitive statement to the media, and we do whatever it takes *not* to escalate the situation. Am I clear?"

Nods all around, including—finally—Canby.

Harrison said, pointedly, "Director Shaley, get me the information I need. ASAP."

"Yes, Mr. President."

"Anyone else care to add anything?"

Senator Blount lifted a hand, a shy student seeking to make a point in class. His blond hair going silver lent him a boyish quality despite his age, though his tortoiseshell-framed bifocals and sagging neck told a clearer story of his sixty-seven years.

The Senator said, "The eyes of the nation, of the world, are upon us, Mr. President. All due respect, sir—spinning our wheels is not enough . . . you have to *do* something."

"I am, Senator—I'm gathering facts. Only then will I make a decision."

The President rose and so did they all. He said, "Get to your posts and we'll convene here again this evening. Tim will text you with the time."

As the senior official in the room, Vice President Mitchell was the one to say, "Thank you, Mr. President."

Turning to Reeder, the President said, "Joe? With me, please."

Reeder followed Harrison out of the room, Vinson and the Vice President right behind them, leaving the others standing there a little dumbstruck, staring at the screen with its image of a battlefield that seemed more field than battle.

The elevator doors slid shut and, as they went up, Vinson said, "Jesus, are the *hawks* getting hard!"

"They have a reason for once," President Harrison said. "Four Americans are dead."

"You're right, sir," Vinson said, quietly.

The elevator door opened and the Vice President made her nodding exit while the Chief of Staff fell in step with the President and Reeder. Harrison paused.

"Tim, you'll be in your office, if I need you?"

The sideways dismissal froze Vinson momentarily. ". . . Certainly, Mr. President."

Vinson headed off to his hidey-hole.

The two men remaining walked in silence until they were inside the Oval Office. As he moved around behind his desk, Harrison waved Reeder to a chair on the opposite side. In previous meetings, they had used the couches and comfortable chairs in the informal central meeting area. The formidable desk said the words to come would be important, official.

"So, Joe—maybe you can use your fabled people-reading skills to tell me if Director Shaley is lying about not knowing who sent our agents into Azbekistan."

Reeder didn't hesitate. "He's lying."

Harrison's eyebrows went up. "You can tell?"

Reeder nodded. "He had his mouth open."

The President offered up a weak smile. "I was being serious."

"So was I," Reeder said. "The man is a professional spy, buttoned-down and hard as hell to read, even by a kinesics expert. That said, he lies for a living, Mr. President. It's a habit with him."

"What does your gut say—is he the one who sent our agents over there?"

Reeder considered that. "If you're asking me if he signed the actual order, I have no idea. If you mean do I think he was aware of it? Damn likely. Shaley has been Director of the CIA since I headed up the presidential detail. In my experience, no one passes wind at Langley without Shaley knowing."

"But what the hell is the motivation here, for Shaley or anyone else, to kill four Americans?"

Reeder shrugged a shoulder. "War is big business. We both know, even if it's not general knowledge, that Azbekistan has some very valuable, as yet unexploited mineral rights." He shrugged the other shoulder. "And, then, Russia always makes a good bad guy."

The President nodded, but said nothing, thinking.

Finally, Reeder said, "With all due respect, Mr. President, surely you didn't bring me in this morning to read Director Shaley—you already knew he was a liar."

Harrison smiled a little. "You're right—he's so opaque he's transparent. I called you in because I know—hell, everyone in this building knows—the Russians killed our agents."

"So the hawks are right."

"They're right. But they're also wrong." Harrison slid a thumb drive across the desk to Reeder. "This is the information we have. Or I should say, that I have. You'll have to find out the rest yourself, Joe. Because it's not the Russians we're after here."

Reeder took the thumb drive. Tucked it away in a coat pocket, then said, "It wouldn't seem to be. Someone on our end sent those four to die."

The President swallowed thickly, then he waved a hand. "Hell, given the situation, I'd have done the same thing the Russians did— what would we do if four Russians showed up in the middle of our war?"

"Our people never even identified themselves as Americans. They may have been taken for resistance."

"Either way, it just doesn't matter. The thing is, Joe, as you heard in the Sit Room, I had ordered that no one be sent to Azbekistan . . . yet someone deliberately disobeyed. I want to know who that someone was—who that someone *is*—before I take any action. Can you do that, Joe? Can you find that person?"

"I can try, Mr. President. But I'm just one man."

"One man will have to be enough. And do it fast, Joe—that sound you hear is the clock ticking. And it may be attached to a bomb."

"Yes, sir."

Reeder rose, but the President said, "Just one more thing."

"Sir?"

President Harrison slid a cell phone across the desk. "This is encrypted, safe, and programmed with my personal number."

Reeder picked up the phone, slipped it into his coat pocket with the thumb drive.

"Report any time, day or night."

"Thank you, Mr. President."

"Don't thank me yet—this is an unenviable assignment and inherently dangerous. Try not to be the fifth American killed in this thing."

Reeder nodded.

"The hawks want war and I'm trying to prevent one. No bullshit, Joe—we're talking World War III if Canby and his cronies get their way. Someone inside this government put this thing in motion. Find him."

"I will, Mr. President."

Reeder turned, walked confidently out the door of the Oval Office, shut it behind him, then let out a long breath. He looked at his right hand and it was shaking.

Emily Curtis, the President's secretary, eyed him with concern.

"Are you all right, Joe?" she asked.

He nodded, forced a smile. "Never better, Emily."

But he knew that she could read people, too, and recognized a lie when she heard it. Still, she just nodded and bestowed a maiden-aunt smile upon him.

As he left the White House, its picture-postcard perfection looming behind him, Reeder was struck by one overriding thought.

Things were bad when the President felt the only person he could trust was an ex-Secret Service agent, no longer in government, name of Joe Reeder.

"America is the land of the second chance—and when the gates of the prison open, the path ahead should lead to a better life."

George W. Bush, forty-third President of the United States of America. Served 2001–2009.

FOUR

At the wheel of her government Ford, Patti Rogers sensed she was embarking upon a wild goose chase; but when Joe Reeder gave her a lead, she followed it up, no questions asked—particularly when she and her task force were so desperately in need of a significant case.

She did not share her misgivings with Special Agent Lucas Hardesy, her ride-along on this trip. The senior agent, with whom Rogers was enjoying an uneasy truce, wore shoes as shiny as his shaved head, and an immaculate off-the-rack suit—a good agent who shouted ex-military even at his most quiet.

Not that his "most quiet" happened very often.

"What's this asshole's name?" Hardesy asked from the rider's seat.

"Let's not *assume* he's an asshole, Lucas," she said, keeping her tone easy, not wanting to restart anything. She always called him Lucas, never Luke; no one on Special Situations did. "We're just looking at the guy who delivered Secretary Yellich's lunch every day—a citizen named Glenn Willard."

"So, then, Reeder knew the woman, huh? Probably in the Biblical sense. And now we're doing this as a favor to him, 'cause he's such a suspicious bastard?"

"You're doing it because I'm buying your lunch today. *I'm* doing it because Joe has better instincts than both of us put together."

Hardesy didn't dispute that. She was driving southeast on Branch Avenue in Hillcrest Heights, Maryland, getting ready to take the right onto Curtis Drive.

Hardesy asked, "What do we know about this Willard who isn't necessarily an asshole?"

"Not much. Miggie called the restaurant Secretary Yellich ordered her sandwich from every day. The owner, Dev Avninder, says Glenn is the deliveryman in question."

"Okay, but who made the sandwich?"

"Avninder himself. He *always* made it himself. He knew sesame was a big no-no in Yellich's diet, and made sure she got exactly what she ordered."

He gave her a grunt of acknowledgment, then: "What kind of name is Avninder?"

"East Indian, I think."

Another grunt. "Phone's not enough. We should talk to him."

"We will. But first, Willard." She made the right onto Curtis, Hilltop Apartments in sight. "Avninder says Willard is a decent employee and a good enough guy."

"You had Miggie run him?"

"Of course."

"And, nothing?"

"Nothing at all."

"Well, we know one thing, boss."

"Which is?"

"How much I'll put up with for a free lunch."

The buildings of the Hilltop Apartments, set at the corners of a huge parking lot, might have been four six-story college dorms. Nondescript white brick weathered to light beige gave the place a worn-out, even weary look. Rogers parked the car and they got out. She was in a cream-color silk blouse and navy trousers, the day cool but not enough so to require the matching jacket.

"Which building?" Hardesy asked.

"Number two," Rogers said, nodding to the one in front of them.

"Security building?"

She nodded again as they strode across the parking lot.

He was reaching in his pocket for his jimmy tool. "One thing I never miss? The Fourth Amendment."

"Don't let Reeder hear you say that," she said.

The Patriot Act, expanded over a decade ago, had pretty much gutted the Fourth Amendment, and the conservative-dominated Supreme Court had upheld the decision. But old-time liberals like Reeder still pissed and moaned about "unreasonable search and seizure." For her part, Rogers—a self-identified middle-of-the-road Republican—liked not having to deal with all the bullshit warrants and assorted other crap that might keep her from saving a life or hauling in a bad guy.

"I'll keep my opinion to myself," Hardesy said, jimmy in hand.

Then, like a jump cut in a film, the door to Building Two flew open and a youngish guy in a business suit popped out. Her hand moved to her sidearm.

The guy's eyes grew wide and his arms went up at the sight of Rogers' palm resting on the butt of the pistol at her hip. In his twenties, his dark hair short, his retro-hipster beard the same, he looked like he might pass out. As the door banged closed behind him, he flinched.

Rogers said, "Glenn Willard?"

Confusion clenched his forehead. "What? No . . . no! Basement flat, in back, on the right." His voice was a shaky tenor. "Cops?"

"Federal agents," Rogers said, her hand drifting away from her pistol.

The guy shook his head, lowering his hands slowly. "Not a surprise . . . DEA?"

"FBI," Hardesy said. "What's that mean, 'not a surprise'?"

"When you get to his front door, just take a whiff. It's not springtime."

"Blowin' smoke, is he?"

"Considering how many 'friends' he has, going in and out of there? I'm guessing he's not just blowing it . . . but you didn't hear that from me."

"Who exactly," Rogers asked, "are we not hearing this from?"

"Joe Boyer."

"You live here, Mr. Boyer?"

"For two years now."

"Willard been here that whole time?"

Boyer nodded.

Hardesy asked, "All that time, dude's been flyin' the Mexican airlines, and doing a lot of entertaining, too?"

With a shrug, Boyer said, "When I first moved in, it was *real* steady—you'd have to push past 'em sometimes, and they reeked of the stuff. Fewer now."

By 2031, only ten states had not passed legislation allowing recreational use of marijuana; but Maryland was one of them, and selling the stuff illegally remained frowned upon.

Realizing he wasn't the target here, Boyer said, "All right if I go? I'm already late."

Rogers nodded, but Hardesy had another question: "Do you know if your neighbor's home now?"

Boyer shrugged. "I wouldn't say he's a neighbor. I'm a floor above him, but we usually go to work about the same time. Not unusual we go out the door one after the other. Haven't seen him today."

Rogers sent her colleague a look that said this interview was over. But Hardesy wasn't quite finished.

"How would you like to get in solid with Uncle Sam?" he asked the guy. "And open the security door for us?"

Boyer looked around to see if anyone was watching. "Why not?"

He slid his key card into the door and opened it for them.

"You have the gratitude of your federal government," Hardesy said, happy not to have to jimmy his way in; but Boyer was already walking toward the Naylor Street metro stop.

Hardesy held the door open for Rogers.

"You want to cover the back?" she asked.

"Other than weed, this guy is clean, right?"

Rogers shrugged. "He's got no record, anyway."

"Probably no need then. Let's stick together."

That made sense to her.

The pair headed down to the lower floor. As they emerged from the stairwell, a young man was locking his door—short dark hair, medium build, polo shirt, decent jeans, Reeboks. The kind of guy who might pass for invisible in a busy office building, say, delivering something.

"Glenn Willard?" she called, her hand not at her hip but hovering.

The young man's eyes flew to her, then widened with fear.

"Federal agents," she said. "We'd like to ask you—"

But then Willard was sprinting down the corridor to a door that led to stairs that no doubt rose to a rear exit.

Just behind her, Hardesy said, "*Shit!*"

Rogers was only two steps into her pursuit when she heard her partner bellow, "Maybe I should take the back after all, huh?"

He said this while heading up the stairs to go around and cut the guy off.

Racing down the hall, she passed Willard's door—*was their man running because of his drug dealing? Or something else?*

Rogers went up the rear stairs and out the door, looking straight ahead, at more apartment houses, then to her left. Turning right she glimpsed Willard slipping around the far corner of the building. She took off like a sprinter at the starting gun.

In good shape from her thrice weekly workouts, she was well up to the challenge, making it quickly to the far end of the building, rounding the corner . . . but Willard was already almost to the parking lot. *Damn!* He had a good fifty yards on her.

She ran harder, closing the distance, but then she heard Hardesy yell, "*Freeze, Glenn! Federal agents!*"

Willard stopped, but he didn't freeze. Instead his hand went behind his back, slipping under the untucked polo to yank out a small automatic from his waistband.

Rogers shouted, "*Gun!*" but she doubted Hardesy heard the warning over the report of his own pistol.

The automatic seemed to fly out of Willard's hand of its own volition, then skittered out of reach as the young man crumpled into a heap on the pavement in an empty handicapped parking place.

Rogers rushed to the fallen drug dealer, her Glock still on him, and Hardesy did, too, from around the front of the building.

At first she thought her colleague had pulled off a trick shot out of one of those old westerns Reeder watched, shooting the gun right out of the man's hand. But it had been pain that sent the weapon flying, not fancy pistol-work: writhing on the cement, Willard got his hands red trying to stop the blood pouring from a wound in his side.

The young man looked up at Rogers as if maybe she were a nurse there to help him. "Son of a bitch shot me," he said, like it had hurt his feelings.

Kneeling next to him, Rogers said, "Shut up and lie still."

She ignored his moans as she dragged latex gloves from her pocket, pulled them on, then took his scarlet-smeared right hand.

"Quit grabbing at it," she said, then pressed his palm back against the wound. "Keep steady pressure."

Pacing nearby, her cohort had his cell out, telling the dispatcher, "Suspect down! Suspect down! Ambulance needed."

As he gave the address, Hardesy was fishing latex gloves out of a coat pocket. When he'd finished the call, he went over, bent down, and collected Willard's automatic, dropping it into a plastic evidence bag like a dog owner cleaning up behind Fido.

Rogers remained crouched near Willard, who was wincing in pain but alert. She asked, "Good idea, you think, drawing down on a federal agent?"

Willard seemed about to say something, but all that came out was a groan.

They didn't have to wait long for the ambulance, but while they did, Hardesy read Willard the revised Miranda rights, after which Rogers—still kneeling, as if praying for the perp—started asking questions.

"Glenn, did you regularly deliver Secretary Yellich's lunch?"

But Willard was too busy whimpering to respond.

She kept trying anyway: "And the Secretary always ordered the same sandwich, correct?"

Not a nod nor a shake of the head. Just whimpering and tears.

"That sandwich had sesame in it, Glenn. And Secretary Yellich was dangerously allergic. Did you know that?"

He passed out.

As the attendants loaded Willard up and in, Rogers and Hardesy gave their statements to both the local cops and an FBI Agent Involved Shooting investigator. This took a while. Before long, the parking lot filled with cop cars whose flashing lights painted the late morning red and blue.

Hardesy said to her, "I told you he'd be an asshole."

"Let's hope he's not a dead one."

"Hey, he pulled on me, so don't look for tears."

"I won't. But we can't talk to him if he isn't breathing."

Finally they had the chance to enter Willard's apartment, the FBI evidence team's work winding down. The apartment wasn't the mess she'd figured, the expected scattering of pizza boxes not present, nor the anticipated scruffy carpeting. The room was surprisingly clean, in fact, and she attributed any disorder more to the evidence team's search than a lack of cleanliness.

The furniture—a leather sofa along a wall, a matching pair of chairs under the living room window, a good-size flat-screen against another wall—was higher-end than she would have expected in an apartment like this.

Granted, the place was redolent of the sickly sweet mixture of dope and incense, but otherwise everything seemed so . . . normal. The dining room, off the entry, had a polished wood table and four chairs with a pile of mail propped against a condiment holder.

Rogers picked up the envelopes, thumbed through—a few bills, some junk, nothing special. She set the stack back down and took a pass through the galley kitchen. Coffee pot and toaster on the counter, sponge and dish soap near the faucet, everything clean and in its place.

Martin Napoli, a tall, balding agent of around forty, strode into the room; he wore an FBI windbreaker and a seen-it-all expression. The Special Agent in charge of the evidence collection team, Napoli was a favorite of Rogers'—good at his job, and he could always make her smile.

"Hiya, Patti," he said.

"Hiya, Marty."

Hardesy and Napoli traded nods.

"Find anything?" she asked.

Napoli gave up a tiny shrug. "You could say that."

"Care to share?"

His expression giving away nothing, Napoli crooked a finger for Rogers and Hardesy to follow him down the hall.

As they trailed the evidence SAIC down the dim corridor, Hardesy whispered to her, "What's he bein' so cute about?"

"It just means he has something."

They passed a bathroom on the right. Neat and clean. A bedroom, door open, was dark but appeared tidy, too.

Opposite was a second bedroom, its door closed. Napoli stopped there, wearing a cat-that-ate-the-canary grin, then twisted the knob and pushed the door open.

The fecund aroma of weed rolled out.

As she and Hardesy stuck their heads in, Napoli said behind them, "Enough grass in here to replace the turf at RFK Stadium."

If this bedroom had a bed, it was buried beneath bursting, stacked garbage bags, the pot aroma so strong that Rogers wondered if she could get a contact high just standing in the doorway.

"My lord," she said. "Marty, any idea how much dope is in there?"

Napoli shrugged. "We haven't exactly had time to weigh it, but my guess? Enough to make a guy carry a gun and make a run for it when federal agents come around."

Nodding, Rogers said, "Anything to tie him to the death of Secretary Yellich?"

"Not unless one of these bags is filled with sesame seeds," Napoli said with half a smirk. "And in the kitchen? Not a bun or a bagel with the deadly little beauties."

Moving away from the odor, she said, "Well, stay at it, Marty. And thanks."

"Always entertaining, Patti, when a call from you comes in. How's your pal Reeder?"

"Getting rich not working for the government."

She and Hardesy headed outside. Afternoon now, it was getting colder.

Hardesy regarded her with narrowed eyes. "So what do you think?"

"Well," she said, "I almost wrote this off as a wild goose chase."

"Yeah, me, too—but I didn't figure it would lead to a half ton of marijuana."

She huffed a laugh. "I guess we know why Willard pulled on us."

"Do we?" Hardesy asked. "Or is Reeder onto something?"

"Always possible with him. We'll have to keep digging. I wonder if taking a huge pile of dope off the street will make AD Fisk smile upon Special Situations?"

Hardesy laughed once. "We may get a day or two out of it."

Her cell chirped—it was Miguel Altuve, their computer analyst.

"I've been going through security video," he told her, "and not just from the day Secretary Yellich died—from the days *before* her death."

"And?"

"And a guy who must be your Glenn Willard *did* deliver her meals regularly . . . but he didn't do it the day of her death."

"You're *sure*?"

"Yeah. The guy subbing for Willard was dressed similarly, similar look generally, but definitely not the same guy."

Her stomach did a backflip. "Do we know who the ringer is?"

"Not yet," Miggie said. "Facial recognition came up *nada*."

"Have you talked to Avninder, the owner of the restaurant, since you got this?"

"Briefly, on the phone. Knows nothing about anybody filling in for Willard. But I figure you'll want to talk to him yourself, and not on the phone."

Nearby, the evidence team was hauling the bulging bags of dope out of Building Two and loading them into a van—they were going to need another.

She told the phone, "Send the file on the restaurant and the owner to our phones. Hardesy can fill me in while I drive."

"You got it," Miggie said, then clicked off.

Turning to Hardesy, she said, "Reeder was right."

"Was he now?"

"Ready for this? Glenn Willard delivered the secretary's sandwich on every day but one. Guess which."

Her colleague's eyebrows rose high on his endless forehead. "Jesus. What are we into?"

She didn't answer that, saying instead, "We kind of missed the noon hour, but I did promise to buy you lunch. And I have a certain restaurant in mind . . ."

Ye Olde Sandwich Shoppe, a hole-in-the-wall joint, sat only blocks from Yellich's DC office. Owner Dev Avninder was in his sixties, the patriarch of a family business he'd opened when he brought his brood to the United States almost three decades ago (according to the file Altuve sent them).

When Rogers and Hardesy walked in, the lunch rush was long over, just a couple of diners at the four tables in the tiny room. The back was taken up with a glass deli case and a counter with register, behind which stood a gray-haired, white-bearded man in suit and tie, with the proud look of a man who'd built an empire, however small. Behind him, younger workers in clean white T-shirts were making sandwiches and otherwise putting together orders, working rather frantically. Lunch hour might be over, but the demand for the little shop's sandwiches wasn't.

"Mr. Avninder?" Rogers asked, flashing her credentials.

The man's brown eyes lost a tiny bit of spark, and his automatic smile for all customers died on its way to his lips. "Yes?"

"I'm Special Agent Rogers and this is Special Agent Hardesy. We'd like a word with you."

"We are very busy," Avninder said.

Hardesy said, "Doesn't really look that way, sir."

"My business is mostly delivery. And my best deliveryman did not show up for work today. We are seriously behind schedule."

Rogers said, "Your best deliveryman—you mean, Glenn Willard?"

Avninder's eyes became slits. "And how do you know this?"

"He's in the hospital," Rogers said. "In the emergency room, or possibly surgery by now."

A hand rose to his lips but didn't quite touch them; his eyes were wide, white all around. "This is terrible. What has happened? Is he ill?"

Hardesy said, "He pulled a gun on a federal agent and got himself shot."

Avninder drew a breath in, quick. "I . . . I don't *believe* it! Glenn . . . he is a good man!"

At his raised voice, a slender girl working the food counter turned in concern. "Papa, what is it?"

"More federal agents, dear—they say Glenn drew a gun, and that . . . that one of them *shot* him."

The girl, her black hair ponytailed back, her white T-shirt emblazoned with the name of the restaurant, looked far less surprised than her father. She peered at them past the register.

Matter-of-fact, she asked, "Was it because of drugs?"

"*Drugs!*" her father said. It was damn near a yelp.

"You knew he sold drugs?" Hardesy asked the girl.

She shrugged.

Shaken, Avninder said to his daughter, "What is this craziness about drugs?"

Rogers locked eyes with the girl, who had ignored her father's question. "And you are?"

"Veena Avninder." She was in her early twenties, pretty, and clearly had a different angle on the world than her father.

Rogers asked, "Did you know Glenn was selling drugs?"

"Yes," she said, not at all ducking it. "That was common knowledge."

Her father's eyes flared. "*Veena!*" Then to the agents he said, quietly, "I did not know of this. He seems a nice young man."

Veena seemed a nice young woman, but she knew about the drugs didn't she?

As if Rogers had spoken that question aloud, Veena said, "But Glenn never sold them here! My father's business is legitimate. We make deliveries to some of the most important people in town."

But that didn't preclude drugs, did it?

Hardesy asked, "What about Glenn's deliveries? Was he delivering more than sandwiches?"

Veena gave a very elaborate shrug that said she didn't know, but suspected he probably was. Rogers wondered if the girl was herself a customer of Glenn's, but didn't press in front of her papa.

Hardesy asked, "Mr. Avninder, has anyone talked to you about the death of Secretary of the Interior Yellich?"

The old man frowned deep and suddenly Rogers had a pretty good idea why Avninder had been brusque when they came in. He seemed to be searching for words, but his daughter beat him to it.

She said, "Other FBI agents stopped by, and my father explained that he himself made the Secretary's sandwiches—she was a longtime, valued customer, who came into the shop at times."

"I knew all about her allergy," her father said. "I told the agents, and someone from the FBI today who called, and I told him, too. She was a fine lady and I looked out for her."

Rogers asked, "You made the sandwich yourself that day?"

"I did. As always."

"It's not possible you were busy, and someone else stepped in to do it, maybe someone who didn't know about the allergy and made a mistake?"

"No! Impossible."

Rogers didn't press it further. "All right," she said. "Did the FBI agents ask you about the other deliveryman the day of the tragedy?"

Avninder shook his head as if trying to clear it. He said, "What are you talking about? For over a year now, Glenn delivered the Secretary her sandwich every day. *What* other deliveryman?"

Rogers said, "Someone substituted for Glenn that day."

The old man swiped the air with a dismissive hand. "No, you are misinformed. Glenn took it as always."

On her cell, Rogers brought up Miggie's security still showing the alternate deliveryman and showed it to Avninder.

Nodding as he looked at it, Avninder insisted, "As I said, Glenn . . ." Then his voice trailed off.

Veena stepped forward, looked at the photo. "That's *not* Glenn," she confirmed. "There's a resemblance, but that's definitely not Glenn."

Rogers asked, "Do you know who it is? Someone else here? Someone who fills in?"

Veena shook her head, then turned to Avninder. "Papa?"

He said, stiffly, ridiculously proud, "I have never seen this person before."

"So, then," Hardesy said, "how did he end up delivering the Secretary her fatal lunch?"

They both shrugged, then looked at each other and shrugged again.

"No idea," Veena said.

"I have no idea also," her father said, at her side.

Rogers exchanged grim glances with Hardesy.

She'd be calling Reeder soon to tell him he was right—Amanda Yellich's death had been no accident. The Secretary of the Interior, a *cabinet member*, had likely been assassinated . . . with everyone writing off her death as just a tragic accident . . .

And the one man who could shed any light on this affair was in surgery in Baltimore, possibly about to die from a gunshot wound for which she and Hardesy were responsible.

Avninder seemed surprised when Rogers and Hardesy ordered two sandwiches and ate them at one of the little tables. They were delicious and, anyway, a deal was a deal.

"When even one American—who has done nothing wrong—is forced by fear to shut his mind and close his mouth—then all Americans are in peril."

Harry S. Truman, thirty-third President of the United States of America. Served 1945–1953.

FIVE

Alone in his Georgetown office at ABC Security—a surprisingly modest space for a CEO—Reeder went over the information on the thumb drive he'd received from President Harrison.

The security firm now took all four floors of the nondescript 1990s-era building they'd moved into a decade ago, occupying space that had sat empty ever since the microfiche company that erected it went belly up. Reeder was constantly pressured by his business associates to upgrade, embarrassed as they were that the home office was shabby compared to the branch ones; but he was comfortable here.

Right now he sat at an old-fashioned oak desk with a window to his back; to his left was a wall of manuals and studies with trophies and awards serving as bookends. The wall opposite was engulfed by a video monitor, and to his right the remaining wall was given to a couch under a surprisingly small but nonetheless client-pleasing display of his national magazine covers and the famous photo of him taking a bullet for a president (who he just as famously hadn't liked).

He was leaning back in his oversize black-leather ergonomic office chair, one of his few indulgences, his gaze fixed on his desk's video monitor. After a third time through the thumb drive, he still had not found one damn thing of real interest.

Included were individual files for each of the missing-presumed-dead CIA operatives, a copy of the President's directive that no one be sent to Azbekistan, and incident reports that detailed prior actions of lead agent Jacob McMann and his longtime partner, William Meeks. The two analysts, Vitor Gorianov and Elizabeth Gillis, were not regulars in McMann and Meeks' circle, but had occasionally worked with them.

McMann and Meeks were good, very good, and none of their previous missions cast any light on why they might have been deemed expendable. But in being ordered to Azbekistan, four top operatives—including Gillis, an exceptional young talent (judging by her file)—appeared to have been knowingly sacrificed.

What other explanation was there, for some unknown party in government intentionally disobeying the orders of the President of the United States? If pawns were needed, why not send less competent agents, to accomplish the same goal?

The answer was obvious: using more clearly expendable people—a mix of inexperienced rookies and burned-out operatives—might have raised troubling red-flag questions. On the other hand, top-flight agents, lost on a mission, would only fan the flames more.

And somebody wanted a conflagration.

After letting his secretary know that he'd be mostly out of pocket for an unspecified period, Reeder left to take a meeting scheduled at Langley. The stone wall at the Agency had gone up fast and high, but thanks to the direct intervention of the President himself, CIA Director Richard Shaley had made himself available this afternoon for a one-on-one meeting. Imagine that.

The Director was seated behind his desk when a male secretary ushered Reeder in. The large office was a study in cherrywood, its rich walls sparsely decorated, almost surprisingly so, although a large framed American flag under glass rode one of the walls, as did the CIA emblem.

Reeder was shown to one of two oversize rust-colored, well-padded visitor chairs.

Behind the Director and on the right side wall were floor-to-ceiling windows whose blinds were semi-shut, providing a surreal view of the Langley campus. The massive, carved mahogany desk—its glass top free of anything but a banker's lamp and two fancy pens in holders—was of another era; but then of course so was Shaley.

An angled ceiling light shone down on the CIA chief, bathing him in an almost divine glow but not reflecting off his mostly bald dome. Meanwhile, the lighting on the guest side of the desk was about the wattage of your average garage door opener. The arrangement was rather obviously meant to intimidate, and Reeder supposed it worked a good deal of the time, particularly with subordinates.

But Reeder didn't work here, and in any case didn't intimidate easily.

The Director was on the phone. His side of the conversation was "yes," "no," and finally, "See that you do." No state secrets were shared.

When Shaley had hung up, he said, "What is it you want, Mr. Reeder? The President asked me to squeeze you in, and I've done so. But I encourage you not to waste my time—as you may have heard, I'm not one to suffer fools."

"Then you'll be relieved to hear I'm no fool," Reeder said. "For example, when I sink down into a well-stuffed chair like this, I know it's not for my comfort but about putting you at a higher level."

The Director sat back and folded his arms. "I have you scheduled for fifteen minutes, Mr. Reeder, and then I have important things to get to."

Reeder crossed his legs but left his arms unfolded. "Fine. Let's start with whether you've accomplished what the President requested of you this morning—do we know who sent your people . . . *our* people . . . to their deaths?"

"If I knew, Mr. Reeder, I'd have reported as much to the President, and you wouldn't be here." His eyes were hooded behind the wire-frame glasses, his mouth an expressionless line. "So what's the function of this visit? Are you running point for the White House? My understanding is that you are out of government."

"I'm here, Director Shaley, because—like you—I serve at the pleasure of the President."

The Director's gaze was cool, but Reeder could tell the man was boiling. "Mr. Reeder, I don't care to be hounded. I have a duty to perform and I'm doing it. It would seem to me your presence here is a sort of . . . veiled threat from the President. Meaning neither him nor you any disrespect, I assure you I know how to do my job."

Reeder didn't let any irritation come to the surface. All those years standing post with the President paid off at times like this.

He said, "Meaning *you* no disrespect, Director Shaley, I have a job to do, too—again, at the bidding of the President. Call it running point if you like. I see it more as fact-finding, and passing along whatever information you may find . . . or have found."

Tiny eyes flared large behind the lenses. "It sounds as if the President is asking me to report to *you*—a civilian."

"If it helps, think of me as a consultant to the FBI—a liaison between two great government agencies."

Shaley shifted in his black tufted-leather chair; maybe it was ergonomic, too. "I've personally checked all the deployment orders for McMann's team."

"And you've found . . . ?"

"Just that those orders were routed through the encrypted in-house e-mail of every single senior agent, including myself."

"But who sent it?"

Shaley looked suddenly very small behind the big desk—one of the most powerful men in government, facing a situation that seemed almost certain to end his career.

"According to our top computer techs," he said, "all of us did."

Reeder mulled it a few moments. Then: "Was somebody just covering his trail? Or is this a statement someone is making? A message that makes you out to be the very kind of fool you don't suffer?"

If the grandfatherly figure was offended by that, it didn't show. "I haven't the slightest idea," he admitted.

"Let's come at this from another angle. Who working in the Company might see a benefit from starting a war with Russia? Motivation, monetary or political."

Shaley shrugged, sighed deep. "Again, I have no idea. You say you're on a fact-finding mission. Well, that's all we *do* here. Apolitically. Our job is to try to know what our potential adversaries in this precarious world are up to. When we're at war, our job shifts, in a way gets easier. Whoever is shooting at our people, that's the adversary."

"Does narrow it down," Reeder said.

"No one here I know of stands to benefit directly," Shaley said. "Not unless they've been bought."

"There's another possibility."

"Enlighten me."

"I said 'monetary or *political*.' This could be somebody with a political agenda who has infiltrated your agency—acting either for himself or as someone's agent."

The Director's eyes narrowed to slits, and there was nothing grandfatherly in his tone now. "Whichever is the case," he said, "we will find that traitor, and I intend to deal with him in my own way."

Reeder held up a cautionary palm. "Not to tell you how to do your job, but I'd keep in mind that your infiltrator will have valuable knowledge. So you might hold off on terminating this party with the customary extreme prejudice."

Shaley nodded. "I will keep that in mind. Now, Mr. Reeder—if you don't mind . . . as you might imagine . . . I have things to do."

Nodding, rising, Reeder said, "I might be able to help you, Director. I have some very good computer techs at ABC, and I also have access to the best computer man at the FBI."

Shaley gave up a mirthless laugh. "Even if I wanted to, Mr. Reeder, I couldn't give you access to internal CIA computer records. And if you had a court order, you know I'd only give you so much horseshit."

"I know," Reeder said, grinning, "but it never hurts to ask."

The slightest smile traced Shaley's lips. "Joe . . . if I might . . . I respect you—you're a genuine American hero. For all I know, you may just be window dressing in Harrison's effort to make this mess go away . . . but this is *our* screwup, the Agency's . . . and we'll fix it."

"Okay, Dick . . ." Reeder could be familiar, too. ". . . but four of your people are dead, and already *were* before you even knew they were in the field."

Shaley said nothing. His eyes were tight, and his hands were fists. And here they'd just started getting along . . .

"I'm just saying, Mr. Director, if you need me, call. Maybe I can do you a favor . . . like help to see your place in history isn't how you paved the way for World War III."

Leonard Chamberlain and Reeder went back a couple of decades. Graying now, soft around the middle, Chamberlain had been called back to Langley and retired to the elephant's graveyard of desk jobs. Back in the day, Chamberlain had been a top field agent, especially during his stint in Eastern Europe; but a stray bullet in Bosnia had ended that part of Chamberlain's career and left him with paperwork and a limp.

Back in DC, Reeder pulled into a convenience store parking lot and got out his cell, scrolling down to Chamberlain in his contacts. He'd considered trying to see his friend while at Langley, but thought better of it. If they met, it should be on Reeder's turf.

The CIA agent picked up on the fourth ring. "Human Resources, Chamberlain."

"Since when are you human?"

"Hi, Joe."

"You can guess why I'm calling, huh?"

"Yeah."

"You know anything?"

"I might."

"Can you be a little more vague?"

"Given where I am right now, is this something you want to discuss on an open cell signal?"

"Best not. Where and when can we talk then?"

"Remind me. Where was that place Superman used to go to chill out?"

"North Pole."

"I'll meet you there in an hour. Dress warm. And keep a sharp lookout for polar bears—the few that escaped climate change."

His old friend was referring to Arlington National Cemetery, Reeder's own personal Fortress of Solitude.

"Will do, Len. And touch base where?"

"Main Street," Chamberlain said.

Main Gate.

"See you there," Reeder said.

In the convenience store, Reeder got himself a bottle of water and, back in the car, sat and sipped at it. His friend knew something or they wouldn't be meeting.

Don't get ahead of yourself, he thought. *Might be nothing.*

But if so, why the precautions?

He was about to start the car when his cell trilled—ROGERS in the caller ID.

She said, "I've got some news on the Yellich thing."

"Good."

"Maybe not . . . but it does indicate you were right."

A wave of something bordering on nausea swept through him—he was pleased she'd found something, but . . . *had Amanda been murdered? Really murdered?*

She filled him in about taking down Glenn Willard, making an accidental major dope bust, and following up with the sandwich shop owner and his daughter.

"So," Rogers said, "it's evident that your friend's death is a homicide. But much more than that, we don't know. Our delivery boy is still unconscious. Lost a lot of blood. And the substitute delivery boy we have no line on. So—how was *your* day?"

He told her about it, holding nothing back—he rarely did, with Patti.

"So," she said, "you're consulting for the President now."

"Yeah, I'm big shit. Hey, I may need to borrow Miggie, if you can arrange it."

"Given who you're working for, I don't see a lot of trouble with that."

"Patti, it can't be common knowledge who my new boss is."

"Then maybe we shouldn't talk about it over an un-secure line. As soon as Hardesy and I are able to interview Willard, I'll get back to you."

"That's a loop I need to be kept in," he said, thanked her, then clicked off.

As he drove the short distance to Arlington, Reeder couldn't help but wonder: *Who the hell would want Amanda Yellich dead?* Secretaries of the Interior didn't normally make the kind of enemies who wanted them permanently gone. He was still mulling that when he parked in the parking lot near the Arlington Cemetery metro stop.

Chamberlain had been circumspect on the phone and Reeder expected the veteran agent would act the same way in getting here.

Taking public transportation, most likely, where you could spot or shake a tail more easily than in a car.

Reeder walked across the street to the main entrance of Arlington National Cemetery. A frequent visitor for years, he had requested and received free access to the cemetery as his only perk for taking that bullet for President Bennett. In the years since, he had spent part of almost every single day here, usually early mornings before the public had entry. When he was after serenity, this is where he came.

Today, the cemetery would provide not only serenity, but security, keeping him and Chamberlain at a good distance from listening devices or prying ears.

Reeder looked back toward the metro station, then checked his watch. He figured Chamberlain should be coming up the stairs any time now.

Then almost as if Reeder had willed it, Chamberlain stepped out of the shadows of the station and onto the sidewalk. The two men made eye contact, but gave no greeting, no indication at all of recognition. Reeder, in fact, stepped back into the shadow of a nearby evergreen.

Chamberlain started across the street, his limp even more pronounced than Reeder remembered—time hadn't been a friend to the man, who also looked heavier since their last get-together. The CIA agent was about halfway across the street when a black GMC crossover sped east on Memorial Avenue, gaining momentum, engine roaring, the vehicle bearing down like a big ebony bullet.

Chamberlain saw it, too, and tried to get out of the way . . .

"*Len!*"

. . . but his bad leg wasn't having any.

Reeder came running out onto the sidewalk by the main entrance, his hand instinctively slapping his hip where the gun he no longer carried used to be.

The car hit Chamberlain hard on the left side and propelled him like a man shot from a cannon, the already broken body smacking off the roof of the car as it flew by; bouncing off, the agent landed on the pavement with a sickening squish, and it would have hurt like hell if he'd still been alive.

In the middle of the street now, Reeder tried to catch the license plate number, as the vehicle squealed off toward George Washington Memorial Parkway; but the GMC had no plates—not surprising. He'd seen a driver and a passenger as the killing car blurred by, but he got a good look at neither, though they appeared to be male.

Several citizens were already on their cells calling 911, so Reeder didn't bother. Instead he got out his phone and punched in Rogers' number. She didn't pick up.

He wove his way into the street through the small crowd of gawkers and finally stopped for a look down at the twisted, broken thing that just minutes ago had been Leonard Chamberlain. The man's skull was smashed, exposing part of the brain that had held information meant for Reeder.

He stood there staring down at his dead friend, his fists clenching and unclenching, making a promise to the dead man, though Reeder's face gave nothing away—he'd trained it not to. But within him motors were turning and guts were churning.

Someone was monitoring Reeder's calls—someone who knew enough about him to see through the Fortress of Solitude reference that translated to Arlington National Cemetery. Someone who'd sent assassins to wait for them when they tried to meet.

Assassins who might have taken Reeder down, too, if Chamberlain hadn't provided such an easy target.

Or maybe not.

Reeder knew that the hit-and-run slaying of a national hero—however much that designation might annoy and irritate him—would attract much more attention than the "accidental" death of a washed-up CIA agent . . . from the media, from the cops, even from the government . . .

Still, the longer this went, the deeper the shit got, and the more likely Reeder himself would become a target. He needed at least to make sure he wasn't an easy one.

Sirens sang their banshee song as he got in his Prius, with no intention of dealing with cops. He would throw away his cell, but not until he had another. Even if someone was tracking him, he didn't want to be cut off from the world.

Back on the other side of the Potomac, he drove past the Navy Yard and parked across from a two-story brick building on Tenth, just off M Street. The pawnshop and tailor still occupied the first floor, but Reeder wasn't here to hock something or to buy a new suit, either.

DeMarcus Shannon, who lived and worked out of the second-floor loft, was a purveyor of products for buyers who wished both anonymity and discretion. The catch was that his business was cash only, but his customers preferred it that way, too.

After making sure the neighborhood seemed clear of surveillance— or black cars that might take a sudden run at him—Reeder headed across and climbed the metal stairs on the north side of the building. When he got to the fire-escape-style landing, he was greeted by a steel door and a video camera.

After some pissing and moaning from a seller who got nervous when the buyer was a cop of sorts, Reeder handed two hundred in twenties through the cracked-open door, and two cell phones were passed out to him. Then DeMarcus opened the door a little wider.

He was a slender, shaved-headed African American who looked younger than his thirty-some years; maybe it was the Washington Wizards warm-ups.

DeMarcus eyed Reeder warily. "You got yourself in the shit again?"

"Only waist-high, so far. Still . . . probably wouldn't hurt if you took a long weekend out of town."

The seller's eyes and nostrils flared like a rearing horse's. "I *knew* I shouldn't do bidness with you!"

Reeder got another hundred out, then a hundred more, and handed the bills over. Then he passed the phones back to the seller. "Put your number in both of 'em. I'll call you when it's safe."

As DeMarcus added a number to the contacts list of each cell, he asked, "What if you don't call?"

Reeder said, "If I don't call, I'll be dead, and it won't matter."

Back in the car, Reeder called Rogers. Again she didn't pick up but he left the new number. He started up the Prius.

He had people to warn.

"No man is worth his salt who is not ready at all times to risk his well-being, to risk his body, to risk his life, in a great cause."

Theodore Roosevelt, twenty-sixth President of the United States of America. Served 1901–1909.

SIX

Patti Rogers, behind the wheel, didn't pick up either call that came in. When she and Lucas Hardesy parked in the ramp at MedSTAR Trauma Center, she finally checked and saw Reeder had tried but left no voice mail. The other number she didn't recognize, but the caller had left a message. As Rogers and her colleague walked toward the main hospital building, she checked it.

"This number ASAP," Reeder's voice said. As usual there was nothing to find in his tone; a man whose specialty was reading people didn't give much for others to work with. But to her the clipped brevity of it spoke volumes.

Reeder had more than one cell phone, and she knew (or thought she knew) them all; but she had never seen this number before.

To Hardesy, she said, "Go ahead on in—I'll be a minute."

Noting her checking her cell, he asked, "Something?"

"Reeder."

"Cool," he said with a nod and kept walking.

On the grass near the sidewalk to the entrance, she punched in the unknown number. Reeder answered on the first ring.

"What's up, Joe?"

His answer was as long as her question was short: the old friend who was CIA, the scheduled meeting at the Fortress of Solitude, the car that had run his friend down, a description of the vehicle and where it was headed. She promised to do what she could.

"But, Joe—this is obviously a professional hit. If we or the locals manage to find the car, it's not likely it'll lead anywhere."

"No argument. It's almost certainly stolen, and'll be abandoned somewhere—with maybe a piece of lint for the forensics guys to work with."

"You're calling on a burner phone."

"Right. I tossed mine. They must have tracked my call to Len—it's the only way that could have gone down. So hold onto this number. For now."

"Jesus, Joe. What the hell's next?"

"Oh, not much. Just keep the President happy and figure out who sent four Americans to their death to foster a war between us and Russia. Same-oh, same-oh."

"Oh, Joe." The phone in her hand was shaking. "This is . . . I mean, we've been through a lot, but . . ."

"I don't mean to involve you beyond some simple law enforcement stuff. This call is just a heads-up."

"But, Joe, if the entire CIA is flummoxed by this thing, how can you . . . ?"

"Don't know," he admitted. "I may have to fall off the grid and go underground for a while."

"I wish there was something more I could say than just . . . be careful."

"*You* be careful, Patti. Remember, these pricks didn't come after me—they took my friend Len Chamberlain out."

"And . . . you think they might try to hurt you through—"

"The people I care about, yes. Consider yourself warned. I'm on my way to try to talk Melanie and Amy into disappearing for a while."

His ex-wife and daughter.

"Okay," she said, "so I'm warned. Do what you need to, but remember to call me in off the bench if need be."

They ended the call.

Hardesy was waiting for her near the information desk. He eyed her as she approached. "You okay?" he asked.

She shrugged. "Reeder. Some problems he's dealing with."

"Such as?"

She gave him the short version, which did not include the reason for Reeder meeting with his old buddy at the cemetery. The mission for the President was not to be general knowledge.

"Christ," Hardesy said, eyebrows high. "Chamberlain was a CIA guy, huh?"

"Just a desk jockey. But they always have histories, those people. So where's Willard?"

"Upstairs. ICU."

They walked to the elevator.

She asked, "How is he?"

"Out of surgery. Awake, I'm told."

They got off the elevator, took an endless corridor walk to the ICU, pushed through the double doors. Glenn Willard was just two rooms down. As advertised, the suspect was awake, hooked to an IV and several monitors, propped up slightly in a bed, a thin white blanket covering him, though where he'd been shot, the bandages made a mound. As they came in, a middle-aged nurse, taking his vitals, gave them an accusatory look.

Holding up her credentials, Rogers said, "FBI," for the benefit of both caregiver and care-given.

The patient, getting his blood pressure taken at the moment, goggled at Hardesy. To the nurse, he said, "That's the asshole who shot me!"

The nurse gave Hardesy a glare, and the agent casually said, "That's who I am, all right. And he's the asshole who drew down on a federal agent."

Now the nurse seemed nervous and she finished up and got out, never having spoken a word. Rogers and Hardesy stood on opposite sides of the patient's bed. The patient looked alert enough.

"Getting shot over some damn dope," Willard complained. "Not even *real* drugs. Stupid."

"We're in agreement," Hardesy said.

"That's not why we're here," Rogers said. "And it's not why we were at your apartment today either."

Willard frowned in confusion. "Then why *did* you come around?"

"We wanted to talk to you about Secretary Yellich. We still do."

"Well, she's dead, right? Heard about that. She was nice, always . . . cheerful, tipped good. Too bad. But what's it got to do with me?"

Hardesy said, "You delivered food to her regularly."

"Yeah. So? Look, I know she was important. Secretary of the Interior, right? Whatever that is."

Rogers asked, "Did you know she had an allergy to sesame?"

"No. I don't make sandwiches, I just deliver them. Like I said, she was a nice lady, kind of foxy for being that old. We joked around and stuff. I liked her. I'm sorry she died. You should check at the sandwich shop, if that's what killed her."

"Thanks for the advice," Hardesy said.

Willard shifted in bed and made a pained face. With Rogers on one side and Hardesy on the other, he had to work a little. They meant him to.

"Hey," he said. "Five days a week I delivered her a damn sandwich and some chips. We exchanged, you know, pleasantries. I gave her lunch and she gave me the money with a twenty-five percent tip. That's the whole story."

Rogers said, "You didn't deliver her sandwich *every* day."

"Sure I did."

"Not the day she died."

"I didn't?"

Hardesy leaned in menacingly. "Now is a bad time to play dumb."

"I'm not playing dumb!"

"Then you really *are* an idiot?"

Rogers gave her partner a quick look.

Willard was shaking his head. "Look, guys, they got me goofed up on pain meds, and most days I'm usually a little lit anyway, you know?"

Rogers said, "We made that leap."

"So for me, time sort of . . . runs together."

"Well," she said, "since you delivered the Secretary's lunch 'every day,' you surely must remember the *one* day you didn't."

His boyish features tightened in thought. "Well . . . I do. Didn't realize that was the day she bought it, but yeah—I remember it. Only, really, I *did* work that day."

Hardesy said, "Somebody else is on the security footage outside the Secretary's office. Much as I would like you to've delivered the fatal sandwich, Glenn, you didn't."

"Somebody took your place that day," Rogers said. "Who?"

Willard gestured with an open hand and tugged on his IV. "Like I said, I *did* work, but . . . my buddy Tony filled in for part of the day."

"Your buddy Tony who?"

"Tony Evans. Anthony Evans."

"Why did he fill in part of the day?"

"You know . . . I had stuff to do. This and that. Stuff."

"*Why* did he fill in, Glenn?"

He shifted in bed a little. "I don't think I want to answer that. Maybe . . . maybe it's time I lawyered up."

Hardesy said, "Might be at that, if we arrest you on an accessory to murder charge."

That got Willard's attention. He managed to sit up some. "I'm no accessory! I told you, I liked that lady. If Tony did something to her, I had nothing to do with it!"

Rogers said, "Then answer the question—why did Tony fill in for you part of the day?"

His eyes squeezed shut as if the pain had gotten worse; in a way, maybe it had. "All right, okay, all right. I had a chance to score some primo chronic at a crazy low price . . . but the guy selling it could only meet me at a certain time."

"Let me guess," Hardesy said. "The time you were supposed to deliver the Secretary's sandwich."

"Well, it was that time of day, yeah. I didn't remember that was *the* day that . . . that she, you know, died."

Rogers said, "So you got Tony to take your place. I would imagine you have lots of friends, Glenn. Why pick on Tony?"

Willard was shaking his head. "No, no, it wasn't that way—he volunteered."

"Volunteered?"

"Yeah, he did! Who do you think told me about the guy with the primo chronic?"

Rogers and Hardesy exchanged narrow-eyed looks.

"Your pal Tony," Hardesy said.

Willard nodded several times. "Tony did, yeah."

Rogers asked, "So tell us about the delivery."

Willard huffed a laugh. "What do you think? I met the guy, I bought the dope. The end."

"Not the dope, Glenn. The sandwich. The owner of the shop says *you* did your regular deliveries that day."

"Oh. Yeah, well. I didn't want to get on Mr. Avninder's bad side—he's a good boss, but he has a temper."

She nodded for him to continue.

"He'da been pissed if I didn't make that delivery myself, so I walked the sandwich out of the shop, gave Tony my Ye Olde jacket and hat, and a bag of sandwiches and chip packs, for lunch-hour delivery, with instructions . . . but not till I was around the corner from the shop. Then Tony made the deliveries, including the Secretary's lunch."

Only instead Tony had delivered murder.

Rogers asked, "How did you meet Tony?"

"He was a customer. I sold him a lid or two at a couple of dance clubs, you know, in the john. We got friendly. He started doing a little dealing himself and I helped him out."

"Did you approach him or vice versa?"

"Him me."

Rogers asked, "Where can we find your friend—Tony?"

"After what he's put me through," Willard said, "he's no friend of mine."

And gave them an address.

On the way back to the Ford, Rogers called Miggie and gave him Tony Evans. Minutes later, with her driving, Hardesy put Miggie on speaker.

"The Skygate Apartments address is right," Miggie said. "At least for the last three months, anyway."

"The guy just moved there?" Hardesy asked.

Miggie said, "Yeah, but the thing is, before three months ago?"

"Yeah?"

"I can't find any indication that this particular Tony Evans exists."

Rogers and Hardesy traded a look. "Thanks, Miggie. Keep digging."

"I brought a shiny new shovel, boss," he said, then clicked off.

Hardesy said, "What's your pal Reeder got us into? A cabinet member murdered, and it was put in motion *months* ago? This shit is getting serious."

"And deep."

They drove awhile.

Then Hardesy asked, "You suppose there's any chance this guy is still at Skygate?"

"Maybe, but I doubt it. I suppose if Evans wanted to keep an eye on Willard, yeah. The addresses are damn close. But after what happened this morning, if he's heard about it . . ."

"It's a long shot he's still around. By now, 'Tony Evans' may not exist."

She couldn't argue with that.

They swung by Skygate Apartments in a Hillcrest Heights neighborhood referred to by some residents as Marlow Heights, after the old shopping center that had long ago been replaced by Iverson Mall.

A vast complex of over a dozen matching three-story buildings fanned around a U-shaped parking lot on the north end, with a swimming pool in the bottom of the U. South of that, along Temple Lane, another dozen buildings squatted like Monopoly hotels all clustered onto one property.

Rogers pulled in near the pool. Night had settled in, but the parking lot fought back with streetlamps and nearby well-lit building entries. The two agents sat in the car and regarded the landscape before them, pool shimmer on their faces.

She said to Hardesy, "Look, even if there's little chance our man is here, we need to be more careful than we were with Willard."

"Yeah," Hardesy said. "That was my screwup."

"Not placing blame. But I'm serious."

He held her eyes with his gaze. "I'm serious, too, boss. Glenn's an asshole but I didn't love shooting him."

She could only smile. "You're going soft in your middle age, Lucas."

"Maybe you're a bad influence."

They got out of the car and crossed the parking lot to Evans' building.

"This time," Hardesy said with a disgusted smirk, "I *will* go in the back way."

Rogers nodded. "Second floor, remember. 211."

"See you there."

Then Hardesy disappeared around the corner of the building.

Unlike Willard's place, no security doors awaited them here. Rogers entered a vestibule with mailboxes on one wall, including one that said **EVANS**. To her left, stairs went up; to her right, stairs went down. She checked the first-floor stairwell, saw nothing, then silently climbed to the second floor, her hand on the butt of the Glock at her hip.

This guy might be a ghost who was already gone. Or he might be nobody, just a drug dealer who subbed for Willard, the sandwich dosed by somebody else. *Or he might be the assassin of the Secretary of the Interior of the United States . . .*

Her colleague came up the stairs at the opposite end of the corridor. They met at Evans' apartment. Each took a position on either side of the door, then traded nods. Rogers drew her gun while Hardesy used a pick and a tension wrench on the lock, which he defeated in under thirty seconds.

Hardesy took a step back and turned the knob slowly, then shouldered in.

The door swung open onto a tidy living room empty but for a camp chair and small TV. They moved in, cautious, quiet. The tiny dining area at right bore only a card table and two folding chairs. She wondered how Evans explained his spartan living conditions to his guests, if he had any. The kitchen beyond had no furnishings, but a coffee pot and a microwave rested on the counter. She edged into the room, opened a cupboard and, touching nothing, found a couple of packs of ramen noodles and a bottle of sesame oil.

Beyond the kitchen was a short hallway to a bathroom and the only bedroom.

Rogers pointed to the bathroom and Hardesy kept his gun trained on the bedroom door while she ducked into the john and almost immediately backed out.

Clear, she mouthed.

She turned her attention, and Glock, to the bedroom, too. *Was that breathing she heard?* She couldn't be sure—might be a breeze pulsing in an open window. Her eyes tightened and her spine stiffened as she eased the door open . . .

On the bed, a man lay spread-eagled on his stomach. He wore jeans and a red-and-black plaid flannel shirt. For a moment she couldn't tell whether or not he was breathing and her mind raced to what their next step would be if the guy was dead.

Then he snort-snored and Rogers almost laughed.

But instead, she said, "Tony Evans! Federal agents—stay as you are!"

"What the shit . . . ?" He started to push himself up, but Hardesy pushed him back down. Then the man in the plaid shirt decided to cooperate and flattened again.

Hardesy frisked him while she covered him.

"Guys!" the guy blurted. "I'm not Tony Evans!"

Hardesy said, "Then who's that sleeping in his bed, Goldilocks?"

The guy craned to look at Hardesy. "Look, dude, what I'm trying to say is, Tony isn't here. You're making a mistake."

"If you're not Evans," Rogers said, "who are you? Where's your identification?"

These appeared to be questions that were too tough for him. All he managed was, "Uh . . ."

"Okay," Hardesy sighed. "We'll sort it out at the Hoover Building."

Rogers put her Glock away and cuffed the prone man's hands behind him.

"I'm not Evans, I tell you! You're fucking up!"

"Somebody is," Hardesy said, and pulled the guy to his knees, hands cuffed behind him, and for the first time Rogers could see their man's face. He wasn't exactly a twin, but he had the same nondescript sort of features as Glenn Willard. The two might be brothers. Maybe he wasn't Tony Evans, but he sure as hell *was* the guy in the security video from outside Secretary Yellich's office.

Hardesy pulled him around and helped him to his feet beside the bed.

"I tell you, Tony's out. Me, I'm just crashing here."

Rogers read him his rights and advised him to use them, adding, "Shut up until we get you back to the Hoover Building. We'll straighten this out there."

They marched the guy out of the apartment and down the stairs to the front door. Rogers had him by the arm and Hardesy was right behind; both agents had their guns holstered now. They stepped outside and down the two stairs to the sidewalk, Hardesy's hand on the guy's arm, behind him but guiding him.

Halfway down the steps, a whipcrack split the night. The suspect tumbled awkwardly to the grass, and Hardesy threw himself at Rogers. With her partner piled on top of her, she was sandwiched facing the man who'd been calling himself Tony Evans. He now had a dime-sized hole in his forehead and his empty eyes were more glazed than any drug could manage.

Getting out from under and to her feet—the dead man in the same spread-eagle posture he'd been in when they first saw him—Rogers scurried to the nearest parked car. Staying low, she called back to Hardesy, "Did you see where it came from?"

He nodded toward the cluster of buildings to the east, the other half of the complex. "Over there someplace!"

"Cover me," she said, and headed into the parking lot, keeping her head down, hugging the shadows, but knowing she'd given Hardesy an impossible job—the rifle shot had come from a good hundred yards away. He could neither cover for her nor effectively return the shooter's fire.

As she ran, keeping low, Glock in hand now, she focused on those buildings, watching for any sign of movement. The trajectory made a shot from a window at any height unlikely. Somebody had been in the bushes or flat-out stood there and fired, and maybe was already gone.

But no vehicle in the parking lot had taken off in the aftermath of the rifle fire.

Then she caught a corner-of-the-eye flash of navy blue—a person running toward the parking lot toward the far side of the complex!

She stopped short and ran hard in that direction. If the shooter made it to his vehicle this chase was over . . .

The distance between her and the navy-blue suspect wasn't narrowing but if he tripped or slipped, she had a chance. She was still a building and a half away when he got to the parking lot, where almost certainly his car would be close by.

She was near enough now to get something of a bead on him—an average-sized guy, black hair cut very close, an African American. He had the rifle in one hand, like a soldier charging up a hill. Then he came to a quick stop behind an older model Dodge and swung toward her, the rifle in two hands now, and pointing.

She threw herself to the pavement. The roar of a motor behind her brought her head up—Hardesy, in their vehicle, was closing fast on the Dodge! He was three car lengths away . . .

. . . when the shooter put one in the Ford's radiator.

She got to her knees and raised her Glock as the shooter worked to rack another cartridge, then the shooter again took aim at the Ford, which swerved and slowed, steam pouring from the hole in its grill.

The guy in navy blue was in her sights when he pulled the trigger at the same time she did, not aiming at her, rather at the oncoming vehicle. The sniper dropped out of sight—*she'd got him!*—but then he scrambled up into the Dodge. Then her eyes went to the spiderweb hole in the Ford's windshield.

The car rolled ever slower to bump up and over a curb, finally stopping.

"*Hardesy!*"

No answer.

Instinct kicked in and she sprinted toward their car, resting now in an apartment building yard on Temple Lane, headlights lancing through the night. In one final taunt, the Dodge gunned out of the parking lot.

Apparently she hadn't hit the shooter, after all.

Hardesy was already climbing out, looking a little shaken and a lot pissed off.

"Son of a bitch shot the Ford!" he roared.

"You all right?" she asked.

"Hell no, I'm not all right! Suspect is dead, shooter's in the wind, and the son of a bitch killed our car! Saving grace is, it's the taxpayers' money."

She let out a breath that was almost a laugh.

"I'm glad you're alive," she said somewhat breathlessly.

He grinned at her. "See how much better we're getting along these days?"

Then he called in a BOLO (Be On the Look Out) on the Dodge while she walked over to where the vehicle had been parked. She clicked on her small mag flashlight and pointed it down: two rifle cartridges lay on the pavement next to a quarter-sized drop of blood. So while she hadn't killed the shooter, she *had* hit him.

"Good," she said to herself.

Hardesy came over. "BOLO is up. He keeps that car, we'll get him."

She pointed at the blood on the ground.

"So you hit him! Atta girl. Meaning no sexist disrespect."

"None taken. The best part is, we have his DNA."

He nodded. "I'll get the word out to hospitals to look out for anyone seeking treatment for a gunshot wound."

"And I'll call in the evidence team . . . and talk to Miggie. Nobody knew we were coming here today but him. And I trust Miggie."

Hardesy was frowning. "Me, too. Obviously someone else set us up. But who, and how?"

"Miggie ran Evans in the computer. Somebody must be doing some electronic eavesdropping."

"Shit. That happened once before, if I remember."

"You remember correct. There are some people in our government who would appear not to be trustworthy."

"You mean, besides Congress?"

They both smiled at that, but not for long.

"Somebody," she said, "is trying to keep us from investigating Secretary Yellich's death."

Hardesy was shaking his head hard enough to clear cobwebs. "What the hell has Reeder got us into?"

Even if she could have told him about the presidential mission, Rogers didn't have an answer.

"Liberty may be endangered by the abuse of liberty,
but also by the abuse of power."

James Madison, fourth President of the United States of America. Served
1809–1817. Known as the "Father of the Constitution" for contributions
to the drafting of the US Constitution and the Bill of Rights.

SEVEN

Melanie Graham, the ex-Mrs. Joe Reeder, glared at the man she'd divorced, who still loved her.

"Jesus, Joe," she said, "when is *enough* going to be *enough*?"

He guessed that was a rhetorical question.

Slender, she was wearing her brown hair very short these days, a change he regretted but hadn't commented on. Her brown eyes burned into him and her teeth were bared, her upper lip curled back.

Okay, so she was pissed at him—at least she still cared.

"You're a very successful businessman," she said, biting off words, "and you're not a kid, and yet you insist on getting yourself involved in these dangerous fixes and then everybody in your life has to uproot themselves for God knows how long until you sort the crap out and try not to get yourself *killed.*"

She didn't get raving mad like this very often, but when she did, Reeder knew there was nothing he could say. He tried anyway: "I'm on a mission for the President—"

"The President! *The President!* How many years, how many damn decades, did I have to hear about one president or another whose life was more important than ours! Goddamnit, Joe, I'm still *tied* to you! We might as well still be married!"

He wouldn't have minded that—normally.

She raved on: "How am I supposed to explain this to Donald? That we're to pick up and pack up and go running somewhere and hide?"

The reference was to her current husband, Donald Graham, a lobbyist. Reeder was standing in what had been Graham's house and was now Melanie's as well. The framed landscapes that were scattered around the room, the floral sofa, the antique table lamps, were all touches his ex-wife had brought to what had been Graham's male domain.

Firm but without anger, Reeder said, "We don't have the luxury of this argument right now. I *said* this was serious."

"It's *always* serious!"

"Not this serious. Just hours ago, they killed Len Chamberlain right in front of me."

About to speak, she froze, her mouth half-open as she processed that. Then: "Not *Len* . . . he was . . . CIA wasn't he?"

"He was. Just a desk jockey these days, but he was doing me a favor. We were about to meet outside the main entrance to ANC when he got taken down by a hit-and-run. Do I have to say it was no accident?"

"Oh, Joe . . . oh my God, Joe . . ." Her eyes softened as her voice trailed off, the back of her hand at her cheek in a loose fist.

"Here's the bad part."

"The *bad* part?"

"Len and I talked only once on the phone, with no direct mention of where we were meeting. The only way someone could have known where we'd be was if they are tapping my phone, *and* know my habits."

"That . . . that could have been *you*," she said, her voice small. She took a tiny step toward him and he caught a whiff of her favorite perfume, Magie Noire. His favorite, too.

He put his hands on her shoulders, gentle though strong. "But it *wasn't* me. In fact, they made no effort to get me, and I was right there for the taking. Len shouldn't have been a threat to anyone these days, just playing out his string in Langley, waiting for retirement."

Her eyes were narrow now in tightened sockets. "Why not go after you, if they had you in their sights?"

He dropped his hands from her shoulders. "I don't really know. Possibly they'd already decided on Len, and knew that a hit-and-run death might be written off, whereas taking me down, too, would make it murder."

She stared past him. "And now you're on the run, keeping a low profile, which means . . ."

"Whoever-this-is might come after my family, whether for leverage or to make me mad enough to come at them straight on, which they'd be confident they could handle."

Her eyes swung back to him, wide with alarm. "Tell me you at least had sense enough to handle Amy and Bobby first!"

Melanie meant their daughter Amy, a junior at Georgetown, and her live-in boyfriend, Bobby, who her middle-of-the-road Democrat dad considered half a communist.

He nodded. "She and Bobby are off to—"

She held up a hand. "Don't tell me where, just that they're safe."

"They're safe. An ability to make that happen is one of the perks of having real money."

She sighed, calming herself. "And now you're here. And Don and I get an unscheduled vacation."

"All expenses paid," he said, risking a little smile. "Look, Len and I were circumspect when we talked . . . but they were waiting for us, anyway. It doesn't get more deadly serious than this, Mel. I need to know the people I love are safe. And, uh . . . I'll need that package I left with you."

Nodding, her expression somewhat dazed, she said, "Donald's study. Come along."

He followed her out of the living room and down a corridor toward the back of the house, past the dining room to a closed door.

Melanie led him inside. No feminine touches here—the dark-paneled, book-lined study was strictly male: wall-mounted flat-screen that overpowered the small room, a two-seater black-leather sofa, a massive oak desk that a window must have been removed to get in.

To one side of the window behind the desk was a painting of the Capitol that at Melanie's touch swung open on unseen hinges to reveal a wall safe. She twirled the dial and soon was withdrawing one of two side-by-side brown-paper-wrapped packages about the size of two bricks.

She handed it over to Reeder, who hefted the thing, then said, "You should take the other one for you and Donald."

She pulled out a second bundle. "How much is there?"

"Two hundred each."

"How far will *that* go?"

"Two hundred thousand."

The dark eyes flared. "Four hundred thousand dollars, and you kept it in a wall safe in our house?"

He managed a weak smile. "Turned out to be a pretty good plan, didn't it?"

She found her own small smile. "It's hard to hate a man who has two hundred thousand dollars tucked away for you."

"Here's that rainy day," he said. "How soon can you and Donald get out of here?"

"If I can get a hold of him . . . probably . . . three hours?"

"Make it faster, if you can. But leave the house casually, okay? Load up the suitcases in the garage, and no word to the neighbors."

She nodded.

"Thanks, Melanie, and . . . I'm sorry. I really am sorry."

She glared at him, and then touched his cheek.

"I hate you," she said.

But it sure sounded like, *I love you.*

Reeder, pondering his next move, had been back in the car maybe five minutes when the first burner phone made itself known.

Only one person had the number.

"We need to talk," Rogers said.

When was a woman saying that to a man good news?

He said, "Something wrong?"

"Just meet us."

"'Us' sounds like more than just you."

"Hardesy's with me."

"Does he know what he's signing on for?"

"Do we?"

Good point.

He said, "Where do you want to meet?"

"Falls Church. Mexican place named Los Primos on Lee Highway—know it?"

"I'll find it."

East of the Capital Beltway on Lee Highway, Los Primos was tucked away in a strip mall across the street from a warren of condos. The place looked to be less than half full, the dinner rush pretty much over.

Ceramic tile on the floor, Mexican music on the sound system, and a couple of cactus plants gave the place its contrived air of authenticity. Rogers and Hardesy were at a table toward the back. When the hostess smiled at him, Reeder nodded toward his friends and went on by her. She trailed him back to the table, one side of which Rogers and Hardesy shared. He sat opposite.

They declined menus and Reeder ordered Chiapas, black. Rogers already had coffee, Hardesy a Modelo. They waited in silence until Reeder's cup came.

He had already noted, on the shoulder of Rogers' jacket, the smudge of blood. Someone else might have thought she'd just spilled something on her navy-blue suit. Somebody had spilled something, all right.

"Whose is it?" Reeder asked her.

But Hardesy answered: "The recently late Tony Evans."

The name meant nothing to Reeder and he said so.

Hardesy added, "He's the delivery guy who brought Secretary Yellich the sandwich that disagreed with her."

"Did he know that was what he was doing?"

Reeder's expression said, *Murdering her?* This was a public place.

Rogers shrugged and said, "Too early to tell for sure, but we did find sesame oil in his apartment."

Quietly Reeder asked, "How did his blood end up on your jacket?"

Just as quietly she told him.

The booths on either side of them were vacant, and the people at the table behind them were leaving. When they'd gone, Reeder asked, "A *sniper* was waiting?"

She glanced around the restaurant herself, then softly said, "Joe, they knew where we'd be, and that we were there to pick up Evans."

Reeder considered the possibilities. "Who on our side knew where you were going?"

Hardesy said, "Only Altuve. *Just* Altuve."

"Miggie's true blue," Reeder said, shaking his head. "But remember—he *did* get hacked in the J. Edgar Hoover Building last year. Maybe that happened again." His eyes went to Rogers. "Or it could be the people who were tracking my cell were . . . *are* . . . also tracking yours."

"Why track Patti's cell?" Hardesy asked.

Reeder said, "Who else would I get in touch with in a tough spot? Who else do I trust?"

"Okay," Hardesy said, frowning, "so you two are tight. But what made a target out of our suspect?"

"Somebody tidying up, maybe," Reeder said. His eyes traveled from Hardesy to Rogers. "Could the shooter have meant to hit one of you instead?"

Rogers shook her head and so did Hardesy.

"Trust me," she said. "That sniper hit the bull's-eye."

Reeder thought for a moment. "What do you know about your suspect?"

She filled him in.

After she'd finished, he said, "With DNA results from the shooter's blood, and/or fingerprints on the shell casings, we may soon know more."

Rogers sipped coffee. Hardesy swigged Modelo.

She asked, "Just what the hell is going on here, Joe?"

"I don't know," he admitted. "What do a poisoned Secretary of the Interior, four dead field agents, an assassinated delivery boy, and a murdered CIA desk jockey add up to?"

Hardesy had no answer, but he did have a question: "Who has the high-tech capability and inside knowledge to tap your phone and/or hack Miggie's computer?"

Rogers took that one. "Someone in the government," she said. "That's what happened last year—a mole who was part of that would-be coup."

"You're right," Reeder said. "And we stopped that coup, but there could be other moles. A lot more."

Rogers cocked her head, which was a question in itself.

"Suppose," Reeder said, "we're dealing with a shadow government. A faction, a large one, within the government."

Hardesy grunted a laugh, then looked across at Reeder and saw the man wasn't laughing. Not at all.

"Since last year," Reeder said, "when that mole hacked Miggie, our cyber-defenses have been improved. But we're still at our most vulnerable to . . . who was it said, *The Enemy Within*?"

Though Rogers was slowly nodding, Hardesy was shaking his head. "This is crazy," he said. "That mess last year has softened your skulls. You're talking conspiracy-nut nonsense."

She said, "The Secretary of the Interior was murdered, as we've established. But till we waded in, there'd been virtually no investigation. Did somebody make sure of that?"

Hardesy kept shaking his head.

Reeder said, "Someone sent four top CIA agents to die in a country on the brink of war where the President himself had made it clear he did not want any American presence."

"Come on, Joe," Hardesy said, but he was weakening. "You know over at the Company the right hand doesn't know what the left hand is doing."

"But does the far right?" Reeder asked. "Or for that matter, the far left?"

Her eyes on Hardesy, Rogers said, "Then there's what happened with Joe's all-but-retired CIA friend . . . not to mention the suspect who got blood on my jacket. Face it, Lucas, only someone with *real* power could do that . . . someone on the inside."

"Not *one* someone," Reeder corrected. "A group."

Hardesy held up his hands in what was not quite surrender. "Wait, guys, wait . . . what if there's no real connection between these events? What if it's all just a coincidence? Isn't it possible we're rushing to make the evidence fit a theory?"

Rogers smirked. "How many dead bodies add up to a coincidence in your book?"

Reeder said, "No, Patti, your friend Lucas here is right. We can't just jump to conclusions."

Her eyebrows went up. "You think *that's* what we're doing? Somebody assassinated a CIA agent right in front of you, and shot a suspect right next to me? And we're jumping to conclusions?"

"Easy, Patti," Reeder said, giving her the faintest smile. "We're both a little rattled by everything that's gone down today. We need to get our feet under us again."

She let out a breath, and nodded.

"If, for instance," Reeder continued, "Amanda was killed for reasons that have nothing to do with what's going on with the CIA . . . and we try to shove the two cases together . . . we could wind up chasing our tails, or worse."

"Worse?" she asked.

He nodded. "We could add to a climate leading to, no exaggeration, another world war."

That sent Hardesy's eyebrows up, but despite what Reeder had just said, Rogers seemed calmer now.

She said, "All right—you're the consultant, the voice of experience, the great American hero—what *should* we be doing?"

"Put Altuve on it. Once Mig realizes he may have been hacked, and can use other means to follow up, have him find out everything he can about Amanda . . . then you two chase down every lead. You may even learn that there's some *other* reason she was taken out."

Rogers was nodding. Then, after a beat, so was Hardesy.

"What's *your* next move?" she asked Reeder.

"The police've had enough time to look at what happened to Len Chamberlain and go through his effects. I want to know if they found anything. And are they viewing it as a traffic fatality or a murder."

"And if we do come up with something?"

"You go to AD Fisk and get your task force assigned to the case."

Rogers gazed at him with narrowed eyes. "I have Fisk. But you have the President. That's one hell of go-to-guy."

Reeder nodded. "He's promised me help, but so far all I can tell him is that someone I talked to on the phone got hit by a car. Not exactly the smoking gun he wants me to find."

"Okay," Rogers said, heaving a sigh. "For now, we dig separately."

Reeder said, "One more thing." He got in his suit coat pocket and handed her the other burner phone. "Use this."

"How scared do you want to make me?" she asked, only half-kidding.

"Very goddamn scared," he said, not kidding at all. "Because if we're right, and there's something big and nasty going on, killing us is easier than dealing with whatever we might find."

He finally sipped his coffee. It was stone cold.

An hour later, Reeder stood in the cool nighttime shadows beside an attached garage in Burke, Virginia. After leaving his car parked three blocks over, he'd taken a circuitous route through backyards and alleys, and felt sure no one was trailing him.

Pretty sure.

His clothes were all dark, a black watch cap concealing his distinctive white hair. Leaning against the side of the garage, he rubbed his hands and wished he'd brought gloves. There were stars, a lot of them, and no clouds, with the cooler temperatures they indicated. Finally he jammed his hands into his jacket pockets as he waited. He had no gun but was carrying his ASP telescoping baton, retracted to its 6.3-inch length, its diameter under an inch.

The quiet of the houses around him was broken by a dog's indignant barking up the block, then silence. Had the dog been roused by someone else on foot? But no one came along. He could see his breath, and was shifting from foot to foot when he saw headlights.

He moved deeper into the shadows. A few seconds later, the mechanical hum of a garage-door opener announced the rising of the door, and a black Chevy turned into the driveway. The vehicle slowed and eased inside next to a Toyota. Reeder stepped out of the darkness and inside, as the door lowered itself, its mechanics whirring, a single overhead light going on, automatically.

The garage was neatly arranged—a workbench along the right side wall, hanging yard tools opposite, shelves of boxed belongings at the far end on either side of an aluminum door to the backyard; three bikes hanging from the rafters, one each for the parents and one for a grown son now in college.

Reeder knew the owner, and this space, very well. He and his friend had often sat at the workbench talking sports, shooting the shit, and sipping beers out of the mini-fridge in a nearby corner. Now it held only Cokes.

Balding, beefy Carl Bishop, detective with the Homicide Bureau that covered the entire DC area, stepped out of his Chevy and reared back a little.

"Jesus, Peep!" Bishop said, finding Reeder right in front of him. "You wanna give me a heart attack, maybe get yourself shot?"

Bishop, a friend for over two decades, had for all that time used the nickname bestowed upon Reeder by his peers at the Secret Service, due to the then-agent's kinesics-schooled ability to read people. Reeder didn't like the moniker much, but pointing that out to longtime friends who used it seemed less than gracious.

"Tell you the truth, Bish," Reeder said, "getting shot is something I'm trying to avoid."

The homicide cop stood there, hands on his hips, in an unmade bed of a suit, his tie a loose noose the hangman hadn't tightened yet. The end, obviously, of another long day.

He said, "Skulking around dressed like a burglar, especially around an armed detective's domicile, does not seem like the best way to stay *un*-shot, Peep."

Reeder took off the watch cap and shrugged. "You call it 'skulking.' I call it waiting."

"To get *shot*," Bishop said, but he was already over his surprise and annoyance. "You want to come in and have a beer? I keep a few cans for my friends who aren't on the wagon." He shut the car door. "Stacy would love to see you."

Reeder doubted that—it was Melanie who'd been tight with Bishop's wife. The petite blonde was nice enough, but he hadn't seen her since the divorce.

"Not a good idea, Bish. This isn't a social call."

Bishop frowned, nodded, and ushered his friend to the workbench, where high-backed stools awaited. They sat facing each other, swung sideways at the bench, Bishop leaning an elbow and folding his hands.

Almost shyly, Reeder said, "I probably shouldn't even be here . . . but I needed to talk to you, away from your desk, and phones are out of the question right now."

"Just tell me, Peep."

"This is probably outside your sphere, but I need you to check up on a hit-and-run out at Arlington."

The detective's eyes widened and it didn't take a kinesics expert to read them. "You're shitting me."

Shaking his head, Reeder said, "No, there really was a hit-and-run out there, and—"

Raising a traffic-cop hand, Bishop said, "Peep, I know. I know. It's been all over the news."

"It has?"

"The hit-and-run itself didn't attract attention. But tourists got cell phone footage of FBI and Homeland agents at the site—two federal agencies send their people to a hit-and-run? That's news. No one is saying who got killed but—"

"Len Chamberlain," Reeder cut in.

The name meant nothing to Bishop. "You knew the guy?"

Nodding, Reeder said, "I saw it happen. He was CIA. The real deal, but lately just riding a desk. He was coming to Arlington to give me information about the slain US citizens in Azbekistan."

"Hell you say."

"Hell I say."

Bishop's expression would have seemed blank to most people, but not Reeder.

The detective said, "What can *I* do to help? You're talking high intrigue. I'm just a simple DC gumshoe. You were there—what did you tell the cops?"

"Nothing. I left. What could I give them that a dozen witnesses couldn't? And if Len was worth killing, then maybe I was a target, too."

Bishop's eyes were wide again. "Jesus, man. What about Melanie and Amy? These don't sound like people who would stop at much."

"They're safe."

"Good. Good." He took some air in, then let it out. "So . . . we're back to the beginning. What can I do to help?"

Reeder held Bishop's gaze. "I'm curious as to what evidence the cops took from the scene."

"And you want me to find out what that might be."

"*If* they found anything," Reeder said. "But be goddamn careful, Bish—the forces in play may already be responsible for the deaths of seven people."

A deep sigh. "Consider your point made, Peep. Look—was this guy Chamberlain bringing you a package? Is *that* what you hope to find?"

Reeder shrugged. "I hope to find anything that gives me some small piece of daylight. We set up the meeting textbook careful, yet Chamberlain is still wearing tire tracks. Whether he had something to tell me, or to give me, I have no idea. But us setting up a meet got somebody's attention enough to warrant killing Len."

Bishop grunted a non-laugh. "Great. Any advice for me?"

"Yeah. Watch your ass."

They just sat there for a moment.

Then Bishop said, "With the feds already on this, I may not be able to get you a damn thing, you know."

333

Reeder shook his head dismissively. "Don't sweat that. I've got people at the FBI who'll help me on that end. But I want to know if the local cops got anything before the feds shut them out."

Bishop was nodding. "I'll take care of it, Peep . . . *and* I'll watch my ass. Anything else I can do for you? We're full service here at Bishop Motors."

"Sure." Reeder slid off the stool. "Lock the door behind me. I'll go out the back and through the neighbors' yards."

As Reeder headed that way, Bishop followed, saying, "Fine, but be careful. The Smiths, three houses down, have a mouthy little blue heeler. It's penned up, but you might soil yourself if you're not expecting that kind of welcome."

"Yeah, I heard him earlier. Sounded like a bigger dog."

"No, just a little son of a bitch, but a big pain in the ass."

Reeder shot his friend an over-the-shoulder grin, his first in many hours, and ducked out into darkness.

"History and experience tell us that moral progress comes not in comfortable and complacent times, but out of trial and confusion."

Gerald R. Ford, thirty-eighth President of the United States of America. Served 1974–1977. The only person to serve as both Vice President and President of the United States without being elected to either office.

EIGHT

Patti Rogers, in her favorite gray suit with a black silk blouse beneath, strode with purpose into the Special Situations bullpen at the J. Edgar Hoover Building. Though she'd barely slept, Rogers had been up early, ready to go—or anyway, ready after grabbing a tall coffee from the Starbucks in the lobby of her apartment building.

First order of business: talk to the team's resident computer expert, Miggie Altuve, who was as good at his specialty as anybody the FBI had.

He was in the office next to hers, at the back, first in, the other desks empty. He was using his private tablet, not his work computer. The small space had windows onto the street, his door always open because he could focus in a hurricane, and anyway, he was always welcome for more input.

"Hey you," she said, strolling in without knocking on the jamb.

"Hey you," he said, not looking up.

While his razor-cut hair was "Werewolves of London"-perfect, his navy suit coat was already draped haphazardly over the back of his desk chair, the sleeves of his white shirt rolled up a couple turns. Formerly a pudgy nerd, Miguel Altuve had lost weight and ditched his wire-frame glasses, but inside this handsome, diminutive man a nerd still lurked. Right now his eyes were red-rimmed—likely his contacts had been in too long—and his dark complexion looked uncharacteristically sallow.

She lowered herself into the chair alongside his desk. "How long have you been up?"

"Twenty-four . . . uh, twenty-*six* hours."

She almost felt guilty, having dropped Reeder's suspicions on Miggie last night . . . using the burner phone of course. *Almost* guilty.

"No sleep at all?" she asked.

"I was working," he said, as if that explained it, and actually it did. "I napped for an hour or two. Hey, I'm fine. My blood is thirty percent caffeine."

"How far did you get?"

"I'm still on Tony Evans."

Her eyebrows tried to join each other. "You spent all night tracing an alias?"

He leaned back in his swivel chair. "That was part of it. But I was also looking into the fascinating life and times of Anthony J. Wooten."

"And just who is Anthony J. Wooten?"

With a sly smile, Miggie said, "He and Tony Evans are one and the same . . . at least according to the fingerprints from the DC Homicide morgue."

She was on the edge of her seat, like a kid at a horror movie. "What do we know about the late Mr. Wooten?"

"Ex-military. Black ops stuff in Afghanistan."

"So, he's CIA?"

"Not so you'd notice. But clearly an asset."

She shifted in the chair. "Okay, back up. How do you even *know* Wooten did 'black ops stuff in Afghanistan'? That's got to be classified."

"Oh, it is. Way down deep."

"Then you found out how?"

He folded his arms, shook his head. "We're in that if-I-told-you-I'd-have-to-kill-you area. Or even worse, if-I-told-you-they'd-have-to-kill-me."

"Or both of us?"

He sighed and thought for a moment. Rocking a little, he said, "Let's just say I know somebody who knows somebody who knows somebody who could get me the answers we wanted." He stopped rocking. "Are you planning to take this to court?"

"Not in the immediate future."

He started rocking again. "Then we're on a need-to-know basis . . . and you don't need to know."

"For now . . . okay. So, Evans . . . or I should say Wooten . . . was, what? A mercenary?"

Nodding, Miggie said, "In that he got paid to do some bad shit, yes . . . but he was never open to the highest bidder. Never was a part of Air America or anything so mundane. He was, it seems, a contractor, but only for very specific employers."

"Then we *are* talking CIA . . . ?"

"Mostly . . . but also the occasional freelance job for employers within the government."

"What kind of employers?"

"Highly placed ones. Generating the kind of classified activities that don't get talked about even in congressional hearings."

She processed that for a while. Then: "And this CIA asset, this governmental handyman, is who befriended Glenn Willard, to gain access to Secretary of the Interior Yellich . . . to *assassinate* her?"

"Sure seems that way."

She stared past him at Washington, DC, out his window. "You're saying . . . *we're* saying . . . that someone within the United States government dispatched Wooten to kill Yellich. That simple."

"That simple," Miggie said. "That terrible."

Her eyes went to his. "You've shared this with no one else."

"Of course not."

She nodded toward the monitor on his desk. "Is there a government computer that has any record of your searches?"

He made a face. "You don't have to be insulting."

She twitched the tiniest smile and rose. "We need to tell Hardesy."

Miggie looked up at her in surprise. "He's in Reeder's inner circle on this?"

"He is. And with you, that makes four of us."

She fetched Lucas from the bullpen, where he and the others were trailing in, and led him into Miggie's office to hear what the computer expert had learned.

When Miggie finished, Hardesy—in the chair Rogers had vacated—was shaking his shaved head, making the overhead light reflect. "Un-fucking-believable," he said.

Standing next to him, arms folded, looking down at him like a teacher checking a student's paper, Rogers said, "You don't buy it?"

Hardesy's smirk was humorless. "No, I don't *want* to buy it." His sigh was deep and sounded like somebody had opened a distant boiler door. "So, there's a rogue element in the government? This shadow group that Reeder posits?"

Rogers said, "Looks that way."

"And they assassinated a member of the goddamn cabinet?"

"Yeah."

He turned up both hands. "To what end?"

"It would be nice to know," Rogers said.

"And nice to know," Miggie added, "who in this rogue group put the Yellich murder in motion. Have to be somebody pretty high up."

"Maybe as high up," Rogers said, "as someone capable of getting CIA agents sent to Azbekistan."

The color had drained from Hardesy's face and wasn't coming back very fast. "Do we think this case is tied to Reeder's presidential mission?"

Her shrug was barely perceptible. "You tell me—or do you still think it's a coincidence, dead CIA agents here and abroad, a mercenary taken out with extreme prejudice, and an assassinated cabinet secretary?"

"You had me at dead CIA agents," Hardesy said dryly. "Okay, let's say I'm convinced. Where do we go from here?"

She let a grave look travel from Hardesy to Miggie and back again. "I go to AD Fisk with what we know," she said, "*and* with what we suspect . . . and ask her to assign our task force to this case."

Miggie asked, "Do we empty the entire bag on her desk?"

"We hold nothing back," Rogers said, nodding.

Hardesy frowned. "Should we run all this past Reeder first?"

She shook her head. "We'll fill him in at the next opportunity. But Wooten's identity only confirms what Joe's already thinking—he knew coming into this investigation that there must be some kind of government involvement, when the President's own directive was ignored. Those four CIA agents didn't just suddenly decide to check out Azbekistan as a vacation spot on the eve of a Russian invasion. No, Reeder's already got a mission from the President, and he's staying off the grid as he carries it out. Meanwhile, we need to get the Bureau to stand behind us on our side of it."

Rogers made a quick call to AD Fisk's office and learned that the Assistant Director was in a meeting, but should be free momentarily.

Soon, seated in Fisk's reception area, she checked the burner phone to see if a text had come through from Reeder—it hadn't—then got out her other phone, which had a text from Kevin about seeing her tonight. The AD's inner-office door opened and a tall man with dark hair came out. Pleasant enough looking, he had a Cost Cutters haircut and generic gray Men's Wearhouse suit that screamed government drone. He gave her the nod that was a stranger's hello and strode out.

Two more minutes passed before the AD's male secretary interrupted her perusal of the *FBI Law Enforcement Bulletin* on her cell phone, to say, "Ms. Fisk will see you now."

Rising, Rogers took in a breath, let it out. She strode into the inner office to find Margery Fisk staring past her, her expression cold. Not welcoming.

But as Rogers neared the aircraft carrier of a desk, AD Fisk met her eyes and said, as if uttering an expletive, "Accountants."

Obviously Fisk was referring to her previous visitor.

Taking the waiting chair opposite her seated boss, Rogers shrugged, smiled just a little, and said, "Accountants."

"GAO's threatening another audit," Fisk said, her voice matter-of-fact, her eyes hooded.

The Government Accountability Office audited, evaluated, and ran investigations for Congress. Another GAO audit would be the first step in the process of stripping the Bureau of much-needed dollars. Theoretically, the GAO could recommend more funds, but Rogers knew that with the economy in a downturn, such a thought bordered on fantasy.

Sensing an opening, Rogers said, "Would it help if we successfully took on the biggest case the Bureau ever had?"

Fisk's smile had a bitter edge. "I believe, Agent Rogers, that John Dillinger is no longer at large."

Rogers kept her tone businesslike. "Suppose, just hypothetically mind you, that there was a rogue element in the US government. A shadow government within the government, manipulating certain events."

To Rogers' relief, the AD neither laughed out loud nor threw a paperweight at her. But the woman did say, "So, you're a conspiracy theorist now."

Rogers had expected a reaction like this, and had decided not to point out to her superior that just a few years ago evidence had finally surfaced clearing Lee Harvey Oswald.

"It doesn't seem to be just a theory, ma'am. I'm confident I can prove it."

Fisk straightened in her high-backed chair. She studied Rogers, as if perhaps the need for a major crime for the Special Situations Task Force had turned the younger agent desperate.

Then Fisk said, "Make your case."

Rogers laid out everything that she, Altuve, and Hardesy knew, as well as what Reeder had contributed . . . without compromising his presidential mission, merely reminding the AD that four CIA agents had been killed in Azbekistan despite their presence in that country contradicting a presidential directive.

When Rogers was done, Fisk said nothing for several endless moments.

Just when Rogers thought she had blown it, her boss said, "About half of the dots you're connecting aren't there."

Deflating a little, Rogers said, "But what about the *other* half, ma'am?"

Fisk mulled that, but only for a moment. "You may not have a convincing argument where your 'shadow government' theory is concerned . . . at least not yet . . . but your case for Secretary Yellich having been assassinated is sound. And obviously that is a very serious matter, a threat to the government itself. We'll start there."

"Yes, ma'am."

"Make this investigation your task force's priority. Get right on it."

She rose, nodding. "Yes, ma'am."

Rogers was halfway out the AD's inner-office door when Fisk called out, "Oh, and Rogers?"

"Yes, ma'am?"

"Good work."

"Thank you, ma'am."

She flew through the outer office, thinking that sometimes a trip to the principal's office wasn't so terrible after all.

When Rogers got downstairs to the bullpen of the Special Situations Task Force, the team was waiting for her, having been assembled by Miggie at her request before she went up to see the AD.

Half a dozen desks, with no cubicles but plenty of space, faced a video screen that took up much of a wall; a small table looking back at them was reserved for Rogers in briefing mode, and she took her seat there. Smaller video screens were here and there around the room, and of course several offices in back—her own, Miggie's, and an unassigned one that had been reserved for Reeder as consultant.

Miggie was sitting at the desk he used when not in his office. Hardesy and his usual partner, Anne Nichols, had desks next to each other. Tall and fashion-model striking, the African American Nichols was as tough as she was stylish, and she was plenty stylish. Today she wore a single-breasted, gold-buttoned black business suit and leopard-print blouse.

The other pair of field agents, Jerry Bohannon and Reggie Wade, made up the more senior team, having been partners for years now.

The craggily handsome, fortyish Bohannon had started dating a woman his own age a while back, his post-divorce second childhood finally over, and consequently had stopped dyeing his hair, the natural gray at his temples giving him a distinguished look. So did his navy worsted suit, solid light blue tie, and blue-and-white-striped white-collared shirt.

The six-foot-four, African American Wade was a seasoned investigator who liked to push the limits of the Bureau's regulations of what comprised the acceptable "look" of an FBI agent. Today he was risking a black vested suit with black shirt and black skinny tie—all that black, yet the style of it said Italian.

The final member of the team, behaviorist/profiler Trevor Ivanek, was a balding human scarecrow with a broad forehead over deep-set eyes. Open-collar dress shirt under a sweater vest gave him the air of the scholar he was. For a man who spent so much time trying to understand monsters, he had a quick, easy wit.

Rogers got up from the table facing the team and rolled out a whiteboard that she'd asked Miggie to call down for. Something this low-tech was rarely used anymore, but it gave her a form of communication that the security camera behind her could not witness.

When she finished outlining what she and Fisk had just talked about, to an audience whose expressions ranged from squinting skepticism to wide-eyed alarm, Ivanek was first to speak up.

"With all due respect, Agent Rogers, you and Mr. Reeder are bucking for a psychiatric evaluation."

Wryly amused, Wade asked, "That your considered expert opinion, Doctor?"

His eyes staying on Rogers, Ivanek said, "I don't doubt that you have outlined some troubling events, chiefly the assassination of a cabinet member. And that seems entirely appropriate for an examination by this task force. But making the leap to a conspiracy within our government is ill-advised, reckless, and even foolish."

Hardesy said, "Then put me down for a psych session, too, Doc. I was standing right next to the black ops operative who got eliminated by a sniper. And I for one find it highly suggestive when four CIA agents get themselves killed where they were forbidden to be by, oh, just the President." He glanced around the bullpen. "Reeder and Rogers are right. We've got players on the inside who've gone rogue."

Shaking his head, Ivanek said, "Conspiracies are fine in fiction, but in the real world they're almost impossible to keep hidden, especially something on this scale."

Rogers said, "But we don't know the scale of it. We could be dealing with a handful of people . . . but *powerful* people."

"Most so-called conspiracies," Ivanek said, "are simply the individual acts of, say, police officers trying for the makings of an easy conviction, or politicos drumming up pseudo-scandals on a major figure from the other side. But sending agents overseas to die and tying it to the death of a cabinet member, even the probable murder of that cabinet member . . . it's strictly Through-the-Looking-Glass stuff."

With a pretty eyebrow arched, Nichols said, "That little party at the Capitol last year—you *were* here for that, right?"

Ivanek nodded. "I was. And ever since 9/11, we have lived in a curiouser-and-curiouser world. I grant you that. But Agent Rogers and Mr. Reeder are still making an ill-advised leap. My opinion is that we begin with the assassination of Secretary Yellich and treat it like what it is: a murder case."

"I have no problem with that," Rogers said. "But I would request that everyone here keep in mind the context that I've provided. If the people we're up against are as powerful as I think, then every person in this room is an insect that could easily be swatted."

Wade shifted his long-legged body and said, "Okay, so we've got a case, and just the kind of major-league case that might just keep our little Sit boat afloat. Where do we start, boss?"

"We'll begin with computer checks," she said, for the benefit of any bugs in the room. But on the whiteboard she wrote: NO USE OF BUREAU EQUIPMENT. WILL EXPLAIN. STRICTLY SUB ROSA. Then she wiped it clean.

"Why?" Bohannon asked, a question that might have been for either the spoken comment or the written one.

Rogers said, "They may have left a computer trail, and we'll get Miggie all over that." But again, as she spoke, she wrote: MOLES. TRUST NO ONE BUT THE TEAM. She wiped the board clean.

"Reeder can be considered a part of this team," she went on, "but he has his own agenda. Our focus is, as Trevor has correctly advised, finding out who is behind the murder of Secretary Yellich."

As she spoke, she wrote: NO PERSONAL PHONES. NO BUREAU EMAIL. Again she wiped the board clean.

Bohannan rose, smoothed his suit coat, and went to the whiteboard, taking the marker from Rogers, and wrote: HOW DO WE COMMUNICATE? He erased that and watched her write: BURNER PHONES ASAP. She erased that, and Bohannon nodded and returned to his desk.

Wade asked, "So, where do we start, boss?"

Writing REAL ASSIGNMENTS on the whiteboard, Rogers said, "Reggie, you and Jerry take another look at Yellich—personal life, her staffers . . . make sure we didn't miss anything."

Wade nodded. Bohannon, too.

"Miggie, these people must have left a trail somewhere. Find it. Follow it."

She wrote: APARTMENT HOUSE SHOOTER'S DNA. FROM DC HOMICIDE.

Miggie nodded as she erased the message.

"Lucas," she said, "you, Anne, and I have a job in the field to do."

She wrote in very big letters, and underlined: WATCH YOUR ASSES. Then she swept the board clean.

When she, Hardesy, and Nichols were in the corridor, Rogers said, "We're going to visit Tony Wooten's parents."

"Do you think they know," Hardesy asked, "what kind of mischief sonny boy was up to?"

Bohannon said, "Name a terrorist who lived at home whose mommy didn't know he was making bombs."

"Good point," Hardesy admitted.

"Don't assume the worst about them," Rogers advised. "Remember, they won't have been informed about their son's death—Miggie's digging is what turned up Tony Evans' real identity, and so far we're the only good guys who know it."

"Understood," Nichols said.

Soon, with Nichols at the wheel of a Bureau Ford, the two-hour drive to Chambersburg, Pennsylvania, was spent going over Wooten's file as e-mailed by Miggie to Rogers' burner, though there was precious little in it.

Wooten had entered the military after getting an associate degree in police science from Harrisburg Area Community College. Rogers figured that (like her), Wooten had intended to become an MP, but (unlike her) never made it into the Military Police. Instead, he'd entered sniper school, at which point his military record became conspicuously sparse; nothing of note beyond an unremarkable tour of duty stateside. It was as if he went to sniper school then just disappeared for eighteen months until his honorable discharge.

Rogers wondered where Miggie had gotten the information about Wooten's black ops in Afghanistan. Were there more off-the-books activities of Wooten's in that part of the world, or others for that matter?

A sleepy burg of fewer than 25,000 souls, Chambersburg depended mostly on tourism—thanks to its rich history, quaint downtown, and Appalachian setting—though with the surrounding communities, the greater metro area swelled to about 50,000 with some decent manufacturing jobs available. Amish and Mennonite farmers beyond the city limits made up part of the population as well. It reminded Rogers of her home area back in Iowa, even down to the fields of corn surrounding the town.

The biggest employer, though, was five miles north—Letterkenny Army Depot, the place from which Wooten's father had recently retired. Amos and Constance Wooten lived in a brick bungalow on a two-lane highway called Edenville Road, where lawns large enough to require riding mowers overwhelmed modest houses like theirs.

Rogers left the car in the driveway and the three FBI agents walked up a brick walk. The quietude reminded her of her farmland home, too—this was just far enough toward the edge of town not to get regular traffic, with only the barking of a dog and the breeze whispering through trees to test the silence.

Rogers knocked on the door and waited. She was just about to knock again when a shadow crossed the thin curtains behind the wooden door's glass.

Another second and the inside door opened, leaving only the screen between her and a slender man in his sixties with thinning gray hair and Tony Wooten's nose. He wore a Philadelphia Eagles T-shirt and new-looking jeans.

"Mr. Wooten?"

"Yes . . . ?"

She held up her credentials. "Special Agent Patti Rogers with the FBI. With Special Agents Anne Nichols and Lucas Hardesy. May we come in, sir?"

"What's this about?" Mr. Wooten asked, understandably taken aback. One FBI agent on his doorstep would be bad enough . . . but three?

"I'd rather not discuss it out here, sir," Rogers said. "May we come in, please?"

With a frown, Wooten swung open the screen and they trooped in. The living room was smallish but nice, homey. Family pictures—son Tony with a younger brother and older sister peered at them pleasantly from over the years—rested on perfectly dusted end tables, a sofa with a knitted afghan hugged one wall, a BarcaLounger sat next to a couple of wing chairs, each facing a flat-screen TV on a stand.

Hardesy asked, "Is Mrs. Wooten at home?"

At first alarmed, then reluctant, Mr. Wooten twisted toward the back of the house. "Connie," he said, barely raising his voice.

"What is it, dear?" came a voice from a doorless doorway onto the kitchen. Plates were clinking. "I'm busy right now!"

Bringing his wife into the mix had brought home to their host how serious a visit this was, and Amos Wooten said simply, "FBI."

A short, stocky, aproned woman, her hair a shade of red unknown in nature, stepped into the room drying her hands on a towel. Her eyes were light blue and very pretty. "Did you say FBI?"

Rogers made the introductions again, ending with, "Perhaps we might all sit down."

The Wootens traded a look and moved to the sofa and sat down side by side. Within moments, their hands found each other. The agents assembled seats around the humble living room.

Every law enforcement officer hated this part of the job, hated it like poison. Rogers had been the bearer of bad news more than once back in her county deputy days, and it never got easier. As a federal agent, she usually came in well after someone had already received the worst news of their lives.

"Mr. and Mrs. Wooten," she said, "your son Tony died last night in Hillcrest Heights, Maryland."

The wife's grip tightened on her husband's hand, her knuckles turning white.

"I'm sorry to have to tell you this," Rogers continued, "but Tony was murdered."

She waited for the tears, the explosion of grief, but instead found herself staring at two people whose wide-eyed confusion said they didn't understand a word she was saying.

Mr. Wooten said, "In Maryland, you say?"

"Yes. Hillcrest Heights. He was living there, but you probably knew that. Did you know that?"

Mr. Wooten looked at his wife, bewildered, and she looked back at him the same way. "There has to be some mistake, Agent Rogers—Anthony isn't even in the country."

Was there any way Miggie might have misidentified the shooting victim? No, the file photo matched. And she was not about to show these parents the photo from the coroner's office. On the burner phone, she called up Tony Wooten's military file and his photo.

She held the phone out to the father who studied it, squinting at it, as if trying to make out a distant figure on the horizon. He gave Rogers a look that asked for the phone, and she nodded and gave it to him.

Soon father and mother were looking down at the photo on a phone that was in both their hands.

"That *is* your son?" Rogers asked.

They didn't need to reply. Tears trailing down the mother's cheeks, and the tremor in the father's hand as he handed back the phone, gave the answer.

Rogers said, "We're very sorry for your loss."

Mrs. Wooten's head tipped forward and a small sob escaped. Hardesy got up and went to her and handed her his handkerchief. She accepted the offering with a nod of thanks, and he went back to his chair.

Mr. Wooten gave Rogers a hard, direct look. "What happened to Anthony?"

"He was shot. From a distance, by a man with a rifle."

Tears welling, the father asked, "Who in God's name would want to shoot our son? In Maryland! He was a good boy—he served his country honorably."

"We were hoping, sir, that you and your wife might have some idea."

Spreading his hands in surrender, the father said, "We told you! We didn't even know he was in the country. We thought he was overseas."

"Where, specifically?"

The barest hint of a smile crossed the man's face, then disappeared into sorrow. "He always said that if he told us, he'd have to kill us."

The echo of what Miggie had said to her a few hours before gave her a shiver.

Mrs. Wooten looked up from her lap and said, "It was all top-secret work for the government."

Great. No help. "What kind of government work was he doing if he was out of the Army?"

Mr. Wooten shrugged and shook his head a little. "Well . . . he was working as a contractor."

"Do you know what he was contracted to do? Who might have contracted him?"

The father shook his head. "Anthony just said 'top secret,' and we respected that."

Another dead end.

"Whatever it was," Mr. Wooten volunteered, "there's a strong possibility it was . . . that it wasn't strictly . . . legal."

His wife drew in a breath and gave him an I-can't-believe-you-said-that look, and Rogers felt her stomach tighten.

Resting a hand on his wife's knee, Mr. Wooten said, "Connie, these people are from the FBI. If they look into our financials for five minutes, they'll find the money. I used to work for the government—I *know*."

"Sir," Rogers asked, trying not to betray the stir within her, "what money are you referring to?"

Mr. Wooten glanced at his wife, who closed her eyes and gave him a tiny nod.

Then he said, "A few months ago, Anthony put some money away for us."

"Away where, sir?"

"In an account in the . . . what are they called? Cayman Islands. Under our name."

"How much?"

". . . Quite a bit."

"How much, sir?"

". . . One hundred thousand dollars."

The agents traded looks.

Rogers asked, "Did Anthony tell you where that money came from?"

Mr. Wooten tried to maintain eye contact with her, but couldn't. "Anthony said his contract work was paying nicely, and he just wanted to put some retirement money away."

Hardesy asked, "For himself or for you?"

"For . . . well, for all of us. Whichever of us needed it more. I have a decent pension, and we don't want for much of anything, so . . . really, I suppose it would eventually go to Anthony. Would have gone."

Rogers asked, "You didn't press him on where he got that kind of money?"

Shaking his head a little, Mr. Wooten said, "Agent Rogers, I'll admit to you that I . . . I didn't really *want* to know."

"Do you have the account information?"

He sighed. Seemed defeated, and not by his guests—by life. "Connie can get it for you. We're going to lose that money, aren't we?"

Rogers shook her head. "I don't really know."

Anthony's mother got up and went to a bedroom in the back of the house, Nichols tagging along with her. Several awkwardly silent minutes passed before the two women returned; Nichols, with a manila folder in hand, gave Rogers a nod.

Rising, Rogers said, "We'll look into this, Mr. and Mrs. Wooten. We will, I assure you, do everything we can to find the person responsible for your son's death . . . Is there someone you can call to come stay with you?"

The Wootens were on their feet, too, standing hand in hand.

"Thank you," Mr. Wooten said. "We'll be fine. Our other children are still in the area, and we'll call them right away. Do you . . . do you have any idea what Anthony was doing in Maryland?"

Rogers knew exactly what he was doing—he was plotting the assassination of the Secretary of the Interior.

"No, sir," she told him, "no idea at all."

"The point in history at which we stand is full of promise and danger. The world will either move forward toward unity and widely shared prosperity—or it will move apart."

Franklin Delano Roosevelt, thirty-second President of the United States of America. Served 1933–1945. The only person to win four presidential elections.

NINE

When he entered the Oval Office, Joe Reeder found the President in shirtsleeves and tie behind that familiar, formidable desk, looking like his best friend had just died. Chief of Staff Timothy Vinson, certainly not the friend in question, stood to Harrison's left side, seething, mustache twitching, a boil in a three-piece suit on the verge of bursting.

Jesus, Reeder thought, this guy is in full-blown Yosemite Sam mode.

Harrison motioned to Reeder to join them, and he quickly did, standing opposite, nodding, saying, "Mr. President."

The commander in chief asked the ex-Secret Service agent, "Are you getting anywhere, Joe? On the direct line, Krakenin is stopping just short of accusing us . . . of accusing me . . . of inciting war. And the back-channel chatter is even worse."

Dubbed "the Kraken" by American media outlets, Boris Mikhailovich Krakenin, President of the Russian Federation, was a notorious saber-rattler. But the Russian incursion into Azbekistan was not just a threat, and the deaths of four CIA agents in the midst of it put both nations at the precipice.

Preferring not to brief the President with Vinson present, Reeder said, "Making progress, sir, yes."

Vinson began to pace a small area near the big desk, words tumbling out of him. "Boris has taken to referring to the Azbekistani government as a 'puppet regime,' accusing us of propping up a handful of insurgents. He doesn't consider his own country's actions as an invasion, oh no . . . just rightfully putting down a rebellion."

"A rebellion," Harrison said dryly, "in the form of a freely elected democratic government going back six years."

"Krakenin," Reeder said, "makes Putin look like a pushover."

Harrison cocked his head. "You know the man?"

"'Know him' overstates it. I met him once, years ago. Secret Service days, when now-President Krakenin was serving in the FSB under General Bortnikov."

These three were well aware that the Russian Federal Security Service was home to many a ruthless bastard.

Harrison asked, "Any thoughts on comrade Boris?"

Reeder shrugged. "Only that he considered Putin a weak sister and Stalin the consummate Russian leader. Some men lead with an iron fist. Krakenin heats up that iron fist in a forge till it burns a nice bright orange."

The President was nodding. "He's a hard-ass of the first order, little doubt of that. But do you think he really wants war?"

Reeder smiled thinly. "Mr. President, with all due respect, you have access to far more worthy analysts than some lowly security-outfit exec."

"With all due respect, Joe," Harrison said, with his own restrained grin, "false modesty doesn't suit you. For decades you've stood at the sides of Presidents, in this very office, and seen and heard so very much. Don't they call you the People Reader? So based on your observations of Boris Badenov, years ago and in his on-air appearances of more recent times . . . what do you think he's up to?"

"Not war."

Vinson's laugh was both immediate and bitterly derisive.

Harrison gave his Chief of Staff a quick sharp look, cutting the laugh off, and Vinson looked on in surly silence.

"What makes that your opinion, Joe," Harrison asked, "considering the man recklessly invaded a sovereign nation, and got four of our agents killed?"

Reeder's tone could not have been more matter-of-fact. "He doesn't want war—he wants portillium."

Vinson frowned and growled, "What the holy hell is portillium?"

Quietly the President said, "The element that lends stability to Senkstone as a plastic explosive."

They all knew what Senkstone was—the most versatile and dangerous munition of its kind yet developed.

Harrison said, "Boris wants the rich veins of portillium, known only to that region, found underneath the otherwise unimpressive surface of Azbekistan."

Reeder said, "Taking over that pimple on the face of the planet is the most expedient way to acquire that scarce element in quantity."

"Science fiction," Vinson muttered.

"Is it?" the President asked. "All of this came to classified light when the Special Situations Task Force discovered the existence of Senkstone."

Reeder nodded. "Boris's people go in, mine as much as they can, until a truly serious United Nations threat comes along . . . which after all could take decades . . . and then retreat to the border with all the portillium they can carry, and generously let Azbekistan have its ravaged land back."

The President, looking rather sick, said, "And with the ability to contrive that much Senkstone, Boris can do . . ."

"Pretty much anything he wants," Reeder finished.

Thanks to portillium, Senkstone's best quality as a plastic explosive was that it was stable enough to use in a 3D printer, and could be molded to mimic anything. Like to match some world leader's eyeglasses for an assassination. Or, shaped in some manner that disguised its purpose, blow up the White House.

Or the Kremlin.

"So," Vinson said, squinting in thought, "the Azbekistan invasion is just a cover for . . . a strip-mining operation?"

"More to it than that, Timothy," Harrison said. "The Russian hardliners will be ecstatic to see Boris flexing his muscles, making it a political win at home . . . and with the Azbekistanis under the Russian boot heel again, maybe, just maybe, the world would let him hold onto that little excuse for a country."

"Okay," Reeder said. "Now—do you want to hear the really bad news?"

"For Christ's sake," Vinson said, "what could that be?"

Harrison knew. He said, quiet again, "That someone on our side knew the exact time of that invasion and sent four American agents to die in it, in hopes of starting a war with Russia—a war that doesn't really seem to suit Krakenin's agenda."

Rising, the President gestured toward the informal central meeting area of couches and chairs, and the three men repaired there. Reeder and Vinson took the couch and the President an overstuffed chair opposite.

"Mr. President," Reeder said, "at the risk of impertinence . . . there's a question I must ask."

"Ask it, Joe."

"Someone on our side knew when the invasion was going down. Agreed?"

"That would appear so."

"Which means that someone had the ability to send our agents into harm's way."

"Yes."

Reeder locked eyes with the President and asked, as if wondering what time it was, "Was that person you, sir?"

Vinson exploded, turning to Reeder, spittle flying his way. "What in the hell . . . ! You have no right to—"

An upraised hand from the President cut Vinson off.

"Joe is a citizen I called upon for a mission, Tim, which gives him every right to question his president."

Reeder said, "And the question stands, sir."

Next to him, Vinson was turning shades of red—suffering succotash . . .

The dark eyes in the auburn face met Reeder's unblinkingly. "Isn't the real question, did I go after the portillium for the benefit of the United States, using those CIA agents as an advance team? And have I been using you to cover my tracks?"

"That's two questions, Mr. President. But that sums it up."

Harrison's smile was a weary one. "If only I were that smart, Joe . . . but the truth is, I never even saw this coming. Satisfied?"

Reeder worked to detect every micro-expression, every body nuance, but nothing led him to think that the President was lying. Of course, US presidents were among the most skilled liars in history.

Just the same, Reeder said, "Yes, sir, I am. Thank you for your frankness."

The Chief of Staff next to Reeder on the couch half-turned to him, agape.

"Now it's my turn for a question," Harrison said. "Are you any closer to finding our traitor? Director Shaley is either stalling or genuinely flummoxed."

Reeder let out some air. "I think with Director Shaley, sir, it's the latter. Of course, he might be taking care of the problem in-house, to protect himself and his domain . . . but I can't honestly say I'm really any closer on that front, Mr. President. Not directly."

Harrison frowned. "Then you haven't got a thing for me?"

"I know more than I did, when we spoke yesterday . . . but not the name of the mole. I have learned something that's . . . troubling."

"Which is?"

Reeder had held this back because of Vinson's presence; but there was clearly nothing not shared between these men.

So Reeder said it: "Secretary Yellich was assassinated."

In a soundproofed room, silence can be surreal. And the three men breathing was the only sound any of them could discern in the uncomfortable stillness.

"But that . . . that was an accident," Vinson said, absent of any of his usual bluster. "A tragic—"

"Murder," Reeder said. "So was the hit-and-run death yesterday of CIA agent Len Chamberlain. I was there and I saw it."

Then Reeder handed over everything that Rogers and Hardesy had turned up in their investigation thus far, leading up to and including the murder of Tony Wooten/Evans. He left out only the information Rogers had gleaned from the Wooten family in Pennsylvania—until Miggie Altuve traced the source of the family's money in the Caymans, reporting that would be premature.

And he also stopped short of outlining the potentially absurd-sounding concept of a shadow government.

When Reeder had finished, President Harrison stared at the floor, shaking his head.

"Five CIA agents down," he said, "the Secretary of the Interior assassinated, her assassin himself liquidated . . . and if I put the pieces together correctly, you're telling me this could all be a plot by the Russians, with help from someone in our government, for a land grab? All to acquire the resources to make an unlimited amount of an undetectable plastic explosive . . . with World War III in the offing."

"It's a genuine possibility, Mr. President," Reeder said.

Vinson said, "Why on earth would any American help the Russians acquire the key to Senkstone?"

Reeder shrugged. "They may not have figured out that part. The goal of the rogue players in our government may well be a hawkish one toward Krakenin's Russia. As for Senkstone, very few people in or out of government even know about it, and fewer still are aware that portillium is the element needed to stabilize it."

Shaking his head, the Chief of Staff said, "I just can't believe it."

"Well, there's an even worse read of the rogue element," Reeder said.

Vinson grunted. "What in God's name could be worse?"

But the President answered his Chief of Staff: "They could know about portillium."

"Know about it?" Vinson blurted.

"Know about it," Reeder said, "and be in Russia's pocket—either as foreign agents or, well, capitalists without a conscience."

Again, silence settled over the sealed room.

Harrison looked hard at Reeder. "Now that the FBI is officially on board, by way of Special Agent Rogers' task force, I want you to work with them. You have a history of being a consultant there—no red flags will go up."

"Yes, sir."

"Get to the bottom of all this . . . and Joe—I need it wrapped up before the first of the week."

Reeder felt as if the leader of the free world had just punched him in the stomach. "Respectfully, sir, that's less than five days for an investigation that could take, oh months . . . even years."

"We don't have the luxury of time," Harrison said. "And I'm depending on you to meet my deadline. The cabinet is scheduled for a weekend at Camp David. The only item on the agenda will be whether the United States will issue a declaration of war against Russia."

And another one to the chin . . .

The President was saying, "The decision can be put off but there's a real possibility that the United States will face war with Russia. I'm assuming you'd like to help forestall that."

With a confidence he wished he felt, Reeder said, "Yes, sir, I would. I will."

The President stood and so did Vinson and Reeder, who shook hands with Harrison. And he even shook hands with the Chief of Staff, who had the look of a man about to go home and build a fallout shelter.

Walking to his car, the sky an ominous, starless dome, Reeder felt the vibration of his cell phone, and checked it: Bishop. He'd given his homicide detective pal the number last night. Within the car, he answered.

"Evening, Detective Bishop."

"Some pile of dog shit you stepped in this time around."

"Getting any on you?"

"Naw. It's you who stepped in it, not me. Remember Pete Woods? The young buck you helped on the Bryson case?"

"Sure," Reeder said. "Good detective, even if he does look about twelve years old."

"Well, Woods drew the Chamberlain hit-and-run, and when I casually asked him what evidence he had, he not so casually told me the feds took everything . . . and made it clear the matter, which is to say the murder, wasn't his problem."

"How did Pete take that?"

"More gracefully than either of us would. He told them nicely that he should get at least a look-see, and the feds told him just as nicely to screw off—that in the case of a federal death, he had no jurisdiction."

"Which agency got the evidence?"

"Even that's more than they were willing to tell Woods. What they did tell him was to butt out."

"And has he?"

"Yup. And normally Woodsie Owl doesn't back down from any-thing. Working that case with you last year must have spooked him some. Now he knows just how deep the doo-doo can get."

"Bish, he's a smart kid, and did the right thing. Now do me a favor."

"Any time."

"Hang up and forget we had this talk."

"Fine. As long as I'm allowed to remember one thing."

"Which is?"

"Which is, you owe me big time."

They clicked off.

The White House's massive black gates allowed Reeder passage and he headed north, toward Lafayette Square. Soon he turned west, toward home. He drove leisurely, replaying in his mind the conversation with the President and his Chief of Staff; but even before he got to the round-about at New Hampshire Avenue, he knew he had a tail. It stayed two cars back but in the same lane—that way if Reeder took a quick right, the tail could follow.

It was a simple Ford Explorer, dark green, a few years old—not some black tinted-glass Interceptor utility, and certainly not a hover-ing helicopter—much too showy, far too obvious. No, this might be a government car, or an ex-police car. Either one meant reinforced bum-pers and more horsepower than his Prius, meaning at least a modest advantage for his new best friend.

Getting Rogers on the burner cell would be the fastest way to find out if the Explorer was a chaperone she'd provided. But also the fastest way for the tail to capture the signal of his burner, and hers.

These people would obviously know where Reeder lived, so trying to lose the tail was pointless, unless he was prepared to go underground immediately. Right now the tail was keeping its distance, though the headlights of other vehicles revealed a driver's silhouette and no passengers.

Reeder took a direct route home. When he pulled up in front of his white-brick, two-story townhouse on Thirty-Fourth Street Northwest, the tail tucked into a spot two houses back, on the other side of the street. Reeder got out, closed his door, and—on the way to the front steps—walked around behind his vehicle, lending him an inconspicuous view of the Explorer. But a streetlight was nearby and shining down on the car reflectively, giving Reeder no look at all of the driver.

Instead of going across the street to confront the tail, Reeder trotted casually up to his red front door, unlocked it, and slipped in. After quickly dealing with the alarm system on the wall just inside, punching in the seven-digit code, he got his SIG Sauer out of the drawer of the little table beneath the security keypad.

He considered going out the back way, cutting through yards, then coming up behind the Explorer to meet his new friend.

But checking the house, even though the alarm had been on, was the priority. He turned on the living room light, moved into the dining room. Everything seemed quiet, appeared undisturbed. Of course if a team had bugged the place, they would have been pros and, like the Boy Scouts in a forest, would've left it as they'd found it. SIG Sauer in hand, barrel up, he edged into the kitchen, elbowing a light on.

At the back door, he considered the strong possibility that the rear of the house was covered, too. If he was the one doing surveillance, he'd sure as hell want someone back there.

After checking the two bedrooms and his home office upstairs, and finding no guests, Reeder returned to the front door. He tossed his suit coat on a chair, then went to the front closet and got his black ABC Security hooded sweatshirt, which he got into. He dropped the expandable baton in his right sweatshirt pocket, and tucked the nine millimeter into the back waistband of his slacks. He pulled the sweatshirt down so that it covered the pistol grip.

He went out the front door, in no hurry, just a guy going out for an evening stroll or maybe to a neighborhood 24-hour joint. This seemed better than heading out the back door into the waiting arms of who-the-hell-knew.

He crossed the street at his townhouse and took the sidewalk in the direction of the parked Explorer. Hands in the sweatshirt pockets, the baton in his right, he figured his brazen approach might spook the tail into taking off, or anyway action of some sort . . . but nothing.

Reeder closed the distance at his evening-stroll pace. As he neared, he couldn't see past the streetlight reflection on the windshield to get a look at the driver. Since that driver might have a gun aimed at him right now, this was . . . disconcerting.

But killing Chamberlain by hit-and-run was one thing, and shooting a well-known, government-connected figure like Joe Reeder was something else again. He liked his odds. When he got to the vehicle and could see through the side window, the car was empty.

Damn!

His eyes swiftly scanned the street for any sign of another person—nothing. Where the hell had the guy gone? Nearest place for coffee was several blocks down—should he check that? He scanned the area again, more slowly now—it was as if the world had ended, only an occasional distant honk of a car horn to suggest otherwise.

He walked to the next corner, crossing to his own side of the street, and came cautiously back—where could the tail have gone?

Across the street from the start of his block, Reeder ducked into the shadows of the house there. It wasn't like you tailed somebody just to park a car, unless . . .

. . . a car bomb?

There were car bombs now that could obliterate blocks, and these people were deadly enough for that. But usually they were more surgical—Wooten had taken Yellich out by poison, Wooten himself got liquidated by a sniper's precise bullet, Chamberlain by hit-and-run. Neat kills, relatively speaking, at least as much as murder is ever "neat."

So, no—no car bomb.

Had the driver left his vehicle to check in with somebody watching the rear of Reeder's house?

A possibility. That meant the driver would soon be returning to the Explorer, either to plant himself for surveillance or to vacate the scene. Little attempt, though, had been made to conceal from Reeder that he had been tailed, and would now be subject to surveillance . . .

Somehow, he needed to get his hands on the driver of that Explorer, and interrogate him. Shake it out of him, or goddamn waterboard him in the townhouse bathtub if that was what it took . . .

Keeping to the shadows, Reeder crossed to the northwest corner of Thirty-Fourth Street NW and P Street, then turned west on P toward the alley that ran behind the townhouses. Occasionally, as he crept along, he stopped to listen, but heard nothing. Not even a shoe scraping over concrete, not the rustle of clothing nor the rhythm of heavy breathing.

As he turned into the alley, a fist flew from the darkness.

Reeder couldn't react quite fast enough and it connected high on his cheek, not on his jaw, as he ducked. Even so, the blow turned the inside of his skull into Fourth of July fireworks, and his balance was gone.

The attacker followed up on that advantage, kicking the unsteady Reeder in the ribs, martial arts–style, sending him to the gravel of the alley. His work apparently done, his escape seemingly assured, the attacker headed back toward the sidewalk.

But Reeder withdrew the baton, extended it with a snap, and whapped the guy across the left calf, getting a yelp out of him and sending him face-first onto the sidewalk with a thump.

Reeder rushed the attacker, who flipped onto his back and sent another kick at Reeder, who dodged it—the attacker's face remaining a smudge in the night, thanks to darkness and movement. A second kick got Reeder in the right forearm and his fingers popped open and the baton jumped out, landing God knew where. Both men scrambled to their feet and Reeder reached behind him for the pistol in his waistband, but the attacker sent out another kick to Reeder's ribs, doubling him over.

By the time Reeder regained his breath, the man was sprinting away, likely heading back to the Explorer. Reeder gave chase, but his opponent had too big a head start, and Reeder's ribs were screaming. Reeder caught up only as the Explorer lurched away from the curb and sped off.

A glimpse of the attacker's face, in the side rearview mirror, didn't really help much. The license plate had been removed—no help there either.

He caught his breath, rubbed his aching ribs, then looked up and down the block. Not a single porch light had come on, the struggle apparently unnoticed. He went back to the scene of the attack, to retrieve the extending baton. He found it quickly, just down the side-walk. But he also spotted something else, something small, making a reflective glimmer off a streetlight.

It was a lapel pin of a US flag, a common enough touch on men's lapels in this town—only this one had a tiny camera. The little high-tech thing had been smashed in the struggle.

But Reeder knew what the lapel-flag camera was. And he knew of only one group of people who wore such a pin.

Agents of the United States Secret Service.

"The most terrifying words in the English language are: I'm from the government and I'm here to help."

Ronald Reagan, fortieth President of the United States of America. Served 1981–1989. Formerly the thirty-third governor of California following a successful screen-acting career.

TEN

Rogers said, "The pin could belong to someone who wants you to *believe* they're with the Secret Service."

Reeder, seated next to her, gave Rogers a blank look that somehow conveyed his contempt for that notion.

They were in the outer office of the Director of the United States Secret Service on the ninth floor of its H Street HQ. According to Reeder, he and Jonathon Briar, the first African American to hold the directorship, had been field agents around the same time.

That didn't seem to be helping as half an hour of waiting turned into an hour. Of course, Reeder hadn't left the Secret Service under the best of circumstances.

"I'm just saying," she said, "that some unknown Secret Service agent jumping you isn't the *only* possible explanation."

"You saw the ID number on the back. He might as well have signed it Secret Service."

Rogers took air in, let it out, then rose and went to the desk, where a brunette guardian of the gates was giving her computer the attention they weren't getting, and said, "Excuse me?"

The woman looked up, narrow-faced if attractive with scant makeup, her dark gray suit and midnight blouse nice enough for Rogers to wonder how much better the SS must pay than the FBI. The guardian's eyes, a lighter gray than her apparel, met Rogers' without a word. That was apparently all the response an FBI agent merited.

"We had an appointment," Rogers said. "It's been over an hour."

"The appointment was made only this morning."

"You do know who Mr. Reeder is?"

The guardian nodded, about as impressed as a maître d' at a really expensive restaurant. "Yes, and I told Mr. Reeder earlier, on the phone, that I would do my best to squeeze him in."

"There's no one else out here."

"The Director is in conference."

Getting that principal's office feeling again, Rogers nodded and dragged back to her seat.

Five more minutes passed and the Director's office door opened and a tall male figure emerged—that same GAO drone in wire-frames and a Men's Wearhouse suit who she'd seen at Fisk's office. This time Rogers didn't rate the stranger's nod of admission that she was a human being. Even the famous Joe Reeder got ignored.

Rogers whispered, "Conference must be over. We *have* to be next."

Reeder didn't give her a nod, either.

But fifteen minutes later he got up and strode to the Director's door.

The assistant said, "Mr. Reeder—you can't simply—"

But he did, with Rogers following right after, pausing only to give the guardian a condescending smile before shutting herself and Reeder inside.

Fiftyish Director Jonathon Briar, broad-faced on a muscular mid-range frame, his navy suit with red-and-white tie blatantly patriotic, actually started a bit when they came in. To the right as they entered, Briar was seated behind a black slab that was more table than desk, two modern beige visitor's chairs opposite, a looming framed portrait of President Harrison on the wall behind him. The large, stark office seemed to be keeping as many secrets as the Service itself. To the left was a meeting area with a low-slung black slab table and various modern but comfortable-looking chairs.

"Jesus, Peep," Briar blustered. "You know better than this!"

Reeder stood at the edge of the desk-thing and stared down at Director Briar.

"You're right, Jon," Reeder said. "I should have barged in here the moment your last guest left. I'm getting complacent."

Reeder was standing between the two visitor's chairs and Rogers was just behind the one to Reeder's left. Briar's eyes met hers and narrowed.

Rogers held up her credentials, but Briar said, "I know who you are, Agent Rogers. Do you mind, Peep, telling me what this is about? Make it quick—I have another meeting in ten minutes."

"Let *them* wait an hour," Reeder said, and tossed a small plastic evidence bag with the smashed pin in it onto Briar's desk. Briar was wearing his own, somewhat smaller lapel flag pin—did it come equipped with a camera, too?

Then Reeder lowered himself into one of the visitor's chairs and waved Rogers into the other.

Briar stared at the smashed pin in the bag. "Where did you get that?"

"It fell off someone who attacked me last night, not far from my home. I can show you the bruises on my ribs if you're interested. You'll note that that's an American flag camera pin, a mangled one I grant you."

"Homeland uses these," Briar said, with a shrug. "Agent Rogers will tell you they're not unknown to the Bureau, as well, and several other agencies."

Reeder reached over and flipped the evidence bag. "Do I have to remind you, Jon, that the SS is the only one who uses that form of ID number?"

"That's not one of ours," Briar said without looking at it.

"It's one of yours, all right. And I want to know who this one belongs to."

Briar smirked mirthlessly. "Has procedure changed, Peep, since you worked here? You know damn well that if an agent loses one of these, he or she is required to report it immediately. No one has."

"Why, do you check the reports yourself?"

"Actually, yes. Every day. Are we done here?"

Rogers asked, "Director Briar, who was it that left this office before we came in? In the wire-framed glasses?"

The Director said, "He's with the GAO. Nothing that concerns you."

"Would he have a name, sir?"

Briar said, "That's not information I'm prepared to share with you, Agent Rogers. You seem to have the Secret Service confused with the Smithsonian."

Reeder gave the Director a long, hard look, then said, "Jon, we were never friends—we never shared duty together. But we were friendly enough, and I've always respected you. When I tell you that I was attacked by someone, last night, who lost a Secret Service pin in the process, doesn't that raise any level of interest?"

Briar gave the evidence bag the barest look. "That's not our pin. What you're reporting is not a Secret Service matter. You might try the DC police, or because that pin probably originated with some government agency, you could discuss it with your FBI colleague, Agent Rogers, here."

Reeder rose. "Thanks for the advice, Jon. It's nice to know that all my years with the Service earned me so much support."

Briar looked up coldly at the former agent. "Sarcasm doesn't really suit you, Peep. But let me suggest something. If that pin did belong to a Secret Service agent . . . and if you were attacked by him . . . someone above my pay grade would have to have put it in motion."

Reeder's gaze was unblinking. "Would have had to put *you* in motion, you mean."

"Assume what you like. But I would suggest you're treading on some important toes. As you say, we weren't friends, Peep, but we were friendly enough for me to suggest that whatever you're up to . . . you may want to find a new hobby."

"Noted," Reeder said, and reached for the bag with the pin, but Briar laid a hand on it.

"I'll hold onto that for you," the Director said.

Reeder gave Briar an awful smile. "That's not yours, remember?"

Rogers stood and said, "But it is evidence in an ongoing federal investigation, Director. With all due respect, please remove your hand."

Briar thought about that for a good ten seconds, then nodded, and let Reeder take the bag.

In the corridor, Rogers asked, "What the hell was that?"

"Briar's a decent enough director," Reeder said. "Anyway, he was a good agent. There's a reason he didn't cooperate with us."

"Because he's covering his own ass?"

"That may be part of it. Mostly, he's scared."

Rogers studied that unreadable face and then asked, "What does it take to scare the Director of the Secret Service?"

"Generally not something as small as that pin."

"That GAO guy is who I saw coming out of Fisk's office the other day. She said he was there on budgetary matters."

Reeder raised an eyebrow. "So?"

"Joe, when I got to the AD's office yesterday, he was there. *Already there!* What's he doing . . . tailing us?"

Reeder thought for a moment, then said, "Worse."

"How do you mean, worse?"

"He's out ahead of us."

Rogers was mulling that as they headed for the elevators, passing various agents and office workers. The older agents sometimes exchanged nods with Reeder, and younger ones all seemed to be whispering to companions, *Is that Joe Reeder? Really Joe Reeder?*

She was about to push the DOWN button when a male hand butted in from behind them and pushed it for her. She turned to look and there he was—the GAO drone.

The drone politely gestured for Rogers to get on first, and then did the same with Reeder, who was giving the man a blank look that disguised alarm bells going off.

The nearly handsome man with the dark hair and wire-frame glasses said to her lightly, "We have to stop meeting like this."

Reeder pushed the first-floor button as Rogers said, "I was just telling my friend here that no matter where we go, it seems you're already there."

The doors whispered shut.

Unperturbed, the drone said, "Life's just full of odd coincidences, isn't it, Agent Rogers?"

Reeder hit the STOP button and the elevator did a little shake and braked. A real alarm bell began to ring now, muffled.

Rogers said, "You seem to know me. Who the hell are you?"

The drone shrugged; his smile couldn't have been more pleasant. "For now, my name's unimportant. I'm sure, Agent Rogers, that with a little effort, you'll soon know."

Reeder came over and grabbed the drone by the arm, crowding him in the small space. "She asked you a question. Who the hell are you?"

The drone, not at all intimidated, said, "Violence won't do you any good in this situation, Mr. Reeder."

The alarm bell rang on.

Reeder let go of the man's sleeve. "Who are you working for?"

"The American people, of course."

Reeder grabbed the drone's arm again. "Listen to me, you son of a bitch . . ."

With surprising ease, the drone plucked Reeder's hand off and flipped it away. His voice came back with a new, menacing edge: "No, Mr. Reeder. You listen to me."

On and on, it rang.

". . . I'm listening."

"Walk away from your investigation, if you want your life back. That is, if you want that life to be a safe one for you and yours."

Reeder backhanded him.

Briefly, something vile flickered on the drone's face, then his pleasant expression returned as he dug a handkerchief out to touch the blood at one corner of his mouth.

The alarm bell did not let up.

The drone's eyes were on Reeder but he was speaking to her now: "Agent Rogers, I believe I have good news for you. I have it on good authority that an Assistant Directorship will be opening up soon. Could well be yours . . . if you and your friend here can find something constructive to do . . . such as: nothing."

The drone punched the button that released the elevator and they started down again.

The alarm bell ceased.

"Not interested," Rogers said, soft but firm.

"Sorry to hear that," the drone said. "A wrong decision can get a person into trouble. The wrong outlook can even get a person killed."

Reeder grabbed the drone's Men's Wearhouse jacket by its lapels, and shoved him against an elevator wall.

Though he was clearly rattled, the drone said calmly, "Agent Rogers is the one at real risk here. You, Mr. Reeder, are a public figure. An American hero, and eliminating you would draw an unfortunate amount of attention. That would be less a concern for, say, your wife and daughter. They can't stay in hiding forever, unless you three are prepared to live in exile."

Letting go of the drone, Reeder backed away, visibly shaken in a way Rogers had never observed in him before.

The doors swished open and the drone knifed through a group waiting for an elevator that had taken a terribly long time to arrive.

Soon Rogers and Reeder were outside in the sunshine, but gloom nonetheless shrouded them.

"Did that really just happen?" she asked.

"That was a very real and serious threat, Patti, made by someone not afraid to carry it out, if need be."

They tucked themselves against the outer wall of the building; the sidewalk butted almost up to the building here.

She asked, "Is he who we're after, do you think?"

Reeder shook his head. "We're looking for more than one rogue player, and your GAO pal seems more a messenger."

She was flushed. "I don't care if Briar *is* the Director of the Secret Service, I'll put him in custody and haul his ass to the Hoover Building into an interview room and—"

"No."

". . . No?"

"We take a frontal approach like that, we'll be lucky to be alive tomorrow. And if that prick knows my wife and daughter are in hiding, he just might learn where."

"You're not suggesting we walk *away*?"

"No. Not at all."

"Then . . . ?"

"We go to ground."

Rogers frowned. "But I need my task force to get anywhere on this thing, and access to my resources at the Bureau, and—"

"Where did you first see our GAO friend?"

"At Fisk's office." She looked at him agape. "Oh, come on, Joe— you're not saying *Fisk* may be compromised!"

"The Director of the Secret Service seems to be. And Fisk is just an Assistant Director."

"She gave me full support on this investigation!"

He just sent her one of those frustratingly bland looks. "How better to keep an eye on you and your people?"

Government employees trouped by on the sidewalk in either direction. Employees of a government that Rogers could no longer trust . . .

She said, her voice sounding as small as a child's, "What do we do?"

His response seemed a non sequitur. "You care about Kevin."

"What? *Yes!* Of course."

"Then we need to get him somewhere safe. You make him vulnerable, and he makes you the same."

She willed herself to say calm. "Okay, so we get Kevin somewhere safe. What about us?"

"The same. Off the grid. Way off. We'll pull Miggie in, too, so he can work his computer magic and help us get the identity of our GAO buddy. That son of a bitch is our way inside to whoever's behind all this."

"What about the rest of the team?"

"For now, they stay on the job. We'll pull them off at some point, and get them to ground, too . . . but for now they make a show of continuing the Yellich investigation, only they won't get anywhere that they share. Otherwise, anything they come up with, anything they accomplish, could be known by the rogue group."

Soon, with Reeder at the wheel of his Prius, Rogers kept an eye out for a tail. After last night, the agent who lost his flag pin would not likely still be on the job, but someone else obviously could be. Right now they were going south on Ninth Street NW.

"We need somewhere to work from," Reeder said, "a shadow HQ for an investigation of a shadow government. And we have to stay in the city, because that's where the enemy is."

"We need a safe house," she said.

"Yes. And that's where we're going."

He drove up the ramp for I-395 and headed east. They rode in silence for a while—she would let him think, even as her own mind was spinning. When he merged onto I-695, she finally asked, "Not the Navy Yard?"

"Not the Navy Yard. Too many security cameras. Someplace better."

He parked on Ninth Street SE, with greenery to their right as he got out of the car and so did she.

"Where are we?" she asked.

"Near where we're going. But it's best we walk."

They skirted Virginia Avenue Park, then turned back down Tenth toward the Navy Yard and into a sketchy area where they passed a vacant lot between two brick buildings. The one on the corner of M Street, a tailor and pawnshop below, had a fire escape up to the floor above.

Reeder took the 'scape, surprising her a little, and she followed him to a landing where awaited a steel door with an overhead security camera . . . and a doorbell. As if the bell weren't there, Reeder pounded on the steel.

In a moment, a voice came over a speaker: "Closed for bidness."

"I got after-hours money, DeMarcus."

"Who that with you?"

She said, "Special Agent Rogers."

The voice said, "You shittin' me, Reeder? You bring *Five Oh* to my door?"

"Five Oh is city, DeMarcus. My friend here is federal, but she isn't DEA or ATF, so don't sweat it."

"Go away, man. I don't know you no more."

"Ten thousand dollars."

The speaker fell silent.

Then: "Fifteen."

"DeMarcus, you don't even know what I'm buying yet."

"I know you brung a fed around."

"I need two minutes. We come to terms and I got ten K for you."

"Like you got that much on you."

Rogers goggled at Reeder as he withdrew a major wad of cash from his pocket like Bugs Bunny producing an anvil from somewhere. He held up the wad with one hand and the fingers of the other riffled through bills.

The door opened. Half-opened, anyway.

The skinny African American guy who peered suspiciously out at them looked to be in his early twenties; he wore Georgetown University gear, though she doubted somehow that he was enrolled.

"Patti," Reeder said, "this is my friend DeMarcus. DeMarcus, this is my friend Patti. You can call her Agent Rogers. Be nice. She's armed."

He grunted an unimpressed laugh. "What you wanna buy?" he asked.

"Oh," Reeder said innocently, "did you want to deal right out here in the open? On your doorstep?"

Their host scowled and waved them inside, stepping aside for them.

The place was a loft, with an office area just inside, a metal desk with computer off to the right and a warehouse of goods to the left— three tall rows of shelves arranged by product: bags of weed, handguns, and cell phones. Beyond was a modern kitchen, like something from a Home Depot showroom, and to the left a spacious home theater area with overstuffed black-leather chairs and a couch facing a massive flat-screen, below which a low-riding doorless cabinet held electronics gear, two massive black speakers bookending the big screen. Down on the M Street end was an elaborate wall mural of classic rap and hip hop, interrupted by two doors—bathroom and bedroom, probably.

The place reeked of weed. A door in the mural opened and a beautiful young naked black girl with a retro 'fro leaned there and called out sleepily, "Come back to bed, Markie—your baby's lonely."

DeMarcus shrugged at them. "Don't mind Sheila."

Reeder was looking in Sheila's direction; he didn't seem to mind one bit.

"*Bidness!*" DeMarcus called back, and Sheila's sigh could be heard all through the loft before she shut herself poutily back in.

They remained near the door in the office area as DeMarcus asked, "So, Joe. What you wanna buy?"

"Nothing."

"Nada?"

"Not a thing. I want to rent something."

"What the hell you wanna rent?"

"This loft."

And Reeder handed the wad of bills toward DeMarcus.

"Like hell," their host said, his brow wrinkled. Maybe he was closer to thirty, she thought. "I got a bidness to run."

"That's why this fistful of money isn't really ten grand."

"If it ain't ten grand, then get you white asses outa my crib."

"It's fifty."

"Say what?"

"It's fifty K, DeMarcus. You old enough to remember when somebody won something, and a guy showed up with a giant damn check for them? Well, nobody uses checks anymore. You'll just have to settle for cash. Here. Count it."

DeMarcus, looking a little dazed, took the wad and counted. It was hundred dollar bills. Presumably five hundred of them.

Reeder waited until DeMarcus's nod indicated the tally was right.

Reeder said, "There's a string attached."

Their host scowled again. "Would be."

"You have to use that to take little Sheila someplace exotic for a week. Belize maybe. Nassau's nice. When you come back, I'll have another fifty for you."

DeMarcus thumbed through the bills; he looked stunned. "A hundred K to rent the place for a week."

"That's right."

"What for?"

"Why, are you afraid we might do something illegal? DeMarcus, the green rents the place and comes with no explanations. You have a passport?"

"Yeah, but, uh . . ."

"How about Sheila baby? She have a passport?"

"Yeah, we did Cancun last year."

"Long-term relationship, huh? That's good, DeMarcus. That's healthy."

"Reeder, I gotta know—"

"That's not healthy. One week, the out-of-country dream spot of your choice."

"When?"

"Now."

"Now?"

"Well . . . soon as you've packed, and broken it to Sheila. She's not going to mind."

"But I . . . man, I got a damn *bidness* to run."

"Why, do you generally pull down a hundred K in a week? You send out word to your customer base, e-mail or text or whatever, that you'll be away for a week. Anybody comes around, we won't answer the door."

"Maybe . . . maybe I should go pack now."

"No maybe about it."

DeMarcus started off, then turned and said, "I don't *really* wanna know any more than this?"

"That's right, you don't."

DeMarcus headed for Sheila's door at the other end of the loft, but Reeder's voice stopped him. "Consider part of that hundred K payment for any burner phones I might need. If I take any weapons, we can settle up later."

"You can have up to five nines," DeMarcus called back, "on the house," and then slipped in the bedroom.

Their host and his lady friend had flown in an hour, but the weed smell remained. Rogers found some Febreze under the kitchen sink and got rid of it as best she could.

Using a burner phone from DeMarcus's seemingly endless supply, Reeder rented a car to be delivered to a restaurant on L Street a couple of blocks north.

"We'll walk over there together," he said to her.

They were each in an overstuffed black-leather chair.

Rogers shook her head. "No need. Hey, you may have forgotten, but I'm a trained FBI agent. Me with *your* famous face is way too conspicuous."

He reluctantly agreed.

"When the car gets there," he said, "you drop the driver off at the rental agency, then go to Miggie's, pick him up, and have him bring as much gear as he can carry."

"Mig'll work from here?"

Reeder nodded. "No one's going to look for him at this address. We'll keep the rest of the task force out on the street while we get things done here."

"Mig should bring some clothes, too, I assume."

"Unless he's into Redskins and Georgetown threads, 'cause probably that's all DeMarcus has. We'll get some of your things when we pick Kevin up. I can cover my needs from some neighborhood bodega and the tailor downstairs."

"You can wash what you have on, too. This place has everything. It's the damn Batcave with burner phones."

Reeder gave her half a smile. "DeMarcus is a smart cookie, as we ancient types say. He stays under the radar, and in the ten years I've known him, never served a day inside."

"Why d'you never bust him?"

"His crimes aren't federal. Anyway, he's a resource. Like the CIA guys say, an asset . . . You better get going, Patti. That rental's due in fifteen minutes. Oh, and grab one of those nine millimeters of Marcus's on your way out."

"Come on, Joe—I already have my service weapon."

"Yeah. And it can be traced."

"The government, which was designed for the people, has got into the hands of the bosses and their employers, the special interests. An invisible empire has been set up above the forms of democracy."

Woodrow Wilson, twenty-eighth President of the United States of America. Served 1913–1921. President during World War I, only President to be interred within Washington, DC, at the National Cathedral.

ELEVEN

Anne Nichols, going up in her apartment building's elevator, knew she owed her mother a phone call. Despite the fresh look of her light blue silk blouse and black flared slacks, the African American FBI agent was dead tired, and wanted nothing more than to get inside her apartment, maybe take a detour to the shower, then crawl between the sheets ASAP.

Nichols and her mother, a Chicago policewoman, usually talked at least once a week. But it had been almost two weeks now, and she was feeling guilty.

For almost a decade, she and her mom had been each other's entire immediate family—her daddy, a CTA bus driver, came home one night and fell asleep in his recliner, never to wake up again. And her older brother, Trevon, died in Iraq. His framed Purple Heart was still on Mom's mantle.

So Nichols felt a responsibility to keep in touch, however busy she might be, and the Special Situations Task Force had been plenty busy over this past year. Still, she knew that her mom wouldn't shame her for not calling, and would rarely call herself, for fear of intruding.

When Anne had gone straight from law school to the FBI, after her mother had assumed her daughter would go into private practice,

Mrs. Nichols had understood without need of discussion that her "baby girl" wanted to be a cop like her momma.

Nichols had the long, slender frame of her father, and a prettiness that her stocky, rather blunt-featured mother lacked. But both women knew they were more alike than not.

On the fifth floor, Nichols walked quickly to her apartment, beckoned by the thought of a hot shower and cool bed sheets. She was just getting her keys from her purse when she noticed the edge of light under her door.

Her tiredness evaporated and she was on the alert—she *never* left the lights on. *Never.*

This was a security building, with a doorman on duty much of the day and a keypad in the lobby. Not an impregnable fortress by any means, but anyone who'd been able to get in here, and into her apartment, was likely a professional criminal . . . or a federal agent.

And considering the rogue element in government that Rogers had warned them about, Nichols could not assume the best about another fed.

She dropped the keys back in her shoulder-strap purse, withdrawing a small automatic with one hand, and the burner phone she'd been given with the other. Tempted as she was to deal with this herself, the wiser move would be to call Rogers for backup.

The automatic trained on the door, her hearing perked for anything behind it, she had just started keying in Rogers' new number when she sensed something behind her.

An anonymous nine millimeter snugged in his waistband, Joe Reeder stood on the fire-escape landing outside DeMarcus's crib, pulling on a cigarette liberated from the half-pack of Benson & Hedges Menthol Ultra Lights left behind by the formerly naked Sheila in the couple's rush to leave. The beautiful starry evening seemed at odds with the storm clouds of the situation, though a March crispness provided a reminder that a chill was coming.

That distinctive white hair of his Reeder had tucked under a Nationals cap, appropriated (like the Georgetown windbreaker) from his host's closet. The door was propped open, a shaft of light cutting the darkness of the wrought-iron landing as he waited for Rogers and Miggie, knowing they should be back soon.

He hadn't smoked in over a year, not even a single cigarette, but he couldn't resist just this one as he tried to calm his jangly nerves. He'd been going over every single aspect of the Yellich assassination and the dead CIA quartet in Azbekistan, looking for possible connections—was Len Chamberlain's murder the connective tissue? He tried to separate what he knew from what he thought, what he could prove from what he surmised.

As soon as he saw headlights swing onto Tenth, Reeder tossed the cigarette sparking into the alley and went down to greet them.

When Rogers parked the car alongside the building, Reeder stepped behind the vehicle so that when she popped the trunk, he'd be ready to grab some of Miggie's gear. With the three of them, a single trip got all of it up and inside. Although Mig used a tablet for most of his searches, the rest of the tech wizard's toys, which were in part to help hide his presence here, would not exactly fit neatly into a shoulder bag.

With the door finally pulled shut, Miggie looked at Reeder and said, "Patti gave me the Cliff Notes version. How about the unabridged edition?"

Reeder motioned for them to move to the comfy chairs and couches facing the big flat-screen and settled in. Reeder brought Mig up to speed quickly but thoroughly.

Then he asked Miggie, "Have you had any luck tracking the money Wooten was paid to take Secretary Yellich down?"

Mig, in gray Hoyas Basketball sweats, shrugged. "Some . . . but nothing that does us any good yet. Shell companies, a slew of them.

Whoever paid Wooten wanted the transaction untraceable. Nothing *is*, of course . . . but tracking it could take time."

"How much time?" Reeder asked.

Miggie shrugged again. "Who knows? Weeks, even months."

"We have four days. Then it won't matter."

Miggie frowned, flipped a hand. "I can only do what I can do, Joe. It's like peeling an onion a layer at a time."

Rogers asked, "What about our friend from the GAO?"

"Your elevator buddy? Well, knowing he's from the GAO—if he's *really* from the GAO—isn't much to go on."

She clearly didn't like the sound of that. "Can't you round up some pictures for me to sort through?"

Miggie huffed a non-laugh. "Patti, there's somewhere north of three thousand employees in the GAO, more than half of 'em male—you want to look at all their photos?"

She frowned. "There has to be a faster way . . ."

"Might be," Miggie admitted. "I've got a couple of ideas. Get back to you on that. In the meantime, what else do we need?"

Reeder held out the plastic bag with the busted flag-lapel camera in it. "Any way to track this?"

Miggie took the bag, removed its contents, studied it. Finally he said, "There's no onboard memory, so it recorded images to a hard drive somewhere else. Meaning . . . probably not. Any idea who it belongs to?"

"A guy who jumped me in the dark."

"Giving me a lot to work with, aren't you?"

Reeder lifted a shoulder and put it back down. "Well, the Secret Service is the only agency I know of that uses these, this model anyway. It almost *has* to belong to one of their agents. If not, why did the GAO drone try to intimidate us right there at the Secret Service?"

Rogers asked, "What do you say, Miggie? Is there a way to track down the right agent?"

Examining the back of the mini-camera, the computer expert said, "There's an ID number . . . maybe match it, *if* I hack the Secret Service. No small feat that, and when the flag cam got smashed, the ID number appears to've been ground into the concrete, and it was a tiny one to begin with . . . but we should be able to come up with several possibilities."

"Good," Reeder said.

As if taking stock for the first time, Miggie glanced around, sniffing some, and said, "You'll need more Febreze than that to cover up that much weed."

Reeder chuckled. "Who says Miguel Altuve can't determine anything without a computer?"

Really taking their surroundings in now, Miggie asked, "What the hell *is* this place?"

Not missing a beat, Rogers said, "The Batcave."

Miggie smirked. "Oh really? Is that how Bruce Wayne made his fortune, selling dope and guns?"

Ignoring that, Reeder rose and said, "Get set up, Mig, and get at it. You should be safe here . . . just don't answer the door."

The smirk morphed into a frown. "You think that elevator clown who threatened you can find us? Him or whoever he works for, anyway? And I don't mean the GAO."

Reeder shook his head. "Probably not, but in this town, what *couldn't* happen? And the friend of mine who loaned us this pad has customers who will *not* be expecting *you*. So don't answer it unless it's one of us. There's a camera—you'll be able to see who's out there."

Miggie nodded, let some air out, said, "Got it."

Reeder turned to Rogers. "Have you taken care of the Kevin situation?"

"No, but it's next on my list."

"Mine, too."

She rose. "Joe . . . I can handle it myself. You stick here, why don't you, and keep Miggie safe."

Miggie volunteered, "I can handle myself."

"He's right," Reeder told her. "This is a fortress. But you'll be out in the world, Patti, and the next time they come at us, it'll be with more than just threats. Consider me your backup."

They took the rental car, Rogers driving, sticking to secondary streets, headlights like twin Maglites searching the darkness. When they were about a mile from her Joyce Street apartment house, Reeder had her pull over. He got out and in back and stayed low. He figured no one would recognize the rental, but understood that all of their residences were likely under surveillance.

A mile later, she pulled into the underground garage of her apartment building, pausing to swipe her card at the entry.

"Anything on the street?" he asked, still ducked down.

"Not that I saw. But these are pros."

"So are we."

"Should that be a comfort?"

She parked and they got out of the car and headed for the elevator, which was close to her stall. They didn't bother trying to evade the security cameras, including the elevator cam, but going up the stairs would only put them in view of more high-mounted cameras. Odds were good no one would be monitoring the security system in Rogers' building— her comings and goings would be the important observations.

They rode up in silence. Reeder had only been to her place two or three times, and not at all since Kevin Lockwood had more or less moved in. Of that he didn't give a damn—as long as she was happy, he was fine with it. His only concern was that they now had another person who needed protecting. Another member of their extended "family."

As she unlocked her apartment door, Reeder backed against the wall to one side, with his hand on the butt of the nine mil in his waistband.

"We've been busy," she said, "so it's kind of a mess," then led him into the immaculate living room.

Browns and greens dominated, giving the place a vaguely military feel. A new sofa and matching recliner, dark green, dominated the middle of the room, angled toward shelves to Reeder's left with a flat-screen and books. To his right, next to the door, hung a framed poster of Kevin and his late friend DeShawn Davis in their drag costumes—"The Plain Sisters," a spoof of the Haynes sisters played by Rosemary Clooney and Vera-Ellen in *White Christmas*. Kevin and African American DeShawn—stage names Virginia Plain and Karma Sabich—posed in floor-length gowns, blonde wigs, and dazzling smiles.

DeShawn's murder had first put Rogers and Kevin in contact. Despite the stressful circumstances, the pair had hit it off and had gradually become a couple. Reeder had accompanied Rogers to one of her boyfriend's performances at the Les Girls club, and the young man, in his drag queen persona, was quite good . . . not that this was Reeder's preferred form of entertainment.

Trying to process this relationship between a woman he assumed was gay and a guy he figured was bisexual only made Reeder's head hurt. So mostly he didn't bother.

Rogers turned toward the back of the apartment, where a hallway led to two bedrooms and a bathroom, and called, "*Honey, I'm home!*" Like this was 1957 and they were a typical couple. In a lot of ways, they were.

"*Joe's here!*" she added.

Towel in hand, Kevin trotted out wearing only baggy shorts and a chin full of shaving cream, his wide grin nearly as white as the foam. "Mr. Reeder! Welcome."

Kevin strode over and, somewhat soapily, shook Reeder's hand.

"Not exactly a social call," Reeder said.

Kevin frowned in confusion, then turned to Rogers and said, "Patti, why didn't you give me a little warning? I'd have cleaned up the place."

The apartment was about as messy as a NASA clean room, but Reeder said nothing.

"Not prudent, calling," Rogers said.

Kevin looked even more confused.

She touched his arm. "I need to fill you in about something." Then she led him by the arm to the couch.

Taking his cue, Reeder said, "I'll just step outside and check in with Miggie."

Rogers nodded and he went out into the hall, then punched the computer expert's cell number into the burner phone.

When the call went straight to voice mail, Reeder tried not to make anything of that. He debated calling back, but then his phone trilled at him—UNKNOWN.

Letting out a breath he hadn't realized he was holding, he took the call. "Yeah."

"Miggie," the phone said. "Saw you called my cell. Figured I better use one of your friend's burners instead."

"Yeah," Reeder said again.

"Everything okay on your end?"

"So far. We're at Patti's. Anybody else check in?"

"Bohannon and Wade are treading water out in the field, each on his own. Hardesy, too. He picked up burner phones from some street source of his and got 'em to Bohannon and Wade. Nothing new from Nichols, although Lucas did get a burner to her."

"Try to call her?"

"Yeah, no answer."

Reeder didn't love that. "What about Trevor?"

"He's the only one Hardesy couldn't link up to and give a clean cell. But, then, you know Ivanek."

Not working with a partner, the profiler would occasionally fall off the grid for a day or even more. Didn't answer calls, check e-mails, nothing. That he'd been out of touch for less than a day didn't concern Reeder, not much anyway—but he wished they'd heard from Nichols.

Reeder asked the computer guru, "You have any luck on the flag-pin front?"

"Unless the guy reports it missing, finding who that cam belongs to is gonna be tough going."

"I figured as much. What about our GAO drone?"

"Well, an employee signed out of GAO and into the Secret Service building yesterday."

Reeder perked. "Do tell."

"Could be our boy—one Lawrence Morris."

"Why 'could be'?"

"Well, *I* never saw him, and what you and Patti gave me was fairly general. Seen one government drone, seen 'em all. I'm sending you a photo to this number. See if it's your elevator buddy."

"Will do. Good work."

"Thanks. Oh, and I'm still digging through Wooten's Cayman Island money."

"And?"

"And one of the shell companies the money was funneled through was owned by Adam Benjamin."

The late billionaire had launched an independent run for president last year.

Reeder grinned at the phone. "So we're getting somewhere."

"Somewhere . . . and nowhere. This transaction was made after Benjamin died. Still . . . considering Benjamin's role in last year's fun-and-games, it's a hell of a coincidence, wouldn't you say?"

Like most law enforcement types, Reeder hated coincidences. But sometimes seeming coincidences were very real clues. "That shell company—does the Benjamin estate own it, or what?"

"No, it was sold as part of his holdings. But this looks like *another* shell company—something called DTOM Holdings."

"Which is what the hell?"

"No idea. Shells within shells, like those Russian dolls." Miggie laughed a little. "Except here you open one doll and there are fifteen inside."

"Then why do you sound so chipper?"

"Why, don't *you* like a challenge?"

Reeder chuckled and said, "Stick with it. I'll get back to you after I check the photo. And keep trying to reach Nichols, too."

"Will do."

They clicked off and Reeder called up the photo. Staring blandly back at him was the bespectacled bastard from the elevator, who was indeed one Lawrence Morris. A name to put with the face was always good. Now, to learn more about him . . .

Reeder knocked on Rogers' door.

"It's open, Joe," she called.

He went in and saw Rogers and Kevin side by side on the new couch. The boyfriend had wiped off the shaving cream, the blue of beard making his profession seem unlikely. His concerned expression didn't surprise Reeder, who walked over to face them.

Looking up at him, locking eyes, Rogers said, "Kevin isn't coming with us."

Reeder frowned. "He really should. Kevin, you really should."

She held up a hand to cut him off. "It's not that we don't value your opinion, Joe, or your advice . . . but this is our issue, mine and Kevin's, and we think it's safer for both of us if only I know where he is."

Reeder nodded. She was right, of course, it was their issue. But he did say, to both of them, "Staying here would be foolish."

They were holding hands. "Kevin won't be here . . . he has friends he can stay with."

Reeder's eyebrows went up. "He might be endangering them."

"Kevin doesn't think so. Joe, other than these friends and a few others, no one really knows about us anyway. We've kept it low-key, these months. It's not like we're posting selfies on Instagram or Facebook."

Reeder shifted his gaze to Kevin. "You're sure about this? You *do* seem to be living together. I don't know how much Patti told you, but we're navigating very treacherous waters right now. I sent my own family away."

Kevin said nothing, just raised a forefinger in "wait" mode. He got up and disappeared down the hall. Reeder frowned at Rogers again, but she just smiled, and raised a hand in her own "wait" gesture.

Kevin was gone about two minutes, but that was enough time for him to finish his shave and put on his shoulder-length wig of brunette curls. Wrapped in a dark blue silk robe, he was Kevin no more—this was Virginia Plain.

Planting himself before Reeder, Kevin—his voice higher, sharper now—said, "Joe, dear, how long have you and Patti been on the radar of these miscreants? Long enough for them to know about Patti and me, despite our discretion?"

"They might know about Kevin," Reeder admitted, "but probably not Virginia."

Startlingly, Kevin's voice dropped to his normal male pitch. "That's right. And until we all can come in from the cold, I'll be in full-on Virginia—clothes, makeup, heels, hair, the whole magilla. Trust me—they'll never know."

Reeder nodded. "I'm convinced. But we're dealing with people who have no compunction about killing, remember . . . and who have resources that stretch into the highest reaches of government. You need to be good and goddamn careful. Patti, you gave him a burner?"

She nodded.

"Kevin—Virginia—whatever. Anything out of the ordinary, anything scares or disturbs you, you get back to us, *now*. Understood?"

"Understood, Mr. Reeder."

"And Kevin?"

"Yes?"

"Goddamnit, it's 'Joe.'"

The beautiful face beamed. "All right, Joe."

Reeder curled a finger at Rogers and said, "Time." She nodded, went over and gave Kevin a quick kiss, and then she and Reeder were out the door.

They were in the elevator, on their way down, when she asked, "So—Miggie?"

He told her what Mig had shared about the GAO drone.

She frowned. "Lawrence Morris—he even *sounds* like a damn accountant."

"Accountants don't generally threaten to kill you."

Then he told her that everybody but Ivanek and Nichols had checked in, and gave her the number of Miggie's new phone.

In the parking garage, Rogers said, "I'm not worried about Ivanek—half the time he doesn't answer when he knows it's you."

"No argument," Reeder said. "But I'd feel better if we checked on Nichols."

"No argument," Rogers echoed.

Anne Nichols lived in a two-bedroom flat in a high-rise on Connecticut Avenue NW, a good neighborhood strewn with apartment houses, south of Melvin C. Hazen Park. The tan-brick building was on the corner, two burning-bush trees guarding either side of the front walk.

At the entrance, up a few steps, Reeder called Miggie and asked, "Any luck reaching Anne?"

"Nope."

"Can you give me the security code to her building?"

"Give me a second."

Keystrokes clicked through the phone, then Miggie gave Reeder the requested numbers.

"Thanks," Reeder said. "You'll hear from us soon."

Reeder ended the call.

He and Rogers moved through the outer lobby, passing the wall of mailboxes and a potted plant that did not really bring the Great Outdoors inside.

Next to the security door, a keypad was waiting for Reeder to punch in the code. The door buzzed open.

The interior lobby, unpopulated at this hour, had a little more space than the outer one, accommodating two potted plants, a couple of overstuffed chairs, and one elevator.

Soon they were on Nichols' floor, moving down the corridor, guns drawn. Reeder kept behind Rogers as she moved down the otherwise empty hall toward the last door on the right.

Not surprisingly, Nichols' door was locked. Rogers knocked and got no response. She tried again—nothing. They traded a look, and Reeder whispered, "You do the honors," and she nodded and withdrew a small pouch of lock picks from a pocket.

They were inside in well under a minute. The living room was dark, and Reeder hit the lights—the place was as stylish as Nichols herself, ultramodern, blacks and browns and whites. Nothing looked disturbed. They traded rooms and yells of "Clear!"

No Nichols.

No sign of her.

Reeder had fought the thought that they might find her dead in here, and that she wasn't, well, that was a relief, at least.

Rogers just behind him, Reeder turned on the overhead light in the galley kitchen, and they both saw it at once—a sheet of copy-size paper on top of the stove.

One oversized computer-printed word, red ink—**COLLATERAL**.

Reeder shook his head. "Jesus."

Rogers got her cell out, called Miggie, and reported what they'd found.

She told him, "Have Bohannon stop by Ivanek's. If Trevor's not home, have Jerry stake out the place."

"You got it."

"And pull Wade in. Give him the Batcave directions. We need reinforcements."

"Sounding like it."

"Meantime, while we're headed back to you, round up the security video from Anne's building. Can you do that?"

"I can do that," Miggie said, and clicked off.

Reeder was leaning against a counter. He said to her, "Did you see one thing out of place? Any damn thing at all?"

"No."

"Whoever took her got her by surprise. Got the drop on her."

"Joe, they could have taken her any time after Hardesy delivered her that burner phone. No one's heard from her since."

He sighed deep. "Let's hope Bohannon gets to Ivanek in time."

He glanced at the one-word note, finding one small scrap of solace.

At least **COLLATERAL** wasn't followed by **DAMAGE**.

"How far you can go without destroying from within
what you are trying to defend from without?"

*Dwight D. Eisenhower, thirty-fourth President of the United States
of America. Served 1953–1961. Former five-star general, Supreme
Commander of the Allied Forces in World War II.*

TWELVE

Lawrence Morris sat at the long narrow table in the expansive private dining room of the Federalist Club on F Street. He had been here a few times, to deliver messages, but had never been admitted past the front vestibule. Tonight, he perched among the chosen, ready to deliver his report when the chairman called upon him.

The chamber, with its rich oak paneling and dark heavy furnishings, seemed a throwback to a day when industrialists openly ruled the nation from behind closed doors. The same was true for the formal table settings with their bone china, impossibly white dinnerware with intricate hand-painted cherry blossoms. Baccarat crystal water glasses, Reed & Barton sterling silverware, hand-embroidered table linen, the outlay fairly dazzled Morris. He knew, for example, that these napkins ran over $150 each, which meant that for tonight's dinner with the six-body board, plus the chairman, plus Morris himself, brought the napkin cost alone to $1,200. Toss in the fine tablecloth, and linens, and it tallied more than the price of his first car. (Working as he did in the Government Accountability Office, knowing what things cost was Morris's specialty.)

The male staff wore tuxedos, the females old-fashioned maid-uniform livery. Whenever staff entered the room, all conversation stopped, and—other than giving orders or responding to questions from waiters—the board members remained silent until they were alone again.

With dessert done, and coffee served, the liveried army retreated to the kitchen. The chairman waited a full minute, then tapped his knife against his water glass, just once.

Every eye went to Senator Wilson Blount, his sharp light blue eyes peering from above the low-riding tortoiseshell glasses, his silvery blond hair barbershop perfect despite the late hour. Even before that single tap of metal on glass, all here were already under his sway. The chairman of the American Patriots Alliance led the way of this joint effort to restore the United States from "*the sniveling weakling it had become,*" as Blount himself sometimes explained it, "*to its rightful place as the world's preeminent superpower.*"

"We all know why we're here, gentlemen," Blount said in his lilting Tennessee accent.

The six board members nodded as one.

Their attire varied in style but not in monetary value—Morris was out of his depth as to the exact price of their wardrobe (tailored suits rarely came up at the GAO). And admittedly he felt somewhat self-conscious in his own Men's Wearhouse number. But actually, Blount's off-the-rack brown suit, which fit his contrived folksy persona, may have cost even less.

Morris recognized two of the board, powerful men with national reputations who occasionally made it into the media—a major hotelier from New Jersey, and a trucking magnate from Wisconsin. The other four Morris drew a blank on, though that was hardly surprising. Anonymity was something the Alliance board cultivated.

They were all low-profile players now, with the one exception—an individual who had unwisely sought the political limelight—conveniently deceased. When the man had refused to step back in line with the Alliance's plans for the greater good, Senator Blount and the board simply distanced themselves from him. No further action was taken, since the natural course of events had resolved the situation.

The chairman swung his eyes toward Morris and so did everyone else. "Your report, sir, if you please."

Morris cleared his throat and stood, nodding to one and all, allowing a tiny polite smile to flicker. Blount had personally given Morris his task and, other than the Senator himself, no one in the room would have the slightest idea of his identity, foot soldier that he was.

Which was fine with Morris. He believed in the American Patriots Alliance's motto: *Serve Country, Not Self.* Someday that would be on currency. What he and all of the loyalists enacted was part of their overall mission to restore the greatness that President Harrison had so recklessly squandered.

Still, this was a chance to make an impression, to demonstrate his value to the movement. Not that he had any illusion that a regular chair at this table might become his—the money and power here were out of his reach. But he would happily serve.

He said, in a firm voice that disguised his unease, "I met with Joe Reeder and Special Agent Patti Rogers after their meeting with the Director at the Secret Service. As instructed, I proffered both carrot and stick."

"And their response?" the chairman asked.

"As you predicted, sir, they were not receptive to the carrot . . . but somewhat so to the stick. They *did* seem to have a sense of the precariousness of their situation—the implications of what further inquiry by them might cost."

"Reeder has two weaknesses," came the folksy drawl. "His pride and what we might call his . . . 'family.'"

Morris asked, "His ex-wife and his daughter, sir?"

"No. They are out of reach for the moment. Efforts are being made to find them, but Mr. Reeder is not a man without his own resources."

Morris leaned a hand on the linen-covered tabletop. "Reeder betrayed emotion, sir. I realize his reputation is one of rather . . . restrained behavior and self-expression. But he laid hands on me—*twice.*"

The other eyes at the table were moving from the chairman to Morris and back again, as the two men exchanged remarks in a tennis-match fashion.

"Joseph Reeder," drawled Blount, "is such a self-righteous soul that the very idea of his character bein' besmirched likely gives him physical pain . . . but he would sooner endure that than allow anything untoward to happen to those he cares about."

"Sir, you . . . you *don't* refer to his ex-wife and child?"

"Well, they're the major part of the mix, of course. But he's become attached to this agent, this Rogers woman. I don't believe it's a sexual relationship. Call it . . . father-and-daughter, or big-brother-and-little-sister. However you might characterize it, she is important to him. So are those he's worked with at the FBI, as a consultant—the so-called Special Situations Task Force."

Morris nodded, understanding the weak spot the chairman intended to penetrate.

Blount asked, "Did our people track the pair after they left the Secret Service buildin'?"

Morris offered an apologetic open-handed gesture. "I'm afraid, sir, within minutes, they went off the grid. If we find them . . . that is *when* we find them . . . what action do we take?"

The chairman leaned back in a chair taller than he was. "For now, nothin'—we'll let 'em flail and flounder."

"Sir."

"They're tryin' to find a way to keep out of harm's way and yet contin-yuh their investigation at the one-and-the-same time. Eventually they will come to perceive the hopelessness of that goal."

"Sir, Reeder is a top investigator, and so is that FBI female."

Holding up a hand, the chairman said, "Keep your powder dry, my friend, and wait. They have not yet grasped the untenable nature of their position. They will contin-yuh to flail around for a time, likely gettin' nowhere a'tall." Blount pointed a thick forefinger at Morris. "But if they get close, we will have no choice but to shut them the hell down. Do you follow?"

Morris nodded. He followed, all right.

These men, the patriots on the board, were willing to make such sacrifices to return America to its greatness. A soldier kills in battle, at the direction of generals. The four CIA agents and Secretary Yellich had not been murdered; they were casualties of the cause.

For something as far-reaching as the ongoing operation, individuals would occasionally have to be sacrificed—for the greater good. That was at the core of the American Patriots Alliance.

Patrick Reitz, the trucking magnate—a heavy man with receding dark hair and a lizard's hooded eyes—shook his head. "Why not eliminate them now? Aren't they a genuine threat to our current goal?"

The chairman's glance at Reitz had steel in it. "You are aware, my friend, that six government employees are already fatalities."

"Nothing wrong with your math, Mr. Chairman. Only . . . why not two more?"

Blount's intake of breath seemed to consume half the air in the room; when he let it out, nearby napkins rustled. "You would have us liquidate an FBI agent, a female one at that, who has generated positive publicity for the Justice Department in recent years? Then there's the national hero who saved one president's life and now is more popular than another one."

"Accidents *do* happen," Reitz said.

The chairman shook his head; there was a finality about it. "Too many red flags have already gone up for us to risk such behavior. Their deaths would bring more questions, more agents. But, yes, we can and will deal with these two, if necessary. For now, we have control of the situation. Killing that pair would relinquish our control. Doesn't that make sense, gentlemen?"

Morris found himself nodding. To his surprise, so was Reitz, and the rest of the board, too.

"That'll be all for you this evenin'," Blount said to the GAO man pleasantly.

Then no one, not even the chairman himself, spoke a word as Morris rose and left like another member of the club's staff, just not as well dressed. He slipped out the door, leaving behind the muffled sounds of the meeting continuing without him.

Alone on F Street, Morris felt he'd done well tonight. The chairman appeared impressed, the other board members, too. Big things were in the air, and in his future, and he was too exhilarated to want the night to end.

He didn't have a significant other in his life right now, and hadn't for a while—these days, he just didn't have time. But tonight, as on many nights, he wanted female company.

He would use (as he had so many times) Aphrodite's, a discreet escort service that could be reached only by text message—911 for a blonde, 912 for a brunette, 913 redhead, 914 Asian girl, 915 black and so on. No haggling, and no hags—these women were all attractive and bright, fulfilling a man's desire like delicious items on a fine restaurant's menu.

Ducking into the recession of a doorway, Morris on his phone sent his message: *911, usual, 30 minutes*.

"Usual" meant the bar within the Hotel Mont Blanc, which happily was just three blocks away. The management knew him and looked the other way; he was a good customer, two or even three nights a week at his most ravenous. And tonight he would be there in plenty of time for his after-dinner delight.

The Mont Blanc, which occupied a former post office, was a reasonably priced hotel by DC standards, rooms in the four-hundred range. Kepler's, the bar off the lobby, was a plushly appointed, dark-wood-and-red-leather establishment catering for the most part to the hotel's guests and foreign dignitaries—a good place for Morris to meet his purchased conquest, with little chance of running into anyone he knew.

They would go up to his room after a couple of drinks, have their romp, then Miss 911 would be sent on her way, unless of course he felt he could manage seconds, with room service cocktails tiding them over till he was able. He would chat with them about their lives, though most would lie to him (college girls—right!), and he would spin his own tale of high government service that had nothing to do with his reality at the GAO.

He checked in, got his key, then turned his attention to Kepler's. Entering the bar, he found it decidedly underpopulated, just as he'd expected. Just as he'd hoped. Three men at a table, their suits worthy of the board members with whom he'd recently dined, were speaking with an apparent Kuwaiti in traditional kandura with a one-button collar and a ghotra worn in cobra style. Oil business, most likely.

At another table, a couple, possibly tourists, were in close conversation. Behind the oak counter, a tall African American bartender in a white tuxedo shirt and black tie smiled at Morris, who sat down at the bar.

The bartender brought Morris a napkin, and Morris ordered a Johnnie Walker Blue.

The bartender's practiced smile became a genuine grin as he poured. "Man knows his Scotch."

Morris sipped it.

"Not your first time here," the bartender said.

"No."

"Thought you looked familiar."

"Yeah. I remember you, too." Vaguely.

Motion at the entry, caught from the corner of an eye, turned Morris that way. A blonde, a pretty blonde in a form-fitting red dress, obvious but enticing, here already! Aphrodite's didn't fool around.

She walked right up to him with fluid confidence and eyed the Johnnie Walker, licking lipsticked lips and saying, "That looks good. Could I have some?"

Morris nodded and waved for the bartender to bring another drink. "Glad to. I'm Lawrence. And you are . . . ?"

"Diane," she said, which was the name the confirmation text from Aphrodite's had promised.

"Pull up a chair, Diane."

The blonde smiled, displaying pretty white teeth, and slipped up onto the stool beside him. Her dark eyes were bright, despite the dim light. Those long legs and that nice rack were fine even for Aphrodite's buffet.

They talked for a while. She was in college—grad school, and she was old enough for that to be true. He told her all about working as the aide to a well-known senator. She pretended to be impressed, just as he had pretended to believe her college crap.

"You know," Diane said, "it's not often a girl gets the chance to spend an evening like this with . . . don't get me wrong . . . someone she would've spent it with anyway."

He gave her a sly smile. "Well, you don't *have* to charge me."

She shrugged, smiling in a chin-crinkly way. "Not up to me, I'm afraid. Aphrodite's has your Visa on file, remember?"

"I remember."

"But I tell you what. Things go nicely, I won't let you leave me that nice cash tip you're planning to."

He laughed a little. "That's nice of you. Ready to go upstairs and have some fun?"

"One more little drink, okay?"

"Sure."

They had that drink and then were walking arm in arm across the lobby when he stumbled a little.

"You all right?" she asked.

"That . . . that second shot isn't settling right."

"Let's get you up to the room."

They were at the elevators now. She was propping him up, strong for a girl, just using one arm as her other hand extended to push the DOWN button.

"No," Morris said, "up."

The doors opened onto an empty car and she hauled him in and hit the door-close button, enclosing them. It took that long for Morris to know he'd been had. He flailed at the woman, whose expression was cold, and he got a fistful of hair.

Then he had a blonde wig in his hand.

"No," the 911's male voice said, "you're going down."

Rogers had been furious at first, when Reeder suggested enlisting Kevin for this duty. But obviously *she* couldn't play the role since the drone knew her all too well, and Nichols was in the hands of the enemy, so . . .

And the information about Morris and his habits that Miggie had come up with made the Aphrodite's sting a tempting prospect. The idea was to flash credentials at the bartender and send him to the backroom till further notice, while Wade took the man's place and kept Kevin safe.

It had begun at Nichols' apartment, with Reeder talking Rogers through it, assuring her that they'd be right there to back Kevin up, should her roommate agree to play.

And he had.

She'd hoped that Kevin might have already disappeared into the world of his Virginia Plain friends, but Reeder had caught him at her apartment, still packing up . . . and eager to help.

Feeling steamrollered by Reeder, she'd faced Kevin privately and said, "You don't have to do this. It's incredibly dangerous, and you don't do this kind of thing for a living like *I* do, and—"

"You may be forgetting," he said, "that despite the trappings, I'm the man in this relationship."

"Oh, Kevin, come on—"

"Then call it an equal partnership. And I'm going to hold up my end."

And that had been it.

Now, back at DeMarcus's pad—with Kevin along but out of drag, and Wade too, no longer in bartender getup—she and Reeder faced each other off to one side.

"You okay?" Reeder asked.

Her sigh seemed to start at her toenails. "As okay as possible when I've just been party to a kidnapping. That's a federal offense, you know. And I'm on the wrong side of this one."

Reeder's expression was blandly blank. "Factor this in: Morris threatened to have you, and everyone else I love, killed. And his people have Anne Nichols. Or are you not in the mood at the moment to save the ol' US of A?"

"Is that what we're doing, Joe?"

"Make it the world then. Nukes on the fly aren't that selective."

She shook her head—not a "no" gesture, more trying to clear it. "I know we're trying to stop something terrible from happening . . . but we're so far out of my law-enforcement comfort zone, I don't know if *I* know what's right and wrong."

"This isn't exactly law enforcement, Patti."

"No kidding!"

"I mean, we're more working the espionage and counterespionage side of things, where the line between what's right and wrong is, well, murky. But it's still a line we have to walk. Or anyway, dance along."

She held his eyes. "Joe, I just watched my boyfriend act as a diversion while Reggie Wade roofied a government employee so we could snatch the SOB. Does that sound like any FBI agent you know?"

Reeder managed a weak smile. "I'm just glad to see you loosening up a little."

That made her laugh, but just a single "ha."

"Kevin did very well," Reeder said. "He's a natural for this kind of work."

"Am I supposed to say 'thank you' for that?" She raised an eyebrow. "He *did* handle himself well, and I think he's a little proud of himself, actually."

"He should be."

Right now Kevin was tucked away in the bedroom where their guest, Lawrence Morris—currently blindfolded and duct-taped into a kitchen chair—wouldn't see him.

"Kevin wanted to lend a hand," Rogers said, no-nonsense, "and now he has. But first chance, I'm getting him the hell out of here."

"Oh yeah," Reeder agreed.

"So what's our next move? A bank robbery, maybe . . . or would that be a step down?"

Reeder gave her a rare half-smile. "They have Nichols, and now we have one of theirs. Let's go talk to our friend from the GAO and let him give an accounting of himself."

"If you take no risks, you will suffer no defeats. But if you take no risks, you win no victories."

Richard M. Nixon, thirty-seventh President of the United States of America. Served 1969–1974. First to resign from the presidency. Also served 1953–1961 as the thirty-sixth Vice President of the United States.

THIRTEEN

Jerry Bohannon, tie loosened, jacket folded up on the passenger seat, was fighting to stay awake. Every law enforcement officer in the world hated surveillance duty, and while this wasn't technically that, it sure as hell felt like a stakeout.

Bohannon was parked in a Bureau Ford outside his fellow agent Trevor Ivanek's place in Dumfries, Virginia. For a change, he didn't have to worry so much about being spotted. All he was doing was waiting for Trevor to come home. There was even a convenience store nearby, so he didn't have to monitor his liquid intake, and was sipping a coffee with cream and sugar right now. Of course, his boss, Patti Rogers, claimed a rogue element in government was up to no good, but frankly Bohannon found that a little hard to buy.

In fact, in this instance, he hoped Trevor *would* spot him, and also hoped he didn't miss the guy if Trevor parked somewhere out of sight, the apartment building having no parking garage.

He got out the burner phone to text Evie that he didn't know when he'd be home. She wouldn't recognize the number, but she'd see his text: *A wn ts # Cs, J*, his personal shorthand for "answer when this number calls, Jerry." The use of that shorthand would confirm it was him at the new number.

Evie was Evelyn Sullivan, the lovely brunette he'd met at a Georgetown bar a little over a year ago. Evie seemed the opposite of Carol, his ex-wife; this forty-something gal had a bawdy sense of humor and a go-with-the-flow attitude that included putting up with his weird work hours—all she ever asked was that she be kept in the loop. Not doing that had been a big factor in the breakup of his marriage.

As he waited, Bohannon sent his eyes up and down the street, which had been dead when he got here and still was. The apartment buildings had cars parked out front, and traffic was light. A couple was strolling at the other end of the block, and a dog across the street was barking at them. That was it for excitement.

Wishing Evie would call, he got out his tablet and went through the information he'd gathered on Secretary of the Interior Amanda Yellich. Her personal life was clean, her professional life exemplary, and the one thing he'd turned up was something of a happy accident.

Earlier in the day, he had visited Yellich's condominium. The building's doorman had told him the condo was empty, the Secretary's things in storage in the basement waiting for some distant family member to claim them.

His FBI badge and a twenty had bought Bohannon ten minutes in the storage room with furniture, clothing, and boxes and boxes of books, the latter including a handwritten journal he almost missed. This he'd stuffed in his back waistband.

Bored in the Ford, he got out the journal and picked up where he'd left off. He took no pleasure out of paging through the dead woman's private thoughts, which were frankly not terribly interesting much less revealing, and just cryptic enough to be irritating. One entry had caught his attention: *JR hopeless case, still in love with his ex.* Could JR be Joe Reeder, and was Reeder's connection to the woman what sparked Rogers to send them digging into Yellich's death?

Good God, was this shadow government Rogers imagined some offshoot of Reeder's love life? Bohannon grunted a laugh.

Just then he came to an entry that made him sit up a little: *My turn to sit out Camp David trip. Maybe I can kick back at home for a change.*

So Amanda Yellich had been the designated survivor, left behind when the President and Vice President gathered with the cabinet at a single location. Now with Yellich dead, someone else would stay behind. Probably meant nothing, but the back of his neck was tingling—this was worth telling Miggie Altuve about.

He was about to send Mig a text when the phone vibrated—Evie was texting: *K*—okay. Quickly he switched screens and typed *AY not CD* and sent it to Miggie. He'd explain more fully as soon as he had a chance to call Evie and say that he'd be late, that in fact this case might tie him up for days.

That was when someone approached his window quickly, probably Ivanek.

Reeder and Rogers went over to Lawrence Morris, who was duct-taped in a chair on the kitchenette side of the big room; he wore a gray duct-tape strip over his mouth and a swath of black cloth over his eyes, the wire-frame glasses on the kitchen table nearby, his buy-two-for-the-price-of-one suit hardly rumpled.

Their guest appeared to still be out from the Mickey Finn that had been administered at the Mont Blanc bar by Reggie Wade, who watched nearby on another kitchen chair, looking loose-limbed in dark gray sweats.

"He really out?" Reeder asked.

Wade shrugged. "Could be. Johnnie Walker and roofies make one sweet cocktail."

"Know anything that might bring him around?"

Another shrug. "Light a match behind his ear, maybe."

A micro-expression passed over Morris's face at the prospect, though with the blindfold, it was hard to be sure, his chin down, touching his chest.

"Well, let's try this," Reeder said, and ripped the duct tape gag off.

Their guest howled. It rang off the brick walls.

Reeder pulled around another chair. "That was your wake-up call, Lawrence."

The man was breathing hard now, chin up, obviously awake. Reeder left the blindfold on the man.

Rogers, standing just beside Reeder, a hand on the back of his chair, said, "Joe—maybe we made a mistake grabbing him."

"How so?"

"What if he doesn't know anything? What if he's too lowly a grunt for the other side to trade Nichols?" She was smiling at Reeder in a way that didn't go at all with her tone.

"Good point," Reeder said, voice solemn, smiling back. "That puts us in a bad place. I don't want to end up with this son of a bitch on our hands."

Reggie, amused, put plenty of nasty into his voice as he said, "That's what they dig holes in the forest for, bossman."

"*I know things!*"

Morris had joined the conversation.

"The only thing that really matters right now," Reeder said, "is where our friend Anne Nichols is. Who has her, and what we have to do to get her back."

"I don't know anything about Agent Nichols."

Rogers said, "You know she's an agent."

The blindfolded man nodded, still breathing hard. "But that's all. I'm what you'd call . . . middle management. I don't know every move. There are cells working various aspects."

Reeder and Rogers exchanged looks.

She asked, "Aspects of what?"

Morris strained at his bonds, leaning forward. "I'm valuable to them! They'll trade for me."

Reeder asked, "Who will trade for you, Lawrence?"

Nothing.

Wade said, "You want me to get the shovel, bossman?"

"*The board!*" he blurted.

Immediately their captive's face drained of blood; his mouth was hanging open like torn flesh. He had said too much and he knew it.

Reeder said, quietly, "What board would that be, Lawrence?"

"They're . . . they're powerful people. And they, they value me. That's all you need to know."

Reeder scooched his chair closer, the feet making a fingernails-on-a-blackboard scrape. He got the anonymous nine mil from his waistband and he racked the weapon, letting the mechanical music of it sing to the captive.

"You and your people," Reeder said, "have sacrificed at least six Americans to whatever this cause is, and whoever these powerful people are. Do you think that hypothetical hole in the forest that my friend here mentioned couldn't become very damn real?"

Lawrence shook his head. "I don't . . . I don't doubt you. But you people aren't the *only* ones who can dig a hole."

"Maybe not," Reeder said pleasantly, "but we seem to be first in line."

Reeder tore the blindfold off and the accountant blinked rapidly as his vision adjusted to the loft's muted lighting. Morris's eyes moved from face to face.

"You were saying, Lawrence," Reeder said. "The board? Would that be a board of directors of some kind?"

Morris drew in a deep breath and let it out shudderingly. He was shaking. He seemed near tears. The information this minor figure had was clearly major.

Very quietly, he said, "A board of directors oversees certain activities."

"That, Lawrence," Reeder said, "is just a little vague."

He drew in breath. Let it out. "It's a group of patriotic Americans. As I said, powerful ones. Movers and shakers, you might say. Captains of industry . . . no, *generals* of industry."

Rogers asked, "A right-wing group?"

"No, no . . ."

Reeder asked, "A leftist group?"

"No, no, you misunderstand. You underestimate. They have their own interests, but those are the best interests of America. These men are above politics, and yet they are the inheritors of everything our founding fathers put in motion."

A little hysteria was in Morris's voice now, the tears ever closer. Reeder hoped the man wouldn't piss himself.

Reeder asked, "Does this group have a name?"

"It's . . . it's rarely spoken . . ."

"Speak it anyway."

Morris swallowed. Barely audible, he said, "The American Patriots Alliance."

Disgust clenched Reeder's belly. How many evil bastards in history had wrapped themselves in the American flag? Or *any* nation's flag?

Rogers asked, "Who exactly is on this board?"

Morris shook his head. "I have a *sense* of who they are, but not . . . *exactly* who they are."

"No," Reeder said, hard, his kinesics skills coming to the fore, "you *do* know them. Or some of them."

Morris stiffened. "If I give you any names, I'm a dead man. And don't threaten me with that hole in the forest again. Just go ahead and kill me. Because I would already be dead."

Now when Reeder read the man, he knew Morris was telling the truth.

"If you don't give us those names," Reeder said, "what do you have to bargain with?"

"Your agent."

Reeder, Rogers, and Wade exchanged looks. *Back to square one . . .*

"If I haven't told you anything," Morris said, "they'll trade. If I talk, they'll kill me, and you have no lever to get your agent back."

"Portillium," Reeder said.

Morris blinked. "What?"

"Portillium—hear of it? Know what it is?"

Morris shook his head. "No. It sounds made up."

Shit, Reeder thought. *He's telling the truth.*

"Well," Reeder said, "it's not a new additive in dishwashing powder. It's a mineral, a very rare one, and almost certainly why the Russians went into Azbekistan."

Morris squinted at Reeder, as if trying to get him in focus. "They . . . went to war for a mineral?"

"Does that strike you as unlikely? Haven't we gone to war for oil? Someone on your board is responsible for sacrificing four CIA agents to that Russian invasion. Either your Alliance is in league with the Kremlin, or they're trying to start World War III."

Morris grunted something that was as close to a laugh as he could muster under the circumstances. "Make up your mind, Reeder! Is the Alliance in bed with Russia, or eager to go to war with it?"

"The frightening thing is, either is possible. Because as you said, these 'powerful people' do whatever it is that's in their best interest."

Another grunt of a near laugh. "You're making all of this up. That mineral, portobello or whatever, you made it up."

"Six Americans dead, Lawrence."

He swallowed. "In war, sacrifices must be made."

"We're already at war," Reeder said. "Your Alliance is at war with the rest of us. They're calling it patriotism, Lawrence, but it's treason. And you're part of it. That's how you'll be charged—for treason."

He could tell that Rogers wondered where he was going with this.

"Murdered Americans," Reeder said almost offhandedly, "including an assassinated cabinet member . . . you'll be executed."

The color left Morris's face again. "Try to scare me all you like . . . I can't give you any names. That's the only thing keeping me alive."

"You think the CIA can't get those names out of you, if I turn you over? They'll waterboard your ass from here to Tuesday, and then drop you into a hole so black you'll never see sunshine again."

"You . . . you won't do that."

"Won't I? I think the boys and girls at the Company would love to have some time with one of the conspirators in the deaths of five of their people."

Morris stiffened. "I'm an American citizen. You kidnapped me. When that comes out—"

Rogers said, "Who says it will come out? Anyway, you're an enemy combatant we apprehended. Under the Patriot Act, we can make you disappear."

"I was just . . . all I want is to be a good American. A patriot."

"Well, Lawrence," Reeder said cheerfully, "you screwed up."

"Sounds like . . . either way I'm dead."

Rogers said, "We can protect you."

Morris began to laugh.

He laughed until tears began to run and Reeder and the two FBI agents did not bother to hide their surprise and discomfort.

Finally Morris, jerking against his duct-tape bonds, said, "You have no idea!"

"No idea what, Lawrence?" Reeder asked quietly.

Morris, laughing near hysteria, was shaking his head. "What you're *up* against!"

Rogers said, "Enlighten us."

Only his head leaned forward now. "They're bigger than you can imagine. Branches intertwining, growing, flowing. The Alliance is everywhere."

"Conspiracies on that level," Rogers said, "are the stuff of madmen and pulp fiction."

Reeder nodded and said, "The late Carlos Marcello had a sign over his door that said, 'Three people can keep a secret if two of them are dead.'"

Morris had stopped laughing, although he came up with one last, "Ha! Wasn't he in on the Kennedy assassination? Those who didn't die kept as quiet as the ones who did."

Rogers said, "It eventually came out."

"Decades later. Special Agent Rogers, that's the kind of thinking the Alliance depends on. You think they don't, they *couldn't*, exist—so they don't exist. In fact, the Alliance teaches its recruits that if someone accuses them, simply laugh it off, using your line of conspiracies-are-nonsense logic."

Reeder could see Rogers still wasn't buying it, and he said to her, quietly, "Nonsense, not necessarily. Skull and Bones, the Bilderberg Group, the Freemasons, the Ku Klux Klan—secret societies, one and all."

She gave Reeder a hint of a smirk. "What next—the Illuminati?"

"Perhaps," he said. "You've heard about these secret societies, you might even think you know something about them . . . but can you name a single member? Tell me their goals? Explain their infrastructure? We guess, but we don't know, because . . . they're secret. The Alliance could be the same kind of thing."

Rogers was frowning. "In this day and age?"

Their prisoner joined in the conversation again. "The Alliance began as a response to the Cuban Revolution in 1959."

That surprised even Reeder.

Morris said, "Recall your history, and the Bay of Pigs? Run in part by the budding Alliance. Kennedy took all the heat when it went south, but that was the first action taken by the American Patriots Alliance."

Reeder said, "To what end?"

Looking at Reeder as if that were a question more worthy of a child, Morris said, "To keep America free of Communism, back in the day. Now? Now, the goal is to restore America's greatness. To put the power back in the hands of the people who know how to properly run things."

Frowning, Wade said, "You mean white people?"

Reeder was shaking his head. "Your loyalty, Lawrence, is to an Alliance playing very dangerous games with Russia. You really think a third world war, in the nuclear age, will make America great again? And if the Russians get all the portillium out of Azbekistan, they'll have weapon-making capabilities beyond the imagination."

The accountant's expression revealed doubt breaking through the rote history lesson drilled into him by his masters.

Rogers asked, "Who is on the board, Lawrence?"

"Even if I gave you the handful of names I *do* know, it wouldn't do you any good. They are too well entrenched, with their followers spread throughout every level of government. *The Alliance is everywhere.* You think you can protect me when you can't even protect yourselves. Already they have one of yours."

"Who *you* will help us get back."

"In exchange for what—protective custody? I wouldn't last an hour. Hand me over to your FBI friends or the CIA to get information out of me, and see how long it takes for you to get the phone call that I had a heart attack in the earliest stages of interrogation."

Reeder said, "Your people will trade for you."

"Will they? Or, once they know I've been captured, will they just kill me, too? I'll be tainted, understand? Sacrifice, remember? You,

Agent Rogers, and your whole team, will be eliminated. Mr. Reeder, you'll merely have your life destroyed, your family dead and yourself possibly in prison. That suicide you encouraged last year could easily become a murder."

Rogers looked at Reeder in alarm.

Reeder, coldly, said to their prisoner, "Then maybe it's in our best interest for you just to disappear into that hole in the ground."

"If you kill me, they will find you, all of you, and kill *you*."

"Big talk from such a small cog."

His upper lip peeled back over his teeth in a rictus smile. "You think you're up against a small cadre of the powerful, but in reality there are thousands of us in government—department heads, middle management, worker bees—a grass roots army working to save America from itself."

"Okay," Reeder said, "then just give us that handful of names you *do* know, and we'll release you. No one the wiser. You can't betray us without betraying yourself, right?"

"Those names, those few names, are my only leverage. I give them to you, maybe I do wind up in the forest. But . . . if you let me go, I will—as you say—*have* to keep my mouth shut to save my own skin. And if you people just drop all this, and go about your business, it will all be over in a matter of days."

Morris meant that the country would either be at war or not.

"If we go head-to-head with Russia," Reeder said, "we might *all* be over."

Morris said, "I'm sure the President will have done the right thing by then."

That gave Reeder a sudden chill—did Morris know some big-picture thing that they didn't? *Did the cog know where the wheel planned to roll?*

Miggie, who'd been working at DeMarcus's desk in the office area, caught Reeder's attention with a wave.

"Give him something to drink," Reeder told Wade, standing, nodding toward the captive. "If he needs a bathroom break, walk him down there."

"I'll have to untie him," Wade said. "He could piss in a bottle or something."

Reeder shook his head. "We've got plenty of duct tape."

Morris was listening to all this with the hangdog expression of the captive that he was.

Reeder and Rogers went over to Miggie, who looked up from his tablet at them in frustration. They spoke low.

"Something?" Reeder asked.

"Someone," Miggie said, and his eyes went to Rogers. "Fisk. She's wondering why we seem to've dropped off the edge of the world."

"Shit," Rogers said.

Reeder frowned at Mig. "She contacted us *how?*"

"She didn't exactly contact us. I hacked my work e-mail, where she sent me a memo. Seems Ivanek's checked in with her, and Bohannon, too . . . but she hasn't heard from the rest of the team and that's making her nervous."

Amused despite the situation, Rogers asked, "You hacked your own e-mail?"

Shrugging, Miggie said, "You guys tell me be careful, I'm careful."

She asked, "Can we get back to Fisk and not give ourselves away?"

"You don't trust her?" Miggie asked.

"I barely trust myself."

Reeder reached for a shelf and came back with another of DeMarcus's untraceable burner phones; handed it to Rogers. "Get her on this, Patti. Best not mention our guest."

"You think?"

With a dry chuckle, Rogers headed out onto the landing and shut the door behind her.

Reeder sat on the edge of the desk and asked Miggie, "Fisk say anything else about Ivanek?"

"Just that he checked in."

"How about Bohannon?"

"Just that he said everything was cool. Jerry knows enough not to tell the AD he's been sitting surveillance for us on Ivanek's place . . . but whether he and Trevor have connected, I got no idea."

Reeder let out a big sigh. "Our communication system leaves something to be desired."

"Burner phones are better than tin cans and string," Miggie said, "but just. Hey, when you wanna go sub rosa, things get harder. I *did* get a text from Jerry, though, on my burner."

"And?"

"He's been looking hard at Secretary Yellich. You told him and Wade to look for anything odd, remember?"

"And?"

Miggie handed his phone over. "And read this."

Reeder did: *AY not CD*

"What's this mean?" he asked the computer expert.

"No clue."

Reeder curled fingers at Wade, who was duct-taping Morris back into the kitchen chair after a bathroom break. The big man came over and Reeder showed him the message on the burner.

"He's your partner, Reg—what do you make of this?"

Wade read it, shook his head. "Typical Bohannon shorthand shit. Maybe a third of the time I have to ask him what the hell he means. 'AY' is probably Amanda Yellich."

Miggie said, "I texted him for clarification but haven't heard back yet."

Reeder turned toward the nearby door. "Isn't Patti done yet?"

Miggie glanced at the clock on his tablet. "It's been a good five minutes, anyway."

Reeder went outside, found the landing empty, and something cold traveled through him. From the top of the stairs, he quickly scanned the area, saw nothing and no one, then rattled down the metal stairs and started for Tenth Street.

Muttering, he walked at a hurried pace, hand over the butt of the nine mil in his waistband, and when he got to the corner, he turned it and about ran headlong into Rogers coming the other way.

"What the hell?" she asked, backing away.

He let out a breath. "Sorry. Panicked a little—worried you'd been gone too long."

"It's nice to know you care. But after I talked to Fisk, I figured I'd better ditch the phone."

"What did you do with it?"

"Burial at sea."

The Anacostia River ran past the Navy Yard, with access to the water just to the west.

They started back.

He asked her, "What did Fisk say?"

"Ivanek's at his desk at the Hoover Building. We'll leave him there, until we know where everybody is."

"Ignorance is bliss, I guess. And Bohannon?"

"He's headed back to the Hoover, too, she says."

They were at the stairs now, and started up.

"So," Reeder said, "for now we leave them on the bench."

"For now," she said.

They went inside. Miggie was at his tablet, Wade guarding the prisoner, who gestured to Reeder with an up-and-down motion of his head.

Reeder walked over and planted himself before the captive. "What?"

The accountant's smile was a joyless thing, but it was there.

"I have a suggestion," he said.

"It is difficult for the common good to prevail against the intense concentration of those who have a special interest, especially if the decisions are made behind locked doors."

Jimmy Carter, thirty-ninth President of the United States of America. Served 1977–1981. Recipient of the 2002 Nobel Peace Prize for his contributions with the Carter Center.

FOURTEEN

Patti Rogers joined Reeder who, hands on hips, stood before their taped-in-a-kitchen-chair prisoner.

Sweat beaded Morris's forehead, though it wasn't particularly hot in the loft apartment. Fear practically radiated off the accountant. Rogers knew the feeling—even the captors here were in a tight, untenable place.

Reeder said, "I'm listening."

Morris swallowed and the earnestness he summoned was almost painful to see. "I wasn't there when your agent was taken. But I have a good idea where she's being held."

"Still listening," Reeder said.

"Then . . . we have a deal?"

"A deal?"

Morris nodded; sweat flew. "I tell you where I think she's being held, and you let me go. You do that because if I were to tell my people I'd been captured, they might consider me compromised, and that could be fatal."

"You give us an address," Reeder said, a faint smile tracing his lips, "and we let you walk? That it? After all, you acted in good faith."

"Yes!"

"No," Reeder and Rogers answered as one.

"Then . . . then what incentive is there for me to help you? And please don't insult any of our intelligence by racking that weapon and threatening me with a hole in the ground. I think we're past that."

Rogers said, "Are we?"

Reeder resumed his seat in the chair that faced the captive. "Here's how this is going to play out. You tell us where you think they have Agent Nichols. We go check it out. If we don't die in the attempt, and actually free her, we return to discuss your future."

"What . . . what *kind* of future?"

Rogers said, "You'll be lucky to have any. Seven Americans have died already."

Morris summoned an air of confidence, though he was trembling. "That's what I mean—you consider me a traitor. From my point of view, I'm a patriot. What I propose is that if you're successful in your rescue, we all go our separate ways, no harm, no foul."

This coming from a man taped in a kitchen chair.

Reeder said, "That's a possible outcome."

Rogers would have rather thrown this excuse for a human down those fire-escape stairs, chair and all. But she would follow Reeder's lead.

"Where?" Reeder asked.

"Burke. Burke, Virginia. It's . . . kind of out of the way."

"What makes you think she's there?"

Morris relaxed within his bonds; he seemed assured of the information he was about to share.

"I was given the task," he said, "of pinpointing government safe houses that are seldom in use. That was a part of my normal work for the GAO—looking for properties that could be sold off by agencies that no longer used them. One of these was a house the ATF used in Burke. 124 Jennings Circle."

Rogers recorded that on her phone.

Morris went on: "The ATF hasn't used it in over three years. The neighbors were getting suspicious, which often compromises a safe-house location. Anyway, I sent that message up the Alliance chain."

"Sounds to me," Reeder said, "like you might be handling any number of former safe houses."

"That's true," Morris admitted. "But the house in Burke was not only the most recent example, it inspired a number of follow-up questions. Something was obviously being planned for that address—my guess? Holding your agent there is it."

Rogers traded looks with Reeder—despite the People Reader's usual blank expression, she could tell he found this promising. So did she. Of course, what else did they have . . .

"We'll check it out," Reeder said.

"And if you get your friend back?"

"Then we'll talk."

"We have a *deal*, remember."

"One thing at a time."

Rogers put the blindfold back on Morris.

"Aw, come on!" the prisoner said.

She said, "Hush," and walked away.

They gathered around Miggie. His tablet had some vintage Latin music going, which he cranked to keep their already hushed conversation private.

"Any word from Bohannon?" Reeder asked.

Miggie shook his head.

Reeder spoke to Rogers: "Nichols is your agent who's gone missing. Take the lead."

Rogers nodded and said, "All right—Joe and I will check out the safe house in Burke. With any luck, we'll extricate Anne. Miggie, you keep digging. Reggie, watch the prisoner. We'll keep you posted by cell. If we go dark longer than, say, four hours, take the charming Lawrence to Fisk and make a clean breast of it."

Wade frowned. "I rather dump him on the street and make noises about how he gave up his crew."

Reeder said, "No. If Rogers, Nichols, and I are casualties, our play is over. Letting the Bureau handle it is the better part of valor."

Rogers shook her head at Reeder. "Joe, our new best friend over there says every sector of government is infiltrated. That would include the FBI."

But Reeder's answer went to Wade. "That's why you'll need to turn Lawrence over in as public and showy a way as possible. Preempt a cover-up. Go to the *Post* and give an interview. Contact every 24-hour news channel. Got it?"

The big man sighed big. "I got it. But why don't you just bring Anne back instead?"

Everybody agreed that was the best idea.

Rogers touched Reeder's arm. "Let me say good-bye to Kevin."

"Sure."

She went back to the bedroom, letting herself in as quietly as possible. The room was just beginning to lighten, the only window allowing in the first hints of sunrise.

Kevin, in dark shirt and slacks, was on the made bed on his side, asleep maybe.

She crept in, shut the door behind her. "You awake?"

He smiled up at her. "Still awake. Can't sleep. Maybe I should have taken my nylons off."

She almost succeeded in not laughing.

"Okay," he admitted, "maybe it *is* a little funny."

She sat on the edge of the bed, found his hand. "Thank you for what you did tonight."

"I kind of enjoyed it. Nice to know I can fool a straight guy like that, not just be some camp oddity."

"But *you're* a straight guy—kind of."

"And you're a straight girl—sort of."

"Made for each other," she said, and leaned in and kissed him a little. He sat up and kissed her more.

Then she put her hand in his short dark curly hair and said, "Now I need you to do what you were *going* to before this sting came up—disappear for a while."

He sat up even more. "I'd rather hang, and help. I proved I can do that, right?"

"No proof necessary. You're all man."

"Except maybe for the nylons."

"And the eyeliner."

"That, too. So you want rid of me?"

"Just till the guns are gone. Just till having you around doesn't worry me and make me lose my edge. You need to doll up and get Virginia Plain's pretty behind out of here. Catch a cab. Grab a bus. I don't want to know where you're headed."

"I've got that phone Reeder gave me. You'll call?"

"I'll call."

She touched his face, so handsome, so pretty, and gave him a smooch and got out of there. She didn't need *her* eyeliner getting spoiled, too.

An hour later, the sun edging up, Rogers—with Reeder in the rider's seat—drove the rental car to the far end of Jennings Circle in Burke, then turned around in the cul-de-sac and eased back the way she'd come. The rental had out-of-state plates, making her just a driver (should anyone notice) who'd taken a wrong turn. She rolled past the house a second time, slow as she dared, before turning off Jennings Circle and back onto Old Keene Mill Road.

"Can you read houses," she asked, "or just people?"

Reeder said, "Good-size, two stories, two-car garage, no cars parked out front. Shades on all the windows, no people, no morning movement. Other houses, cars are backing out of garages, curtains being opened, people stirring. Either it's vacant . . . or it's exactly what Morris said it was: a safe house with a new tenant."

One cul-de-sac later, she turned up Honey Tree Court. She pulled to the curb and parked. "What's the play?"

"If it's a safe house—there's going to be a shift change in keepers, right?"

"Right."

"That's when we hit them."

She blinked at him. "When there are *twice* as many bad guys on site?"

Reeder didn't blink at all. "That's a negative way to talk about employees of our federal government."

"My bad."

"Shift change, they'll be least expecting trouble."

"Trouble being the two of us. Just how the hell are we going to keep an eye on the house till the next shift? We're just a little obvious, strangers sitting in a car."

He pointed to the woods that separated the backs of houses on this street from those on Jennings Circle. "We go native and try to find an angle where we can see the front."

"How many you figure, six? Maybe eight?"

"Not more than six. More than that in a suburban home, all adults, probably all or mostly male, would get the neighbors suspicious again."

They got out of the car, walked up the block, making an odder couple than even she and Kevin did, Rogers in a business suit and Reeder in jeans and Nats windbreaker. Not an average-looking suburban couple out for their morning walk. Not hardly.

Three houses up, they cut between two and ducked into the woods. If some helpful neighbor spotted them and called 911, she and Reeder would have to flash their credentials and hope for the best.

Unfortunately, the best was likely a SWAT team that might further endanger Nichols.

Or had Lawrence sent them chasing their tails to buy time? This might be a vacant house, as Reeder said. Worse, could Lawrence be leading them into an ambush? Through this strip of suburban woods, they moved like animals dodging civilization, trying to stay low, the sun glinting off leaves and dappling them with shadow and light. Finally they found a vantage point behind the house next door providing a partial view of the presumed safe house's front yard.

Reeder said, "I'm going to the far side of the place, and see if I can get a look at the driveway."

She nodded.

He said, "Keep your cell handy—text you when I see an opening. I'll just type GO, okay?"

"By the way . . . have you given any thought to all the things that could go wrong with this?"

He shrugged. "Vacant house, ambush, maybe Lawrence is sending us next door, to alert those in the real place? Or this is the *right* house and, being slightly outnumbered, we get very dead? Those kind of things?"

"We have another option."

"Which is?"

She held his eyes. "Call Fisk. Bring the Bureau in."

"But Lawrence says the Alliance is everywhere, and that could include the Bureau, like you said. Not necessarily Fisk herself, but just a team member on the response unit, and we're screwed. No, Patti, this is us. Strictly us."

She let out air. "Sweet-talker."

That got the world's tiniest grin out of Reeder, before he crept away through the underbrush, skirting trees. There was something military about it, and Rogers suddenly flashed on the nature of their self-appointed mission.

If this was indeed the right house, the guards inside were not necessarily Alliance, but might simply be agents, like herself, like her team, agents who likely thought they were doing their job, nothing more, nothing less.

But *her* job right now was getting Nichols out of harm's way.

She unholstered her pistol, checked it, re-holstered it, then settled in on her haunches to wait, staying alert. The sun kept climbing, and her legs were tight, near cramping, and all the ways that this could go south kept careening feverishly through her mind.

Occasionally, she duckwalked through brush and got behind a tree to rise and stretch, eyes never leaving the house. Then she would reposition herself and crouch again, careful not to attract attention. She checked the time now and again, and—endless minutes turning into mind-numbing hours—she wondered if they really were staking out a vacant house. She hadn't seen so much as a hint of movement beyond a window and it was nearing noon.

She was about to text Reeder that maybe Morris had played them and they should abort when something moved past the half-open blinds on the second floor. She perked, her discomfort and boredom gone. Moments later, a hand separated blinds and a big slice of male face appeared, eyes slowly scanning the woods.

Then the blinds snapped shut.

Was that where Nichols was being held? An upstairs bedroom?

She texted Reeder: *2nd-floor window*

Reeder's response was one letter : *K*

Texting shorthand learned from his daughter, Amy, no doubt. Rogers twitched a smile, then focused on the house so intently she might have been trying to hypnotize it.

Then the phone in her hand vibrated and when she looked at the screen, she saw:

GO

She rose like something that had grown very fast, the phone dropped in a pocket, her pistol coming out and up. Two houses down,

Reeder came out of the woods just as she did. Simultaneously they crossed the joined backyards and took posts at opposite corners at the rear of the target house.

When Reeder disappeared up the far side of the house, she went up her side, stopping at the front corner, making sure she was low enough to keep well under the living room windows. She peeked around the corner—on the other side of the house . . .

. . . a nondescript tones-of-gray Ford, an obvious government car, was just pulling into the driveway. Reeder remained out of sight. That wouldn't change until whoever was in the car parked it and got out.

Then she heard the garage door going up. *Damn!* She was at the wrong side of the house and if she couldn't make it across the front yard, and time it right, the door would close and the new shift of captors was in.

Or worse—Reeder might wind up in that garage alone with however many armed agents were in the Ford.

As soon as the passenger side door passed her position—only two of them, driver, rider—Rogers took off quick and low, bisecting the front yard; as she passed the front door, it stayed shut. At the same time, Reeder came around the garage side of the house, low but not as fast. He didn't have the nine mil in hand—instead, it was that extendable baton of his, looking like he was running a relay and about to pass it off. He pointed inside with the unextended weapon, hesitating as the Ford rolled inside.

The garage door motor indicated the vehicle and its inhabitants were about to be shut inside, and she hurtled under before the drawbridge came completely down. The front doors of the Ford opened, *snick, snick,* and an agent in a dark suit got out on either side.

Was the house soundproofed enough that those within wouldn't be alerted to the arrival of their relief team?

"Turn around slow, gentlemen," Reeder said, positioned behind the driver toward the left rear of the Ford. Rogers was behind the passenger, at the vehicle's right rear, and both she and Reeder were training guns on the men, although Joe had his nine mil in his left hand and the baton in his right.

The two agents turned, nice and slow, hands shoulder high. No stupid moves. Not from this pair. *Smart* moves, though . . . ?

Her man, who she didn't recognize, was maybe thirty, dark hair, wedge-faced, blank-eyed.

The driver was older, forty anyway, with graying dark hair, pock-marked with a reptilian smile.

"Peep," the driver said to Reeder, pleasantly but a little too loud.

"I can hear you," Reeder said. "Make sure no one in the house can."

"Kinda in over your head on this one, aren't you, Peep?"

"Patti, this is Robert Clayton—Homeland."

She nodded just a little. "Mr. Clayton."

"You're on the wrong side of this, Peep," Clayton said. "But you can easily get on the right side. You could have Agents Nichols back, no problem, and we can negotiate our way out of this unfortunate situation that we find ourselves in."

"Define 'we.'"

His chin came up slightly. Pride? "You, and I, and some of the most patriotic Americans who've ever lived."

"Well, some are going to die." Slowly Reeder approached the man. "But you don't have to be one of them, Bob, if you arrange to have Agent Nichols turned over to us without any further fuss."

Clayton's scowl was somehow reptilian as well. "Who do you think you're talking to? You make a move on us, the two inside will execute the prisoner, and—"

Reeder hit Clayton with the baton, right along the side of his head. The Homeland agent chased himself to the cement, sprawled there out cold in a crisply pressed suit.

That'd got Rogers' attention enough for her charge to risk a leap at her, right into a swing of the barrel of her pistol, which caught the agent much the way Reeder's baton had his partner. He did a limp-puppet fall, clearly out before he landed.

Rogers said, "So, there's two more inside."

Reeder said softly, "Unless Clayton is cleverer than I give him credit for." He nodded toward the nearest unconscious fed. "Use their own cuffs on 'em, bind their feet with their neckties, collect their pistols and cells."

She nodded and did that while Reeder stood covering her by facing the door into the house, the nine mil in his right hand now, the baton tucked away.

Throughout, the only sounds were the rustle of clothing and light clink of the cuffs as she bound the unconscious men—nothing came from within the residence. Leaving the two men on the floor of the garage, one on either side of the Ford, they moved quietly inside—the connecting door unlocked—and found themselves in a mudroom, washer and dryer to their left, a bench and empty coat-hanger pegs to the right.

Gun in hand, Reeder walked them into a nice if characterless kitchen—stainless steel appliances, big island in the center, long counter—and she followed him. Dead soda cans were arranged on the counter like a little tin army—big-time agents tended to be tidy—and the smell of bacon lingered. No take-out bags visible in the wastebasket. Cooking for themselves.

A male voice echoed down a stairwell: *"What's with Clayton and Simpson? Should've been here ten minutes ago!"*

From a nearby room, another male voice said, *"Maybe he's getting carryout for a change!"*

"If so," the stairwell voice said, *"cheap-ass probably won't bring us any!"*

Downstairs said, *"Why, you want to spend another half hour babysitting?"*

". . . Ten minutes, you call him."

"Ten minutes, I call him."

The kitchen took a left and emptied out into a dining area that opened onto a living room where a ginger-haired agent in his shirt-sleeves lounged in a comfy chair with his feet on an ottoman. His back was mostly to them as he sat watching an old Bruce Willis movie on TCM, a can of Diet Coke on an end table between him and a couch.

Also on that table was a Glock.

Off to the left, just opposite the front door and entry area, an unenclosed stairway rose.

The openness of the room allowed Rogers to come around behind the agent and grab away the weapon before the guy knew up from down. He straightened, startled, looking toward where his gun had disappeared, and then on the other side of him another gun did appear, its snout touching his temple.

Reeder, whose weapon it was, whispered, "Clayton and Simpson are here. Tell him."

The agent swallowed, nodded, and called, *"Hey, they're here!"*

Which was true in a couple of ways.

"About damn time!" the stairwell voice said.

Rogers was already over at the bottom of the stairs, crouched down alongside where she couldn't be seen. When the upstairs agent's feet tromped down to meet the downstairs, she jack-in-the-boxed up and showed him the gun. Wearing a rumpled-looking, end-of-shift suit, he had a pale, doughy baby-face and tiny dark raisin eyes that opened comically wide. He had a gun, too, but Rogers yanked it from his waist-band before his mind had started to work.

She used his cuffs to secure his hands behind him.

"Take a seat," she said, and nodded toward the couch.

He went there and sat, his cuffed hands behind him clearly uncomfortable. On the TV, Bruce Willis was smirking.

Reeder was perched on the ottoman now with his nine mil trained on the ginger agent, who was sitting up, hands in the air.

Rogers came over and said to their hosts, "Just you two?"

Both captives nodded. Nothing forced about it. Still . . .

She found the upstairs empty until she got to the bedroom at the end of the hall, the door open.

In dark slacks and light blue blouse but no shoes, the tall, slender, model-lovely African American woman was on the bed, on top of the covers, pillows propped behind her. She had her hands cuffed in her lap and her ankles were bound with white cloth possibly torn from a sheet, which might have been the source for the white blindfold and gag, as well.

"Anne, Annie, it's okay," Rogers said, moving quickly across the room, holstering her weapon. "We're here."

Gently Rogers removed the blindfold, revealing a small gash in the center of a purplish lump near the woman's left temple. This was the only overt sign of violence's aftermath, and had probably occurred when Nichols was taken captive.

"You're safe," Rogers said, undoing the gag.

Her voice a hoarse whisper, Nichols said, "I screwed up, Patti. I really screwed up."

"Course you didn't. Let's get you out of here."

Rogers peeled off her suit jacket and snugged it around Nichols' shoulders as the agent slipped off the bed and got unsteadily onto her feet.

Reeder appeared in the doorway.

"Our two friends are cuffed and quiet," he said, jerking a thumb over his shoulder. "How is she?"

Rogers was drunk-walking Nichols across the room.

"Bad knock in the noggin. Annie, you need an ambulance?"

"No. No, no. Let's just go."

"Okay," Reeder said. "I'll check in with Miggie, though."

He got Altuve right away and reported that they'd be back soon. "Tell Reggie to be ready with a first-aid kit. Have you heard from Ivanek?"

As he listened to Miggie's response, Reeder looked up at Rogers and then shook his head.

No Ivanek yet.

Reeder asked the phone, "What about Bohannon?"

He listened and then his face went hard, then soft.

"Be back as soon as we can," he said, then clicked off.

"What?" she asked, she and Nichols at the door now.

"Agent Jerry Bohannon," Reeder said.

"What about him?"

"Dead."

"The time is near at hand which must determine whether Americans are to be free men or slaves."

George Washington, first President of the United States of America. Served 1789–1797. Commander in Chief of American Revolutionary forces.

FIFTEEN

Reeder said, "Bohannon was executed. No attempt to make it look like anything else this time."

Her arm still around and supporting Anne Nichols, Rogers gaped at him, horrified. "*What?*"

"A mob-style double tap. Your people looking into any mob-related activity lately?"

"A few things, but . . ."

"So maybe I'm wrong, and this is somebody's half-assed idea of covering up their latest kill."

Rogers looked stricken. "Where was he . . . ?"

"Still sitting surveillance outside Ivanek's place."

Nichols was quietly crying now. Rogers was shaking her head, saying, "I thought Jerry was on his way back to the Hoover Building."

"So did I. For now, we have to stick a pin it, and get the hell out of here. See if you can find what they did with Anne's shoes and get her into them. I'll tidy up downstairs."

"You're not going to kill anybody are you?"

"I'll try to restrain myself."

It went quickly. The IDs of the captured minders were all Homeland. From the two downstairs, their hands already cuffed behind them, Reeder collected cell phones, and escorted them to the front closet and shut them in. The pair was too professional to squawk.

Shortly in the garage, Reeder was surveying the still unconscious Clayton and Simpson when Rogers and Nichols joined him.

Rogers helped him haul and dump the two Homeland agents into the trunk of their Ford, then the two women waited while Reeder fetched the rental vehicle from one street over. When he'd pulled into the driveway, Rogers ushered Nichols out and helped her into the back, then shut the garage door with an electric-eye opener she'd liberated from the Ford.

Reeder held the driver's side door open for Rogers, who paused and said, "Those four kidnapped Anne. We just leave them behind for their people to pick up?"

"When somebody notices they haven't checked in, yes. With luck that may be next shift change, but it's more likely they have periodic call-ins."

Her face was as clenched as a fist. "Clayton mentioned the Alliance. Probable that all four of them are part of that. They need to be arrested, Joe."

"Who by? Us? The people who assaulted four federal agents?"

She blanched.

He said, "Who do we trust enough with that call? I've now tangled with both Homeland and Secret Service, and we know somebody in the CIA betrayed five of their own. Only thing we can do is get out of here."

They did.

Within an hour, they were back at DeMarcus's crib. Reggie Wade handed off a first-aid kit to Rogers, and she and Nichols disappeared into the bedroom and shut the door. Morris, duct-taped to his chair and blindfolded, head slumped forward, was snoring gently.

Wade smirked at Reeder. "Little man had a busy day."

"Sorry about your partner, Reg. He was a damn fine agent."

"That he was." The dark eyes glistened. "And a better friend."

"When did *you* last sleep, Reg?"

"Do I look like I got that good a memory?"

Reeder reached a hand up to set it on the big lanky man's shoulder. "Go sack out on the couch awhile."

"What, and dream about somebody double-tappin' Jerry like he was some Mafia scum? No, Joe, I'll keep my eyes open, you don't mind."

Reeder nodded. He went over to Miggie at DeMarcus's desk, Wade following, and asked, "What's the cop chatter on Bohannon?"

Miggie said, "Calling it a pro kill. FBI agent with a history of mob investigations."

"What was Jerry doing still in front of Ivanek's? Fisk had called him back to home base."

There was something sorrowful about Mig's shrug. "Guess the killer got him before he left."

Reeder asked, "Ever hear back from Jerry about his Yellich text?"

Miggie shook his head, and Wade sourly offered, "And I still haven't figured out what he meant."

"Hell."

Miggie said, "It gets worse."

"How's that possible?"

"Fisk is losing her shit. She wants all of us reporting back to the Hoover Building, like, yesterday."

Wade asked, "Could somebody have whispered in her ear about our buddy Lawrence?"

"We made a few ripples," Reeder said. "But now we're making waves."

Miggie said, "Fisk says if we're not all back in her office by five p.m., she'll start issuing arrest orders."

"Not surprising. With such widespread government infiltration, anybody can be pressured. We hear from Hardesy yet?"

Mig nodded. "Right before you got back. Should be here soon."

"Where the hell's he been? What's he been up to?"

A knock at the loft's door made all three turn, and their prisoner's head came slowly up, his rest rudely interrupted.

Miggie said, "Might be you can ask him yourself."

The anonymous nine in his hand, Reeder went to the door and checked the monitor—Hardesy was out on the fire-escape landing, moving foot to foot, like he needed a restroom. Reeder let him in, shut and locked the door behind them.

"You had us worried," Reeder said.

Hardesy was in a black windbreaker and black jeans, ready for ninja duty if necessary. "Had to take care of my family. I sent my wife and daughters away—don't ask where."

"Wouldn't think of it."

"What have I missed?"

Taking Hardesy by the arm and starting to guide him toward the sofa in the home-theater area, Reeder said, "You might want to sit down for this, Lucas. You've been out of the loop for a while . . ."

Reeder told him about Nichols' kidnap and rescue, and Bohannon's murder, news of which turned Hardesy blister pale.

"Jesus," Hardesy said. Then, alarmed, he said, "Where the hell's Trevor?"

Miggie said, "At the Hoover Building, apparently. Ignorance is bliss kind of thing."

"Hell with that," Hardesy said, leaning forward. "They're fucking kidnapping and killing us! Trevor needs to be warned, or gotten the hell out of there."

"No," Reeder said firmly. "He's behind enemy lines. Warning him is exactly what *could* kill him."

Wade asked, "Then what's our next play?"

Reeder said, "We get Nichols somewhere safe for the duration. She's too traumatized to be helpful."

The big man smirked. "What about Sleeping Beauty over there? You're not *really* gonna cut him loose."

"Don't know," Reeder admitted. "Still working that out. Listen, I need to step outside for a bit."

The others exchanged curious glances, but nobody asked him what this was about. Everybody knew Joe Reeder had his secrets and his reasons.

From the landing, he slowly scanned the neighborhood. Mid-afternoon was pretty quiet around here, street people, tenants, merchants, denizens of a poverty-stricken area that got rougher when night fell. He trotted down the wrought-iron stairs, strode behind the building and into the shadowed recession of the tailor shop's back doorway. He withdrew the phone he'd been given by President Harrison, took in half a bushel or so of air, let it out slowly, and made the call.

The President said, "Joe."

"Sir."

"Have you the information I need?"

"Not all of it, Mr. President. But there *is* a rogue group within the government. It calls itself the American Patriots Alliance."

"I've heard that term. I've been assured it's a conspiracy theory from the tinfoil hat crowd."

"Well, I'm not wearing one and I can tell you it's very real. It became necessary for me to recruit help and I'm working with Agent Rogers and her Special Situations team . . . one of whom has been murdered. That brings the total dead to eight."

Silence for several endless seconds.

Then the phone said: "I'm waiting for the helicopter to Camp David now, Joe. How soon can I expect an answer on the identity of the traitor or traitors?"

"Well, it's definitely traitors, sir, but the opposition here seems well aware of what I'm up to. Another of our agents was kidnapped, although we were able to free her."

"Lord."

"Sir, I've encountered compromised agents from both the Secret Service and Homeland. I hate to say this, but . . . right now nobody's watching your back."

"Except you, Joe."

"Not me, because I'm not there with you. And you will surely hear some things designed to destroy your confidence in me, and of those I've recruited."

"My confidence in you will not be shaken, Joe. But if you're asking for more time, there isn't any. War with Russia, as unthinkable as it may sound, could be just a few days away. Think Cuban Missile Crisis."

"I'll do everything I can, Mr. President. And I'm surrounded by real American patriots."

"That's all I can ask. All I could hope for. Joe, I have to go—the chopper is waiting." The famous voice turned unexpectedly wry. "I could say something dramatic, I suppose . . . like you're the thin red-white-and-blue line separating us from all-out war. But you don't really need that kind of praise, or pressure."

Reeder smiled. "No, Mr. President."

They clicked off and Reeder went back up to the loft. Rogers had joined Hardesy, Wade, and Miggie in the massive wall screen's viewing area of black-leather overstuffed seating.

Rogers was in a chair and Reeder perched himself on its plump arm. "How's Nichols doing?" he asked.

"I dressed her head wound," Rogers said. "She's really been through it. Exhausted, in shock. I gave her something to help her sleep. That's what she's doing now."

Reeder touched Rogers' sleeve. "When was the last time *you* slept?"

"Earlier this week," she said. "You?"

"Not in recent memory, and I'm afraid it won't be soon. But let's take an hour. Everybody pick a chair. Reggie, you take the couch."

There was mild objection, but it was easily overruled by Reeder. They each found a place to rest, and Rogers—who'd stayed in that chair—said, "I don't see any place for you?"

"I have something to do," he said.

Reeder went over to the kitchenette area, where Morris appeared awake; anyway, he was no longer snoring. Reeder removed the accountant's blindfold, pulled up a chair and sat.

Very quietly, he said, "Let's talk about you, Lawrence. And keep your voice down. My friends are trying to catch a few Zs, like you did."

The captive wore a hurt expression. "You said you would let me go if I helped you. Did you get your agent back?"

"We did. Thank you for that. But I promised you nothing, just that we'd revisit your situation. That's what we're doing now, Lawrence. And I'm afraid, for now, the answer is no."

Morris tugged at his restraints. "You bastard! You lying bastard!"

Reeder raised a lecturing finger. "If you wake my friends up, I'll let you go, all right—*and* spread the word you talked."

All the energy seeped out of Morris. "Maybe . . . maybe you should do that, and I'll . . . take my chances . . ."

"You did help us, and that was a good start. But you're a tool of a treasonous conspiracy, complicit in half a dozen murders or more. If you'd *really* rather not die, whether by lethal injection at the government's hands or by some imaginative means courtesy of your patriotic pals, you could cooperate further."

Morris said nothing. He was looking at Reeder but not really.

"Give me something that matters," Reeder said. "Want your freedom? Give up those board-member names. Outline their plans in this current scheme. Then testify against them. Be a hero, not a traitor."

The prisoner's voice went whisper-quiet, and Reeder doubted it had anything to do with not disturbing the napping agents on the other side of the room.

"You have to know," Morris said, "that I would never live to testify. They'll kill me. They'll kill you. *All of us*. How do you think they've been around for seventy-five years without becoming anything but a rumor or another crazy conspiracy theory?"

"You need to give me those names."

"No. If I give you those names, and you act against them, I'm dead. You're dead. These are not men you can move against. Perhaps you could disrupt what you described as their latest 'scheme,' but—"

"Okay. Let's table the names. What do you know about what the Alliance is up to right the hell now?"

Eyes widened, narrowed. "Frankly, not much. Like the Middle Eastern terrorists, the Alliance only provides its cells with that cell's part of a plan. That way no one can give away the bigger picture upon capture."

"Then you have no idea why four CIA agents were sent to Azbekistan to die?"

"I only know they were supposed to be the spark for a new conflagration with Russia, after years of this tepid President's inaction."

The hair on the back of Reeder's neck bristled. "Why in God's name? We've been at peace with them for decades."

"Complacency and peace are not the same thing, Reeder. Nor is appeasement valid diplomacy. While we've been 'peaceful,' Boris Krakenin has been rebuilding the Soviet war machine, preparing the Russians for world domination. Harrison has done nothing to protest Russian incursions, or to prepare America for this obvious coming war.

We're soft, lazy, and this is a president who *needed* to be prodded into doing the right thing."

Well, at least Reeder knew what flavor of Kool-Aid their guest preferred.

"Why kill Amanda Yellich?"

Morris shrugged. "Above my pay grade. I was told nothing about it before or after. *Was* she assassinated? If so, it must have been something to do with this weekend."

Reeder stiffened. "What about this weekend?"

"Again, no idea. I just know that everything needed to carry out this current objective—from the Azbekistan sacrifice to today—had to be taken care of by this weekend. Apparently, for some reason, Yellich's death must've been part of that."

Reeder recalled Bohannon's text: *AY not CD*

Camp David.

He went back over to the TV area and said, good and loud, "*Everybody up!*"

They roused, mostly from deep sleeps, with Wade's lengthy torso stretching as he said, "What was that, fifteen minutes? Thanks for the sack time, bossman."

"It was twenty, and we need to talk. Five minutes for bathroom breaks and rounding up coffee."

Everybody did that.

Reeder stood near Rogers in her comfy chair. Everyone had coffee but Hardesy, who had Diet Coke. All eyes were on Reeder. Every butt was on the edge of its seat.

Reeder said, "One cabinet member always is held back when the full cabinet is otherwise at one location . . . like it will be at Camp David this weekend."

"To protect the line of succession," Rogers said, matter-of-fact.

Reeder sent his eyes around touching everybody else's. "What if Amanda Yellich was that cabinet member?"

Miggie's eyes popped. He rose, held up a "wait" forefinger, and went back to his tablet. Within a minute he returned.

"This you're going to find interesting," Miggie said, his eyebrows up. "It was indeed supposed to be Yellich."

Everyone exchanged glances.

Reeder asked, "Replaced by whom?"

Mig shook his head. "A very tight lid on that, my friend."

"So Yellich was the designated survivor," Hardesy said, frowning. "So what?"

"So," Reeder said, "the Camp David trip has been planned for some time, and the Russian invasion just *happened* to fall the week before. Forcing the President's hand. Making the already-scheduled Camp David meeting something suddenly of great import. You think that's a coincidence?"

"I would say no," Rogers said dryly.

Reeder, the wall screen at his back, paced. "For some reason, Amanda not being at Camp David is key."

"But she was *already* not going to be there," Rogers said. "If the Alliance plan has something to do with Camp David, why kill someone who isn't even going to be there?"

Reeder stopped pacing and swung toward his audience. "Let's go back to *why* she wasn't going to be there. She was the cabinet member selected to stay home. To protect the line of succession."

"Okay," Hardesy said, "I get that part. But why swap one stay-at-home cabinet member for another?"

"Lawrence says the Alliance has people all through government, including at the highest levels—what if one of them is the cabinet member charged with staying away and protecting the line of succession?"

"Getting them what?" Rogers asked.

Wade said, "The presidency, if everything shakes down right."

"*How?*" Rogers asked. "You would have to take out a certain number, ahead of that person! Who can guess how many cabinet members would have to die, picked off one by one or maybe in one fell swoop . . ."

Rogers was staring into nothing now, having trailed off.

Reeder said, "Exactly right, Patti. And this weekend, everybody's at the party, from the President on down."

The loft fell silent.

"Crazy," Hardesy said finally. "Impossible. No way to pull it off."

"Mass killings have become a way of life in this country," Rogers said hollowly. "And you know what they say—if you're willing to trade your life, you can kill anyone."

"At Camp fucking David?" Hardesy exploded. "Get serious—it's a goddamn fortress."

Sitting forward, Wade said, "Joe, Lucas is right—it's a fortress with the most sophisticated electronic surveillance equipment in the world set up in those surrounding woods, not to mention a small army of Secret Service agents, and a whole mess of Marines. *Nobody* could get in there. If anybody even *tried*, they'd see 'em coming from a mile away, easy. Two miles."

"There's more than one way to do this," Reeder said, and everyone's eyes were on him. "President Harrison will be in a chopper when he's coming and going. Same for Vice President Mitchell. Possible there might be a small window where both copters are in the air at the same time. If you're the Alliance, and you've truly infiltrated everywhere, you might know the itinerary and simply blow them both out of the sky with rocket launchers."

Reeder's ominous suggestion hung in the air like stubborn smoke.

Finally Rogers asked, "But how could anybody get away with that? Or with any kind of assault on Camp David? It's not like a fame-seeking nutcase walks up and shoots the President and dies on the spot—these people want power, not to be apprehended."

Reeder's small smile was large with dread. "Azbekistan has the country on edge, everybody from the man in the street to talk-radio demagogues to United States Senators calling for war over the deaths of those CIA agents. How hard would it be to—"

"Blame the Russians," Rogers said, answering her own question.

"It might well be stage-managed to make that happen," Reeder said with a shrug. "Russian missiles, Russian arms to take out any motorcade leaving Camp David? Not beyond the realm of possibility."

No one spoke for a long time.

Then Rogers said, "Just to recap, we think a secret society has already killed eight government employees, may be angling to manipulate the line of presidential succession, and is risking starting World War III in the bargain. And there doesn't appear to be anything we can do about it. That a pretty fair assessment?"

"I'd say so," Reeder said. "Of course, you did leave out the part where we have a prisoner who can at least semi-legitimately claim we kidnapped him, and an Assistant Director of the FBI who thinks we've gone rogue, and wants to arrest us, which will almost inevitably lead to assassination or prison. So I'd say doing nothing is not an option."

"We could call Fisk," Rogers said.

Reeder gave her a sharp look. "Do you trust her?"

"We have to trust *somebody*."

Hardesy said, "Down the rabbit hole, and you want to cozy up to the Queen of Hearts."

"Let's say, sake of argument, that Patti's right to trust Fisk," Reeder said to everyone. "What do we tell her? That we've kidnapped a GAO accountant who says there's an alliance of would-be patriots manipulating the government from within? Better add the booby hatch to the assassination-and-prison list."

She nodded toward their duct-taped guest. "We have proof."

Reeder asked, "But if Lawrence is right, and protecting his life is a virtual impossibility, *then* what do we have? We need more before we go to Fisk or anybody else."

"I don't disagree," Rogers said glumly. "So what *do* we do?"

Reeder's head tilted almost imperceptibly. "We put our friend Lawrence on ice somewhere till we can use him. Nichols took a hell of a blow to the head, so we need to get her off the front line—"

"Do *I* get a vote?" came Nichols' voice from across the loft.

Barefoot, a square bandage on her head wound, she had slipped into a pair of DeMarcus's jeans that came mid-calf, belt cinched tight, and a Georgetown T-shirt knotted under her breasts.

"Anne," Reeder said, "it's not a democracy. But come join us."

She did, finding room on the couch. "Joe, you may be in charge, but you really don't have much choice. I've heard most of this discussion, and it's clear this is the big game and you can't afford to keep me on the bench."

He raised a hand in a "patience" gesture.

Then he said, "Patti, you'll recall the cabin where we met up with my daughter Amy and her boyfriend, at the windup of the Supreme Court investigation?"

"Of course," Rogers said.

Reeder's late friend Gabriel Sloan—Rogers' onetime FBI partner—had left the family cabin in the Virginia's Blue Ridge Mountains to his goddaughter.

"Miggie, Patti will help you pull that location up on a map. You and Anne take Lawrence there. You three should be safe . . . but take plenty of firepower."

"So I'm on guard duty?" Nichols asked, frowning.

"Come on, Joe," Miggie said, almost whining, "I'm more than just the fastest computer in the East, you know."

"Anne, our prisoner is the only proof we have right now of this conspiracy. Mig, I need you on call for whatever we might need on the information side. Not that you both won't still be in the line of fire. We have no way of knowing how on top of us these people might be . . . Everybody cool?"

Both agents nodded. They didn't look cool, but they nodded.

Reeder wandered over to the prisoner. He said, "Lawrence, buddy, you need to give us something. We're going to make every effort to keep you alive, but if something goes wrong . . . in which case we'll have lost these two fine agents in addition to your sorry-ass self . . . we need a way to verify without you. Give us something we can use."

"If I'm dead," he said, with a ghastly smile, "I no longer have any skin in the game. Good luck to you, though."

"Sometimes you're a hard man to like, Lawrence."

"If I give you something now, they'll track me down and kill me—with the rest of you."

"Not if we take them down first."

Morris began to laugh, tears quickly flowing. "You just don't get it, do you? Even if you knew every name on the board, and arrested them, the movement would go on. Those chairs will always be filled. Joe McCarthy, Barry Goldwater, various media moguls, Gregory Bennett post-White House, the Blount dynasty, there's *always* a board of directors for the Alliance."

"Turn a bright enough light on, Lawrence, and watch the roaches scatter."

"To their hiding place. And you don't really get rid of them at all, do you?"

"*Hey!*" Miggie called from across the room.

Reeder rejoined the team in the home theater area. Miggie said, "I just got an e-mail from Ivanek."

"How did you manage that?" Rogers asked, frowning. "He's out of the burner loop."

"I've been hacking my work e-mail every hour or so, remember. Mostly I'm seeing Fisk memos saying come in toot sweet. But now here's Ivanek."

Rogers asked, "He's at work?"

"Think so," Miggie said. "Anyway, the e-mail is from his office account. He says Fisk has gone ballistic and he would 'respectfully like to know what the hell is going on?'"

Reeder said, "If I call him, how fast can it be traced if we're on the move?"

Miggie said, "Maybe two minutes, tops. Keep it under a minute and you should be safe enough."

"Okay. Lucas, you and Reg help get Miggie loaded up in your car."

"You got it," Hardesy said, and he and Wade followed Miggie to the computer area to start packing up gear.

Reeder said to Rogers, "You and I, plus Reggie and Lucas, will investigate the Alliance as best we can. In that history lesson he blurted, Lawrence mentioned some current players."

"Ex-President Bennett," Rogers said, nodding, "and the Blounts. And young Nicky is on that presidential succession list."

Wade, hands on his hips, towering over them, said, "We're maybe five minutes from our pictures being on TV with a BOLO warning sayin' we're armed and dangerous. You think we can get close to any of the Blounts or Bennett without getting arrested or maybe shot down?"

Reeder shook his head. "We don't talk to them. They're already on red alert, you can bet."

"Who, then?" Hardesy asked.

"We talk with people who know them, people who study them."

Rogers said, "Journalists, you mean?"

"Well, we'll start in-house . . . with our own profiler—Trevor Ivanek."

"Peace, above all things, is to be desired, but blood must sometimes be spilled to obtain it on equable and lasting terms."

Andrew Jackson, seventh President of the United States of America. Served 1829–1837. Defeated the British at the Battle of New Orleans during the War of 1812.

SIXTEEN

Trevor Ivanek, bony and brooding in a black suit with no tie, sat at his desk in the bullpen of the Special Situations Task Force at the J. Edgar Hoover Building, feeling very alone.

The room was already more than the team needed, the big open space more than accommodating their desks and, at the rear, the private offices for Altuve, Rogers, and sometimes Reeder. But it had never felt *this* big, or this empty, to him before.

Night was peeking through the blinds—*how long had he been here? Three hours? No, four.*

Not so long ago, with everyone here, Rogers had used a whiteboard to suggest, out of security-cam eyeshot, that a possible rogue element in government meant that paranoia was a fact not a condition. There had been talk of burner cell phones being distributed. But he hadn't received one.

Possibly that was his fault. He'd made himself scarce last night and this morning, troubled by what Rogers had outlined and wondering where he fit into it. His work as an FBI profiler, for going on ten years now, had taken a toll. He'd never been able to sustain a relationship with the opposite sex, or any sex for that matter—the nightmares of his days made his evenings nothing worth sharing.

Finally, after dealing with some of the worst monsters on the planet as part of an FBI Behavioral Science unit, he'd requested a transfer to something less . . . intense.

The Special Situations Task Force, however, had proven anything but a less intense environment. Serial killers seemed like pikers compared to those who had sought, last year, to arrange a coup by outlandishly murderous means. And now Rogers was saying that a shadow government, with similar intent, might be attempting to manipulate world events with federal employees used as cannon fodder.

While he waited to hear from Rogers or anyone else on the team, he sat reading, on his tablet, *A Brief History of Secret Societies* by Barrett; taking a crash course on what they might be dealing with.

He'd spent the morning wandering the National Gallery of Art, one of many local museums where he could drift along and chill. It wasn't that he was hiding from Rogers and the rest—more that he wanted to decide if he was up to being part of this, this . . . *intense* task.

Beneath his cool, rather scholarly manner a jumble of nerves hid how well he understood his own psychology and that of others. He imagined he could rival Joe Reeder in people-reading skills, though that had never been put to the test.

Night was here, and now what? Back to his Dumfries apartment maybe, where Rogers or other team members might be more comfortable getting in contact with him, should a government facility like the Hoover Building seem too likely to have been compromised.

He'd just decided to gather his things and his thoughts and leave for home when something remarkable happened: Assistant Director Margery Fisk herself walked in the door.

In the year-plus the Special Sit Task Force had been on the job, he could remember only once before when AD Fisk had descended from the heavens, several floors above, for a direct visit.

In a black business suit and a white silk blouse, her short curly hair as perfect this time of day as at the start, Fisk granted him a nod and a thin smile. She glanced around at the otherwise empty bullpen. He was just about to ask her where the hell his team was when she spoke.

"Where the hell is your team?" she asked.

She was standing before him now, a teacher looking down at a questionable pupil.

"They're in the field, Director. I haven't heard from Agent Rogers or any of the others. And I admit I'm concerned."

She came around, borrowed a chair from the desk next door, and sat beside him. Leaning forward a little, staring past him, her hands knitted in her lap, Fisk had already moved from stern taskmaster to worried boss . . . or even worried fellow agent.

"I'm concerned, too, Trevor . . ."

Calling him Trevor was clearly an attempt to put him at ease, and encourage a sense of familiarity between them. And he did have a history with Fisk, a positive one—she'd allowed him to transfer here from the Behavioral unit.

She was saying, "I've left message after message, e-mail, text, voice mail, and no one has checked in. What do you make of that?"

He tilted his head. "Frankly, I know Agent Rogers is concerned about security."

Fisk frowned and smiled at once. "You mean this notion she has that there's a 'rogue element' in the government? That seems highly unlikely, don't you think?"

Considering the subject of the book he was reading, Ivanek wasn't sure. But he told her what she wanted to hear: "Most unlikely."

"But I do understand what her concern might be—she made a most convincing case for Secretary Yellich's death to've been murder. And considering Yellich's high position, that murder might well be considered a political assassination."

"I can see that, ma'am."

"I have the utmost respect for the Special Sit Unit. It is, in a way, my baby. I've been working hand in hand with Patti Rogers to keep you folks funded, which is no small trick in these lean times."

"I can imagine."

She smiled in a chin-crinkling way, patted him on the shoulder, and rose. "Let's make a pact."

"A pact, ma'am?"

"Make me the first person you call when you hear from Patti, and I'll do the same."

Then she was gone, heels clicking down the corridor.

Was she sincere? Should he suspect her? He wasn't sure.

He sat thinking about that for a good ten minutes and was about to finally leave when his cell vibrated. He checked the caller ID.

Rogers.

In the loft, Rogers met Hardesy and Wade at the door—Lucas had waved her over, as they stepped back inside after a trip hauling Miggie's gear out and down.

"Feds," Hardesy said. "I even know one of the guys. Two blocks down across from that rental of Reeder's."

"Damn," she said. "Did they see you?"

Wade shook his head. "No. And I didn't make any others. Course if they bust the door down any second, I reserve the right to change my opinion."

Rogers felt a little sick. This left them in a nearly indefensible position. They had the high ground, but nothing else—certainly not enough firepower, the six of them against the rest of the FBI. Not great odds.

"So," Reeder said, joining them, "they're closing in but they don't know where we are, exactly."

Rogers asked, "Are we sure of that?"

Reeder nodded, confident. "No one in the government is aware of my relationship with DeMarcus, and I sent him and his girlfriend away with off-the-books cash."

"Guy I recognized," Hardesy said, "is Bureau. So this is Fisk."

Rogers said, "Do you blame her? Far as she knows, we're MIA."

Reeder raised a hand. "Let's not assume that Fisk is the only one looking for us. The Alliance likely has access to the same assets as Fisk, and *they* don't want to save or arrest us."

"We can't wait them out," Miggie said, from his nearby computer post. "Sooner or later they'll probably canvass the neighborhood, and even if they don't, and just pack up and go at some point, we're kept out of the game, till then."

"And," Rogers said, "we can't afford that."

Reeder said, "So we get in the game now."

All eyes were on him.

He said, "All of our personal vehicles are out. Fisk has the makes and licenses and so, almost certainly, does the Alliance. So let's discuss alternate transportation. Sooner we change rides the better. Thoughts?"

Wade said, "I can get a car for Hardesy and me. I've got a friend out of government I can trust."

Miggie said, "I've got a *vato* owes me a favor. He'll get me a ride."

Rogers clamped eyes with Reeder. "You have somebody in mind for us?"

Reeder shrugged. "What about Pete Woods? He's a cop, with no love for feds, and he seemed trustworthy enough when we worked with him last year."

"Yeah, well, *we're* feds, remember?"

"He likes you."

"I *have* a guy."

"But not a ride. I'll get you the number. Also, we need to protect Morris in case Alliance guns are out there—they'd probably kill him on sight. So we disguise him a little. No glasses."

"That's not enough," Rogers said.

Wade grinned. "How about I shave his head Hardesy-style?"

"*What?*" came a voice from the kitchenette.

That gave everybody a needed laugh.

"We can't use the side stairway," Reeder said. "Too exposed. We take the rear stairwell to the back of the tailor shop and out into the alley. We need to stagger the times. Don't want all three vehicles back there at once, and Lucas, you and Wade will have to transfer Miggie's gear."

"This is when I wish I were hourly," Hardesy said, "not salaried. Think of the overtime."

"And," Wade said, "the lack of anybody tryin' to kill us."

Reeder took Rogers' phone, punched in Woods' number, and handed it back. She stepped away. Meanwhile Wade went over and started unwrapping their prisoner, who was moaning and groaning about the new hairstyle awaiting him.

After three rings came: "Woods."

"Pete, Patti Rogers. Remember me?"

"I remember you *and* your charming partner. Is this call because I gave that Bureau guy crap at that hit-and-run at Arlington?"

"No. Your instincts were correct."

"Yeah?"

"Joe and I need a ride. We've got the Bureau on our tails, because we're looking into a government scandal, and dodging assorted bad guys who want us dead."

". . . Sounds dangerous."

"It is. Wouldn't blame you saying no. If you say yes, bring your umbrella, 'cause it's a shit storm."

". . . My helping you would really rub the Bureau raw?"

"It would," she admitted.

"Count me in," Woods said. "Where and when?"

She told him where, then clicked off. Wade was hauling Morris toward the bathroom, the man's hands still duct-taped together. Morris was swearing at Wade, whose laughter echoed.

Turning back to the rest of her team, she said, "Our ride will be meeting Joe and me in one hour, three blocks over. Mig, arrange for your ride to pick you up at Eleventh and M, just a block away, which gives you less exposure with our buddy Lawrence. Call your friends and see if they can pick you up in that same one-hour window. Lucas, you and Reggie have your ride pick you up right out back, so you can transfer Mig's stuff."

Hardesy said, "It's Reggie's guy. I'll go interrupt his barber-college lesson so he can make the call."

Hardesy did that, and Mig made his call, too. Within ten minutes both confirmed their rides were set. Within twenty minutes, Wade was hauling out a bald-headed Morris, who looked near tears, some shaving-cream splotches here and there, like the last of melting snow. Now everybody's laughter echoed.

Except Morris.

Who was given Washington Wizards sweats from the DeMarcus Collection, and some Air Jordans that required several extra pairs of socks to make fit. With his newly shaved noggin and no wire-frames, he looked nothing like the Men's Wearhouse–wearing accountant.

While they waited, Reeder, Rogers, and her team helped themselves to extra nine millimeters and handfuls of magazines. The laughter generated by Morris had faded, as everyone knew that these weapons could very well have to be used against others like themselves—government agents on the side of the angels, or anyway Uncle Sam.

Wade and Reggie went first, out the back way. When no sounds came of gunshots or struggle, Miggie, Nichols, and the Daddy Warbucks-ish Lawrence Morris went out that same way. Again, no sound of trouble followed. Five minutes later, Reeder and Rogers took the side stairs and left the Batcave behind.

She fell into step next to him as they took off toward L Street at a fast walk, hugging the buildings and avoiding the glow of the streetlights. At Tenth and L, they turned east and Rogers glanced over her shoulder. A male figure stepped out from under a tree in the block between Ninth and Tenth.

"Bogie on our six," she said, "block back."

"Could just be out for smokes or snacks," Reeder said. "Bodega across the block."

"We could stop and ask him."

Reeder picked up the pace a little. "Or not."

Behind them, a male voice called, "*Hey!*"

Like he'd seen a friend or maybe needed directions. Reeder whispered, "Just keep going. Don't look back."

She obeyed, but building footfalls behind them said their new friend was running now.

"*Hey!*" he called again. Then, abandoning pretense, he yelled, "*Halt! Federal agent!*"

"Go!" Reeder said, and they went, running, with him just a step ahead.

"*Stop or I'll fire!*"

Shoes pounding the sidewalk, the eyes of the homeless on them from the recessions of doorways, they hurtled along. Up ahead an unmarked white van had paused at the mouth of a parking lot—*were they being herded toward their own capture?*

Twelfth Street lay fifty yards ahead, and she didn't know if they could even make it to the corner. Behind them, and the agent pursuing them, a car engine's throaty purr built to a roar. Now a vehicle was in pursuit, too!

They reached the white van, Reeder running with a hand on the nine mil in his waistband while she fumbled with her hip holster to get at her own weapon.

But no one jumped out of the van.

Still twenty-five yards from Twelfth, the two fled the agent whose approaching footsteps were small punctuation marks in the throbbing of the car engine that still built and built . . .

That was when an uneven patch in the pavement sent her down, and she hit her right knee on the sidewalk, as if she'd stopped to pray, which might not have been a bad idea; then she pitched forward and her hands burned, skidding and skinned by the rough concrete.

Reeder went back for her, helping her up. As he did, their eyes met and for once she could read him as well as he could her: *they were screwed*.

As Reeder pulled her to her feet, Rogers finally saw the car that went with the engine roar: a dark green Dodge. No outrunning that.

But the vehicle veered, forcing the pursuing agent to dive out of the way, slamming him into the rear of the white van, his pistol flying and hitting the cement somewhere, bouncing clunkily away.

Then the car was squealing to a stop next to them, Reeder with the nine mil out now, Rogers too, when the passenger door flew open, and from the driver's seat, Pete Woods leaned over, shouting, "Ride's here!"

Reeder got the rear door for her, helped her limp in, then climbed in front, all in a blur.

Woods peeled away as Reeder's rider's side door slammed, the vehicle flying north on Twelfth.

The Homicide detective behind the wheel was in his early thirties, slender, collegiate-looking with steel-framed glasses that made the sharp green eyes seem even sharper. Reeder had caught him at home, as reflected by the dark brown sweatshirt and tan chinos.

"Did I just almost hit a fed?" Woods asked.

"You complaining or bragging?"

"Not sure yet. Care to tell me what you got me into, exactly? Those broad strokes you gave me are feeling a little too broad."

"Get our asses out of here and we'll see."

They sped along, Woods working the side streets to put some distance between them and anyone in pursuit.

Reeder craned to give Rogers a concerned look. "Nasty spill you took."

"Concrete chewed me up a little, spit me out some. At least I didn't tear my slacks."

"Good you have priorities."

Woods asked, "Am I going anywhere in particular?"

"For right now," Reeder said, the nine millimeter in his lap, "away from anybody trying to kill us."

The young detective's eyebrows lifted. "Well, at least I have a goal."

Rogers got out her cell and punched in Ivanek's number. It took four rings for him to answer, and she could picture him staring at UNKNOWN in the caller ID, wondering if it was safe to answer.

"Yeah," his voice said.

"You need to get out of there. We're compromised from within."

"Fisk?"

"I'd like to think not. The rogue gov element grabbed Anne, but we got her back. Bohannon—executed. Mob-style."

"Good God."

"We've got less than a minute, Trevor, before they trace this call. Join us off the grid."

". . . where? When?"

"Washington Monument. Half an hour."

"That's an awfully wide open area."

"Exactly," she said, then clicked off.

Frowning, Woods glanced back; they were on a residential side street. He said, "Washington Monument—really?"

Reeder said, "It's a good call. We'll be out in the open, yes, but so will anybody coming at us. And something as public as that might discourage the bad guys from hitting us."

"This," Woods said, "might be a good time for you to tell me exactly what bad guys we're talking about."

In the half hour it took to get to the monument, Reeder gave the detective chapter and verse. The young cop reacted with squints and gaping glances, but never once interrupted or commented. He had been through the coup attempt last year and knew Reeder was to be believed.

While Reeder filled the detective in, Rogers kept an eye on her cell. Already there was a text from Kevin saying he was safe. Then Hardesy and Wade texted in, confirming they'd got away clean. They were nearing the Mall by the time Miggie reported in. He, Anne Nichols, and their newly bald charge were not yet at the cabin, but were well and safely on their way.

After Woods parked his Dodge up Independence Avenue, the trio walked toward the National Mall. The night was brisk but not quite cold, the foot traffic on the sidewalk sparse and touristy. Thanks to clever lighting, the obelisk that was the monument glowed against the darkness, beckoning them like a ghostly forefinger.

They took one of the gently circular walks radiating across the flat surrounding landscape to the city's tallest structure. Encircled by flags that flapped lazily in the slight night breeze, so tall it hurt to crane your neck for a real look at it, the Washington Monument seemed to have nothing obviously to do with the Father of the Country but nonetheless stunned in its odd singular majesty.

Tourists gawked and milled respectfully, but none looked overtly like federal agents or for that matter undercover conspiracists. If either of those two groups knew enough to disguise themselves as sightseers, that meant this meeting place was known to the opposition and the Special Situations Task Force was done before it started. Only slightly out of place, she and Reeder and Woods lingered near the monument's base, their eyes more on the walks around them than the building, as if they were waiting for someone. And of course they were.

Finally Ivanek, looking like a wandering undertaker in his black suit, moved down one of the sidewalks toward them. The skeletal profiler, eyes intense under that cliff of brow, approached Rogers and Reeder with a wary smile. Without having to be told, Woods headed off to watch the other side of the monument.

Ivanek grunted something that was almost a laugh. "I guess this is a fitting meeting spot at that."

"Oh?" Rogers said, as somewhere in her mind she wondered if Trevor, the loner among the task force members, might have gone over to the other side.

Ivanek glanced up at the towering marble-and-granite structure. "This is Secret Society Central—what this thing and George Washington have in common is Freemasonry."

"Let's stroll," Reeder said.

They walked slowly around the structure, pretending to be just another trio of rubberneckers, as she filled the profiler in on their situation. When they'd returned to their starting point, Trevor stood with hands on hips.

"So," he asked Rogers, but his eyes then traveled to Reeder, "where do we go from here?"

Reeder answered with a question. "What contact have you made with Fisk today?"

Ivanek told them, concluding, "I couldn't read her, Joe. Maybe you could have. She just seemed like Fisk. If she's one of them, nothing she did or said was different . . . I mean, her task force disappeared on her and wasn't checking in. How else *would* she act?"

Rogers and Reeder exchanged glances and nods.

"Your prevailing theory, then," Ivanek said, folding his arms, "is that the President and Vice President will be taken out when they leave by Marine One and Marine Two?"

Reeder said, "With rocket launchers that lay the blame on Russia, yes."

Ivanek winced in thought. "But Marine One and Two are equipped with antimissile tech, and anyway, they routinely fly decoy helicopters, in shifting formation. If *I* were getting rid of the top two men, I'd find a way to do it before they left the compound."

Rogers said, "Why's that?"

"They have security second-to-none at Camp David," Ivanek said. "It's designed to protect against an attack from without—an invasion. Of course, if they were hit from *within*, and since we think the government has been infiltrated, then—"

As if someone had spit in her face, Rogers felt the warm flecks of moisture just a microsecond before she realized Ivanek had been shot and another micro before she heard the report of the rifle. Ivanek collapsed to the pavement, hiding what she knew would be a massive exit wound, the entry wound small and wet and red-black.

She fell to a knee as if to check him, but that wasn't the case since the profiler was clearly dead. Her gun was out of its holster and in hand and pointing at a flat area with its flapping flags and backdrop of trees, a vast world of night that meant she was aiming at nothing at all.

Reeder was just behind her, also taking a knee, also ready to return fire, but where? And at whom? Around them, chaos ruled, tourists screaming on the run, mothers and fathers clutching children, even ones as old as ten or eleven in their arms, and running blindly into nowhere. Woods came around, keeping low but moving fast, his gun out as well, as he yelled, "Where'd the shot come from?"

As if in answer, Woods got hit in the chest, and fell back, his gun leaping out of his hand as if the thing had gone suddenly molten.

Reeder scrambled over to Woods, on his back, kicking like an upended turtle. Rogers scuttled over. Around them a terrible near-silence had descended. Sightseers who hadn't run into the night were splayed on the ground or behind whatever minimal cover they could find. Others could be heard running, but that seemed far away.

Then another shot cracked the night as concrete dust kicked up less than a foot away. *Was this the same son of a bitch who'd killed Tony Wooten right next to her at the Skygate Apartments?*

Staying low, moving fast, she and Reeder dragged the detective around to the far side of the monument.

"One shooter, you think?" Rogers asked.

Reeder said, "Better be."

Then they heard the sirens.

Rogers said, "Time to go?"

"Time to go," he said.

She leaned over Woods. "How bad?"

"Hit the vest," the detective said, wincing, hurting. "Kevlar's never . . . never a bad accessory for . . . a night out with you two."

"Can you stand, you think?" Rogers said. "We need to move."

"What about the sniper?" Woods asked.

Reeder said, "Those sirens had to send him scurrying. But we can't let your brothers-in-blue pick us up, either."

The sirens were screaming. She and Reeder probably had a minute, maybe two. Maybe.

Rogers said, "We'll help you up—we've got to go."

Woods pawed at the air. "Get out of here, you two. I got this. I'll . . . I'll say you called to give yourself up to . . . to somebody neutral, and we came here to pick up another of your crew. Who somebody shot. Now. Get to the bottom of this shit. Here. Take my car." He got his keys out and handed them over.

She gave him a quick nod of thanks and her eyes told him to take care. Then she and Reeder, his arm around her, were just another couple hustling away to safety.

On the way to Woods's car, they stayed alert for a tail, hugging trees and bushes as much as possible. Not knowing where that sniper had gotten himself to made things tense.

At the Dodge, Reeder opened the driver's door for her and she got behind the wheel.

"Where to?" she asked.

It wasn't like there was anywhere they could go.

"I need some rest," he said. "And so do you. We stay up much longer, our judgment will go to hell. But I don't know if we dare go to a hotel or motel. And we can't risk driving far, or for long, in this car. No matter what Woods cooks up to cover us and himself, somebody— maybe a lot of somebodies—will be looking for this vehicle."

She started the engine.

"I know somewhere," she said.

"There are plenty of recommendations on how to get out of trouble cheaply and fast. Most of them come down to this: Deny your responsibility."

Lyndon B. Johnson, thirty-sixth President of the United States of America. Served 1963–1969. Twenty-four years in Congress before becoming Vice President under John F. Kennedy.

SEVENTEEN

They stayed off the interstates, avoiding as much as possible traffic-cams and other security cameras. As Rogers drove, Reeder got Miggie on the burner.

"Everybody safe?" the computer expert asked.

"Patti and I are fine."

Quickly he told Miguel what had happened at the Monument.

"Oh, hell," Mig said hollowly. "First Jerry, now Trevor . . . God. What next?"

"We do our best not to join them. Your end?"

"Everybody's okay. No sign of a tail. Should be at the cabin soon. Nichols is sleeping in back right now."

"Both of you need to get some rest. Sleep in shifts, when you get to the cabin."

"That's what we planned. GPS says you're on the move, too."

"We are. Patti and I'll find somewhere we can sleep before we drop. But tomorrow I want to make a visit, first thing."

"Anywhere special?"

"Just the cabinet member left behind for this Camp David trip, now that Amanda Yellich is off the list."

A pause filled itself with cell-phone crackle.

"Joe, I told you before how tight a lid the Secret Service keeps on that."

"And you're just the guy to pry it off."

Another crackly pause.

"I'll get back to you," Miguel said, and clicked off.

Reeder slept for fifteen minutes and then the burner in his hand vibrated.

"Turns out the held-back cabinet member," Mig said, "is a familiar name."

"Secretary of Agriculture," Reeder said. "Nicholas Blount."

"Jesus! If you *knew* that, why—"

"I didn't. Just an educated guess, based on Lawrence mentioning the Blount dynasty. If procedure hasn't changed, Nicky will be at home or perhaps some summer or winter place."

"His home," Mig said. "Chevy Chase, 6900 block of Brennon Lane. Do I have to remind you a spate of agents from your alma mater will be on hand?"

"No, but see if you can define spate."

Miggie tapped on his tablet.

Then: "Six—three two-person teams rotating over twenty-four hours."

"After the attempted coup last year," Reeder said, "I expected more. But then a contingent of agents would only attract unneeded attention. Hey. Is my pal Lawrence asleep?"

"No. Wide awake and pouting."

"Enough dashboard light to see his face?"

"Sure."

"Ask him if Wilson Blount is the Alliance chairman. And as you do, watch his face close—you're going to read him for me."

"Do my best . . . *Lawrence!* Reeder wants to know if Senator Blount is the chairman of the Alliance board."

Reeder could make out Morris's muffled, "Hell no."

"Hear that?" Miggie asked.

"Yeah. Did his eyes go up and to the left?"

"His left or my left?"

"Yours."

"Yup. For half a sec, I'd say."

"Thank Lawrence for me . . . I'll check back in the morning. That concealed gun cabinet in the cabin is—"

"I remember where it is."

They clicked off.

Rogers, at the wheel, had gathered most of the conversation from Reeder's end and what she could hear of Miggie's.

She asked, "So Blount is the chairman? Based on some minimal eye movement on Morris's part?"

He gave her half a smile. "Wouldn't exactly hold up in court. But it makes sense. The Senator is who angled to get the qualifying age for the presidency lowered last year, and now we learn that his young son is the one cabinet member not at Camp David right now."

"It's thin," she said, "but credible. So we talk to Nicky Blount? How do we get past your Secret Service buddies?"

The sky was already showing patches of pink light in the east.

"Working on it," he said.

Then he fell asleep.

When he woke up, Rogers was pulling into the entry drive of an underground garage using a keycard. Reeder twisted and saw a street sign: **WOODMONT AVENUE**.

Once they were settled into a space away from cameras and potential passersby, Reeder asked, "Are we anywhere special?"

"Bethesda. The Landow Building. Offices and retail, and very little traffic this early on a Saturday."

"And you have a keycard for a parking garage in Bethesda *why*?"

"Gabe Sloan and I—not long after we were first partnered up—stopped some domestic terrorists who wanted to blow this place up for jihad or something. The owners asked us how often our work brought us to Bethesda and we said fairly often, and . . ."

"They gave you each a permanent parking pass. I got a few perks myself on the job. Who knows about this?"

"The late Gabriel Sloan. How long should we sleep?"

"Make it two hours."

"Okay." She set the dashboard alarm. "I'll take the back. That seat you're in reclines. Try not to snore."

He grinned at her, and it felt good. "Same back at you."

Sleep didn't take him immediately, possibly because of the catnaps he'd caught on the ride. He worked out a tentative plan to get in to see Nicky Blount, and wondered if he was too geared up to fall asleep again, and then did.

When the dash alarm buzzed, Reeder quickly leaned over and shut it off. He rubbed his face, his neck. He hadn't realized how exhausted he was. Standing post all those years had taught him to survive on little or no sleep. But he was older now.

Rogers was still deep asleep, and snoring a little, but gently. He decided to let her sleep a while, then got out of the car and called Miggie.

Mig, Nichols, and their sullen charge were at the cabin and fine.

"But I'm still keeping an eye on various e-mails," Miggie said, "including, and especially, Fisk's. The Bureau has finding us high on its priority list, and the AD has other agencies in on it now."

Reeder gave up a wry chuckle. "So we're wanted dead or alive."

"Well, I wouldn't go that far . . ."

"I would. The more agencies she brings in, the more infiltrated ranks we're dealing with. Listen, I need some names."

"Any names in particular?"

"Just those of the Secret Service agents assigned to Nicky Blount today."

Silence followed, with just crackle enough to say the connection hadn't been broken. Getting Secret Service assignments was no small task, even for a hacker of Miggie's magnitude. Reeder was asking a lot.

Then Mig's voice returned: "Get back to you."

Reeder made another call. He was wrapping it up when Rogers exited the rear of the Dodge, yawning, stretching, saying, "What the heck time is it?"

"Almost nine," he said. "I shut the alarm off to let you sleep in."

"So I got two hours and twenty minutes instead of just two hours. You're a prince, Joe. Talk to Miggie yet?"

He told her about their conversation.

Smoothing her clothes, Rogers looked around the parking facility and said, "We better get out of here. Even on Saturday, people are coming already."

"We need to leave this car here," he said. "It'll be hot by now."

"And, what, *walk* to Nicky Blount's?"

"I've taken care of that. Let's find a place for breakfast. Need to kill a little time, and I could eat."

"I could, too," she admitted.

They found a nearby hotel restaurant to have breakfast and he explained that a fresh and secure car would be delivered to them within the hour. Told her he had a friend with a used car lot who did business with ABC Security, and would drop off a nondescript vehicle.

"Trust this guy?" she asked.

They were in a booth, both drinking coffee.

"My people cleared him, couple years ago, when he was falsely linked to a chop shop. Remember last year when I sneaked Chris Bryson's widow and son out of town? That's where I got the car for them."

The vehicle, dropped at a corner Reeder had designated, proved to be a Buick Regal, nice enough but a good ten years old. He had her drive again. They'd gone less than a block when she asked, "You think these Secret Service agents could be Alliance?"

"I've already tangled with one SS agent, so as much as it makes me sick, we have to think that way. Doing otherwise might be suicidal. Minimally, I need to know who we're dealing with."

They were taking a second pass past Nicky Blount's two-story red-brick Cape Cod, its flat yard bulging with impeccably trimmed bushes, when Miggie called back.

"Agents on duty are Chad Holmberg and Ronald Parker," Mig said. "Their shift goes to noon, so should be no surprises."

"Ronald Parker, huh?"

"That's right—know him?"

"Stood post with Ron, back in the day. Could be a break. Know anything about Holmberg?"

"Spotless record. Came on a couple years ago."

"Thanks, Miggie. How's your happy mountain home?"

"It's got everything but a ski lift. Our guest keeps complaining to the management, though."

"His hair will grow back someday."

Miggie was laughing a little as Reeder clicked off.

Rogers pulled around the corner and parked on Cummings Lane.

She leaned on the wheel and gave him a furrowed-brow look. "Only two agents?"

"It's the Secretary of Agriculture, Patti."

Shaking her head, she said, "But there's some kind of conspiracy going on and—"

"Who knows that?"

"Us. The conspirators."

"Bingo."

Her eyebrows lifted and lowered. "Do we have anything particular in mind? I could knock at the front door and ask if they've seen my missing dog."

"Before I knew Ron Parker was on the job, I was thinking we'd go in the back way with our guns out and try not to shoot anybody. Killing a federal agent is a hard one to walk back."

"*That* was your plan?"

"I didn't say I was proud of it, but sudden and swift has its merits. I doubt Nicky is leaving the house for work much less play—they'll have him on lockdown till the Camp David meet is over and everybody's home."

"So how does this Ron Parker fit in?"

"That's the *new* plan."

"What is?"

"He's a smoker."

He explained what he had in mind.

"That's not a plan, Joe. You could easily wind up behind bars or dead."

"But you'll still be on the outside, and can link up with Mig, Lucas, Wade, and Nichols, and go on with the fight."

"I don't like it. Not one little bit."

But she got out of the car with him, and took a walk around the block, checking to see if any agents they didn't know about were posted or on patrol, and watching for anybody not resembling well-off suburban parents or kids. Finally they cut between two houses. All the backyards on the block were connected, with plenty of trees to pause behind, and no fences.

They moved through the shadows of the well-shaded, country club–tended backyards until they were in back of the Cape Cod, finding an American beech whose thick trunk was plenty for them to stand behind. The beech and the expanding reach of its considerable branches, grasping the sky, took up much of the space back here. White steps went up to a back porch at right, next to which was a concrete patio with a glass table with central umbrella, six chairs, and a gas grill. For now the yard was deserted. Kids were playing two doors down, yelping and squealing.

Reeder had the anonymous nine in his waistband, and another tucked similarly in back. Rogers had her hand on the butt of her holstered Glock.

They waited. Ten minutes. Twenty. Now and then, Rogers glanced at him, but he didn't bother returning it. His eyes stayed on those back porch steps and the little landing.

Secret Service agent Ron Parker, his short blond hair going white at the temples, his blankly average features a blank slate, stepped out from the porch onto the landing and casually shook out a cigarette from a pack already in hand. His eyes traveled, but nothing watchdog-like was in it—just a boring morning with only some sunshine to recommend it. Parker blocked the light breeze with his left hand while he lit the smoke with his right.

Reeder gave Rogers a glance that said a dozen things, but mostly to stay out of sight, then stepped from behind the beech, his arms spread away from his body, hands raised just slightly.

The Secret Service agent on the little landing reacted not at all. Had Reeder's hands not been up, Parker's response would have been otherwise, and almost certainly deadly. For now, the agent's ice blue eyes gave away nothing, his face as blank as Reeder's usually was, while Reeder was sending his old friend a small, somewhat apologetic smile.

Then Parker let out air and glanced behind him at the house, before slowly walking down the handful of steps and meeting Reeder at the edge of the patio. It was hardly noticeable when the agent's eyes skimmed past his unexpected guest to slowly scan the woods behind the houses.

"Peep," he said. "Been a while."

They might have met accidentally on a street corner.

"A while," Reeder admitted.

"Did you figure to do your old pal a solid," Parker said, his smile as small and faint as Reeder's, "and give yourself up? Who can't use a gold star in their file?"

"Consider it a white flag," Reeder said, "not a surrender. So what have you heard?"

"That you and the Special Situations bunch are off the reservation, you mean?"

"Not off the reservation at all, Ron. I'm working for the President. Again."

"Really. Can you prove that?"

"Is that something I'd lie about?"

Both men just looked at each other with their patented blank expressions.

Glancing across the yard again, past the beech and the thicket beyond, Parker took a long drag on his cigarette, then let the smoke stream out. "You're not alone, are you?"

"What do you think?"

"Probably Rogers. She's head of Special Situations, and you two cracked the Supreme Court case a couple years back. Congratulations, by the way."

"Appreciate it."

"So, then—why don't you tell me why you're here before *my* partner comes out to see whether I set myself on fire or something?" He stubbed the cigarette under the toe of his shoe.

"I need to have a word with Nicholas Blount."

Parker barked a laugh. "I don't care how far back we go, Peep, that ain't happening."

Reeder's reply would have been much the same had their roles been reversed. "Ron, I'm standing here talking to you, and not barging in with a gun in my hand, because I trust you."

That appreciably threw Parker. "Yeah, well, that's good to hear. The part where you trust me. The gun part, though? Not so much. Let's say you walk away and I never saw you. That's the most I can give you."

"Do you trust your guy Holmberg?"

Parker's eyes narrowed. "You know my *partner's* name? What the hell—"

"Never mind that. Have you worked with him long enough to trust him? Because not everybody in government right now can be. Trusted."

Just barely, Parker glanced back at the house. "I trust him. He's young and he's new but he's straight."

Parker meant what he said, or did if Reeder could trust his kinesics training.

Reeder asked, "Trust him with your life, though?"

"That's the job, isn't it?"

"What I'm saying, Ron, is—if you trust him, I do, too."

"I said I trusted him."

Not a single micro-expression of doubt.

"Okay," Reeder said. "Go tell your trustworthy partner that a former agent, who's wanted for questioning by the FBI, is in the backyard. And that you want him to look the other way just long enough for you to tell Nicky Blount that I want to talk to him about the American Patriots Alliance. Got that? The American—"

"I've heard of it. One of those Illuminati nonsense deals."

"If you say so. But tell him. If Nicky doesn't want to speak to me, I'm gone. Vapor. My word on it. But if Nicky does come outside to talk to me, you let him do so. You can watch from the porch, but out of earshot."

Parker had started shaking his head already. "No deal, Peep. Look, man, we stood post together and I trusted you with my life and you did the same with me. I'll even take your damn message in to Nicky . . . but if he does want to talk, you come inside to do it. No way I'm letting him come out here in the open."

Reeder understood that. A lot harder to protect Nicky outdoors, especially when Reeder had brought backup. "Fair enough, Ron . . . and thanks."

A smirk cut the otherwise blank face. "Don't thank me yet. First I have to sell Holmberg. He may think it wasn't tobacco I been smoking out here."

Parker went back inside, and Reeder waited. If this didn't go as he hoped it would, he'd have a choice between battling two of his brother SS men or just holding his fists behind him for the cuffs. He hoped, when she saw him go inside, that Rogers wouldn't overreact; she might do something rash. He'd take that risk to talk to Nicky Blount.

A distant siren was just giving him second thoughts when the back door opened and Parker waved him to the steps. Parker held up a hand to freeze Reeder at the bottom, then said, "Guns stay outside."

Very professional now, coolly so.

Parker nodded toward the grill and Reeder got the point, opening its lid and putting both his handguns in, and the expandable baton.

"Cell, too."

Reeder did so, then lowered the lid.

From the top of the steps, Parker said, "You have ten minutes, Peep, and only because Blount wants to grant you that. Then you're gone. An hour after that, I report spotting you in the yard. Got it?"

"Got it. Thanks."

Inside the good-size enclosed porch, Reeder stood for a frisk without having to be asked. Parker, of course, found nothing. Then the SS agent led Reeder into a spacious, gleaming-white, ultramodern kitchen, with a center island that might have come with its own zip code.

Waiting in the kitchen on either side of that island were two men: tall, blond, blandly handsome Nicholas Blount in a button-down blue shirt, jeans, and running shoes; and—in a pristine gray suit Reeder might have worn back in the day—a sharp-eyed, trimly athletic-looking man of thirty or so who had to be agent Chad Holmberg.

"Secretary Blount," Reeder said with a nod.

"Mr. Reeder," Nicky said.

Then the piercing hazel eyes of Senator Blount's youngest son went first to Holmberg then to Parker, at Reeder's side.

"Gentlemen," he said, with a hint of Southern drawl, "if you'll excuse us?"

Parker said, "Sir, I wouldn't advise that."

"I must insist."

Holmberg and Parker exchanged glances that seemed to say nothing but spoke volumes to Reeder.

The younger agent said, "I'll just step into the living room, Mr. Secretary."

Holmberg left, but Reeder had no doubt he'd just stepped outside the room, and would stay nearby. But at least a closed door would separate their conversation from the agent.

Parker gave Reeder a hard sideways look, then said, "I'll be just outside, if I'm needed."

Where you can catch another smoke, Reeder thought, almost letting a smile slip, though blocking the exit did make sense.

The two men faced each other across the island.

"We know each other well enough, I think," Nicky said, the drawl still lightly in evidence, "for first names . . . don't we, Joe? You did me a favor once, being discreet when you could have embarrassed me."

Nicky Blount had been in the Verdict Bar when Justice Venter was shot and killed; at the time Venter's law clerk, Nicky had (to put it bluntly) pissed himself.

"And you were very helpful in the investigation," Reeder said. "So we aren't adversaries . . . unless you're part of the sub-rosa organization we're about to discuss."

"I'm not," Nicky said with a single head shake. "I'm aware of the Alliance, of course, though the vast majority of Americans either haven't heard of it, or write it off as an urban legend . . . Coffee? Or iced tea maybe? I have a pitcher, if—"

"Thank you, no. We have limited time."

That simple statement was loaded a lot of ways.

Nicky sat at the island and Reeder took the stool across from him.

"I love my father," Nicky said.

What might have seemed a non sequitur was a remark—an opening salvo—that Reeder did grasp. For one thing, it confirmed that Senator Blount was a key player in the Alliance; so did the concern for his father that Nicky's words underscored.

"When we first met, Mr. Reeder . . . Joe . . . I was just a green kid, new to DC and its ways."

"We're only talking two years, Nicky."

He nodded. "I don't claim I'm on top of every twist and turn in this town. But I'm not naive—I'm not who you met, even if it wasn't so very long ago."

"Okay. How many twists and turns *are* you on top of?"

Nicky's shrug was casual but his eyes were grave. "Well, I know what kind of murky waters I'm swimming in. I've seen deals made, favors traded."

"Politics," Reeder said.

"The President assigned you," Nicky said, "to look into who sent those four CIA agents to their deaths, isn't that right?"

Reeder didn't answer.

His host's smile was not without charm. "Joe, I *am* in the cabinet. I *do* know things. You really think you can deliver on that mission, when you're running from your own people?"

"Kind of a challenge," Reeder admitted.

"Anyway, there are more pressin' matters." Nicky shrugged again. "As I say, I love my father. And in his way, I know he loves me. But my father's two greatest loves are power and heritage. And those two loves come together in the obsession to see one of his sons in the White

House." A sigh. "Nathaniel, of course, was the chosen one. And he might well have been president by now, Governor of Mississippi and all, beautiful wife and three lovely kiddies, but then . . . well, you know the story."

As former Louisiana governor Edwin Edwards had once proclaimed, "The only way I can lose this election is if I'm caught in bed with a dead girl or live boy." In Nathaniel Blount's case, it had been the latter—two at once.

And while Nathaniel's governorship had somehow survived, his presidential plans were deceased.

Nicky said, "What you may not know, Joe, is that one of those young men was underage, and required my father making quite the series of deals with various and sundry devils. Nothing new for him, of course."

"One such deal being," Reeder commented, "the lowering of the age to serve as president."

Nicky slid off his stool. "All this talk has me dry. I'm gonna have some of that iced tea. Join me?"

"Sure."

"It's sweetened. I know you Yankees don't like it that way."

"I'll survive."

Nicky got them glasses of tea on ice, talking all the while. "Another devil of a deal was having the right people whisper in President Harrison's ear gettin' me on the cabinet when that openin' came up last year. Papa made it clear these things had cost him dearly, and made it crystal clear I was to keep my pecker in my pants and there would be no more weed, either, else there'd be hell to pay."

"The end game is to get you into the White House."

Nicky, seated again, nodded. "But not necessarily by the will of the people."

Something cold crawled up Reeder's spine. "By the will of the Alliance, you mean?"

Another nod, a glum one. "Havin' a Southern boy like myself as Secretary of Agriculture is certainly helpful, and it's an impressive item on my résumé, but it's not the kind of power my Papa wants . . . *needs*. He assumes if I were president, he could control me. That the Alliance would have their man in the most important chair in the world."

"He's admitted this to you?"

Nicky sipped his tea, gestured with his free hand. "In so many words. It was only this past year that he revealed the Alliance itself to me . . . making it clear I was not to be in any way affiliated with the group, not on the board or for that matter even just a member in good standin'. I had to be my own man, he said."

"Meaning *his* man."

"Oh, yes, and of course, when the time comes, the Alliance's man."

Reeder sipped his tea, hating the sweetness. "Knowing what you know, Nicky, you *could* be your own man."

"Possibly. There are moments where I think that's a distinct possibility, Joe. But I also know the power my father wields over me. My weakness is that I do love him, and that I want him to love me . . . laugh at that if you like."

"Not laughing."

A loose-limbed shrug. "I hope I could resist his influence. But right now, I'm worried. Worried that I'm Secretary of Agriculture not because Tennessee is a farm state, but to get me into the line of succession."

"You're way down that list," Reeder said, "but that *has* occurred to us. We think we're looking at a plan to take out the President and Vice President at the Camp David meeting."

"What if it's more than that? Everyone's *there*, Joe, but me— *everyone but me!* If a bomb drops on Camp David . . . you're *looking* at the President."

The silence in the kitchen was like the terrible stillness after a bomb blast itself.

Calmly, Reeder said, "We realize that. And if Harrison and the VP are taken out, the rest of the Cabinet would be targets in the fleeing motorcade. That's how we read it."

Nicky's smile was a terrible thing. "But what if people from *within* staged a coup? Some of us know that that almost *did* go down last year."

Reeder shook his head. "At Camp David? The Secret Service would never let that happen."

But hadn't he fought an SS agent in that alley?

Nicky was saying, "The Alliance has people marbled through the government like fat in a rib-eye steak. Men and women in government service with their own take on patriotism—almost certainly *including* certain members of the Secret Service!"

Reeder fought back nausea.

Nicky pressed on: "Who better to kill the President and Vice President and every cabinet member above me in the line of succession? Who better than the very people assigned to guard them?"

"Some tainted people might be in the Secret Service," Reeder admitted, "but surely not in the presidential detail. That's the elite of the elite—the men and women willing to put their lives on the line. To take a bullet."

"Like you did. For a president you disliked."

"Hated!"

Nicky shook a forefinger at him. "And if you shared the Alliance's beliefs, who would have been better placed than you to dispatch a bullet rather than take one? Someone like that, maybe several, who *knows* how many, are 'guarding' President Harrison right now."

"Come forward with what you know about the Alliance," Reeder said. "Right now! We'll arrange for every media outlet to carry it, and that would nip in the bud any goddamn Camp David coup."

"No," Nicky said.

". . . No?"

"We're talking about my father, and my suspicions. I know things, but I don't know of any plan to do a damn thing at Camp David or anywhere else."

"Plausible deniability," Reeder said.

"It goes beyond that, because all I have are those suspicions. Guesses. And a man can't testify to those, not that I would. All I can do is point you in the right direction and hope to hell I'm either wrong . . . or that you can stop this insanity. By the way, I don't even *want* to be president, puppet or otherwise."

The two men were staring at each other when Parker stepped in from outside.

"That's ten minutes," the agent said. "Time to go, Peep."

"Behind the ostensible government sits enthroned an invisible government owing no allegiance and acknowledging no responsibility to the people."

Theodore Roosevelt, twenty-sixth President of the United States of America. Served 1901–1909.

EIGHTEEN

By the time Reeder finally emerged from the Cape Cod, Patti Rogers—
tucked behind the beech, Glock in hand—had just endured the longest
fifteen minutes of her life . . .

. . . Reeder talking to his old Secret Service buddy before giving
up his weapons and cell and going inside, the SS agent smoking on
the little landing until going in himself, and finally Reeder coming out
with Parker, shaking the man's hand, retrieving guns, baton, and phone,
then trotting across the yard to her while Parker watched. If Reeder's old
pal drew his sidearm with the apparent intention of shooting, Rogers
would have shot the man, federal agent or not. Maybe the guy would
be wearing a vest. But maybe not.

Then they were moving through the connecting backyards again,
hugging the trees, and they didn't talk until they were in the Buick with
her back behind the wheel.

"Well?" she asked.

"First, drive. Parker's giving us an hour and we better start using it."

She started the car. "Anywhere special?"

"Not here."

They were out of Blount's immediate neighborhood before Reeder
said, "Gaithersburg. Know where it is?"

"Yes," she said.

That was a suburb of about sixty thousand, northwest of DC.

"What's in Gaithersburg?" she asked.

"Nothing, I hope. No Alliance troops or FBI, either."

"Why Gaithersburg of all places?"

"Why not? Avoid the Capital Beltway. Fisk'll be having traffic-cams scanned."

"You think?"

"Sorry."

As she got her bearings and headed northwest, he filled her in on his conversation with the young Secretary of Agriculture.

"Well," she said, "suspicions confirmed, but how much good does it do us otherwise, if Nicky won't come forward?"

"It's his father," Reeder said. "Took balls to go as far as he did."

She couldn't argue with that.

He set his cell to speaker, then placed a call that was answered on the third ring.

After hearing Hardesy's "Yeah," Reeder asked him, "Where are you two?"

"Reston, at my college roommate's place. He's out of town and that's fine with me."

So they were safe in Virginia. There were worse places to be.

"Can you get your hands on some firepower?"

". . . Could be I can call in a favor. What might we need?"

"Anything with some punch that isn't a handgun but can be used on the move. Controllable. Nothing producing random gunfire, like a machine gun."

A long pause, then: "See what I can do. What then?"

"There's an Applebee's on Frederick Road in Gaithersburg."

"We'll find it. I assume we leave the weaponry in the car."

That had some sarcasm in it, but Reeder's response did not: "Not your handguns. How long you need?"

"Travel time, getting to my source . . . let's say three hours."

"Try to shorten it," Reeder said.

"Give it a try," Hardesy said, and they clicked off.

Eyebrows up, Rogers asked, "Firepower? No machine guns?"

"You don't want the President taken down by friendly fire, do you?"

She stared at him so long and so hard he had to tell her to get her eyes back on the road.

"Please tell me," she said, "that you're not talking about storming Camp David."

"I'm open to other suggestions."

"Good God, Joe! Isn't that a little over the top?"

"So is Nicky Blount's father leading a coup to overthrow the government and leave his bouncing baby boy as the only one standing. Nicky turns out to have more going for him than I would ever have guessed, but I still don't want him to be the next president."

She was shaking her head, the concept rattling around in her skull like something broken. "And we don't trust the presidential protection detail *why*?"

"It's likely at least some of them are Alliance."

He seemed so goddamn calm! But her heart was racing. She didn't realize how heavy her foot was on the gas till he advised her to slow down and engage the cruise control, which she hadn't because of the serpentine way she was traveling.

Finally she said, "Do I have to tell you that place is a military installation? A fortress not only protected by the Secret Service, but staffed with Navy and Marines? You *know* that, and yet you're still contemplating, what, *shooting* our way in?"

"Someone has to protect the President. With the Secret Service infiltrated, who else is there but us?"

She drove numbly for a minute or maybe an hour.

Finally he said, "There's one other way. We can drive up to the checkpoint and I can ask to be put through to Harrison. But how likely is that request to go directly through? Someone on the inside who's compromised would have us taken care of. And anyway, we're basically the FBI's entire Most Wanted List right now."

"Jesus. If there were only some way to warn the President."

Reeder was so quiet and blank, she could read him.

"Joe?"

". . . I have a direct line to the President right now. A cell phone he gave me."

"What?"

"But alerting him at this point doesn't make sense, not until we have an actual plan of action. Telling him that people around him aren't to be trusted could backfire. It's not like he's trained in kinesics."

She gaped at him. "You have a phone that's in the President's pocket? And we're not using it?"

"Not yet. The less time he has to think about it, the less chance he'll give himself away."

"I don't know, Joe . . ."

"This has to be my call."

She smirked at him without humor. "I remember. It's not a democracy."

"Not even close."

They drove in silence for an hour or maybe a minute.

She said, very quietly, "Think Miggie can find us a way in?"

He raised his cell phone. "My next call."

With Miggie on the speaker, Reeder asked, "Security at Camp David—what can you tell us?"

"What you already know," the computer expert said, clearly taken somewhat aback by the query. "That it's good and goddamn tight, as one might expect."

But Mig was already tapping on his tablet in the background.

"Kind of hoping," Reeder said, "for something a little more detailed."

". . . It's a self-contained system, not online. No way for me to hack it."

"None?"

"There's an underground control room, multi-person team inside, pretty much in the center of the compound. They manage all the electronic equipment from there. Motion detectors, infrared, the works. And no way for me to sneak into the system."

"Not good news," Reeder admitted. "What else?"

"Besides the Marines, the Navy, and the F-22s?"

Rogers said, "They have planes?"

"They can get them with a finger snap," Miggie's voice said. "Two different occasions, F-15s intercepted small planes near Camp David that got too close to President Obama."

Reeder asked, "You see a way in? Use your imagination."

"Not that I see," Miggie said, "*or* imagine. Maybe if you had someone inside . . . but from the outside? Suicide."

She and Reeder exchanged glances: *they did have someone inside— the President himself.*

"Miggie," Reeder asked, "is the tunnel still in use?"

"Tunnel?"

"Runs between Aspen Lodge and the command center. Anyway, it did back when I was on the presidential detail."

Miggie's tapping again could be heard, then he said, "Yes . . . yes, it is. Don't know how that helps, but it's still functional, according to what I can access."

"Can *any* part of the system be shut down without tripping all the alarms?"

"There's a way to shut off a single sector, but it has to be done from the control center—*if* you had someone inside."

"Suppose we did," Reeder said, "and a sector could be cleared. What's the best approach?"

A long pause, broken by a sigh. "From the woods on the southeast."

"Through the golf course."

"Yes. If no one is playing, that's where there'll be the least security . . . but also the least *cover*."

"Late enough in the day, shouldn't be anybody playing. President Harrison is a morning golfer."

Mig asked, "How would you know that?"

"I know where the shadows fall, different times of day. Seen pictures of Harrison playing golf there. Old habits die hard."

"But sometimes fast. Anyway—the second tee, Joe. I've got a feeling you know it."

"I do."

"Section A-22. That's the only sector that needs shutting down. Your inside guy can report it as a system check and buy you maybe, oh . . . ten minutes? But you'll really have to hustle."

"Oh yeah. That's over a mile through woods, unless we take the fairway, which would mean no cover."

"But it's also the shortest path to Aspen Lodge, and your tunnel."

"Thanks, Mig."

"Are you really going to try this, Joe? Isn't there some better way?"

"Feel free to call me back with one," Reeder said, and clicked off.

"You can't be seriously contemplating this," she said, her gaze fixed on him again.

"Eyes on the road. I'm going to mull it some. When we sit down with Wade and Hardesy, I'll tell you what I've come up with."

In Gaithersburg, with Hardesy and Wade not due for a while, Rogers located the Applebee's, then drove around the area checking to see if they'd been made by any government agents. She knew the kind of vehicles they drove and the way they dressed and even how they had their hair cut. If somebody was on to their meeting, she had a good chance of knowing.

Finally satisfied, she pulled into the restaurant parking lot and backed into a place at the rear with the alley behind them, giving them two channels of flight. The lunch rush was over, though enough extra civilians were around to give them some cover—not that it was very likely the Buick could be on the FBI radar.

They stayed in the car and waited for Hardesy and Wade. No reason to go in and expose themselves any longer than necessary.

She turned to Reeder. "How's that mulling coming?"

His shrug was barely perceptible. "Let's just say there's zero margin for error."

"Meaning everything goes exactly right, or we check into a federal penitentiary."

"Not necessarily."

"Oh?"

"They may kill us."

They lapsed into silence and the next thing Rogers knew, Reeder was nudging her.

"They're here," he said.

She sat up, yawned, stretched. "How long was I out?"

"Not even half an hour."

"They made good time."

"Or they struck out on the guns."

Hardesy and Wade were backing in next to them in a nothing Kia. They all got out and met in front of their vehicles. The two agents looked somewhat on the bedraggled side, Lucas in his black wind-breaker and jeans, Wade in the dark gray sweats.

Reeder asked, "Any luck?"

Hardesy said, "Two AR-15s. Wish I had four."

"Two'll do. Semiauto?"

"Yeah. My guy is a friend, but he's not *that* good a friend. Fully auto's more than we can hope for, given our circumstances."

Reeder nodded. "Let's go in and stop looking like a drug deal. I have a few things to run past you."

Hardesy gave Rogers a look and she just shrugged.

They asked for and got a table in a back corner. The place was maybe half-full. Wade and Hardesy ordered food, Reeder and Rogers coffee, their breakfast still holding them.

Wade summoned a smile. "Ever try jailhouse food?"

By the time their beverages arrived, Reeder had given them the gist. Nobody was smiling now. Then, covered by clatter and conversation around them, he went over the plan in detail. Wade and Hardesy's food came and neither touched it.

At one point, Hardesy said, "I don't know if I'm prepared to shoot a United States Marine or sailor or even a Secret Service agent. Some may be Alliance-turned traitors, but others sure as hell won't be."

Reeder sipped his coffee. They might have been discussing an office football pool.

"I've considered that too," Reeder said. "The thing is, they'll be trying to kill us."

Hardesy shook his head glumly. "I'm just saying I don't know if I can drop them."

Reeder showed nothing at all in his expression. "They are military sworn to protect and defend their country and their president. Ready to give their lives for that. Those who are uncompromised, and that may be most of them, are in a war where they're being unwittingly used by the enemy."

Wade was nodding gravely. "The Alliance."

"The Alliance," Reeder said. "Any brave men and women who go down will be dying for their country."

Rogers sighed. "Maybe, but that's a roundabout way of looking at it."

"No doubt. And since I first considered going this route, killing our own has weighed heavily. The Secret Service, the Marines, they are all battle-ready, which means bulletproof vests. We're not using any kind of armor-piercing ammo, correct?"

Hardesy shook his head. "No. Nothing like that."

"Good. Then just aim center mass. Knock them down. We're hoping not to fire on anyone at all—a faint hope, I realize, but none of us wants to kill anyone who isn't a bad guy. Hit them in the vest, and that should put them out of commission, nonlethal."

Hardesy glanced at Wade, who shrugged. The ex-Army sergeant still looked skeptical, however, obviously loathe to fire on his own.

Rogers said, "We all need to make our own decisions on this one. Joe, in this case, we *are* a democracy. This is well out of our task force's mission statement—it's more a suicide-mission statement."

That got wry smiles out of everyone, even Reeder, no surprise considering the dark sense of humor of just about every law enforcement professional.

She continued: "So sit this out, with my blessing—just keep it to yourself. Because Reeder and I *are* going."

"I'm in," Wade said, no hesitation at all. "I owe my man Jerry Bohannon as much."

Finally Hardesy said, "I hate this, I *really* hate this . . . but I got nothing better. And I'm not going to be part of letting a fucking coup go down on our watch. I'm in, too."

When dishes had been cleared and coffee cups filled, Hardesy said, "Trouble is, this all hinges on an inside man, Joe, to shut down a security sector. And we don't have anybody."

"Sure we do," Reeder said.

Wade asked, "Who's he talkin' about?"

"Just the President," Rogers said.

Reeder got out a cell phone.

Goggling at him, Hardesy said, "You're just going to call the President of the United States on the *phone*? The plan hinges on *that*?"

Reeder said, "It's a special phone he gave me."

Hardesy's eyes narrowed and he said, "Your mission for the President—to find out who got those CIA agents killed overseas."

"That's right. Lucas, maybe you could take care of the check. Reggie, Patti'll give you the keys—transfer those weapons to the Buick's trunk . . . discreetly, okay?" Reeder stood, pushing back his chair. "And if you'll excuse me . . ."

In the parking lot, Reeder made the call while Rogers listened on.

After delivering a condensed version of the events and situation that had led to this moment, Reeder said, "Yes, Mr. President—I would select the Secret Service agent you trust most."

Muffled talk.

"Yes, sir, I'll text you when we're in position. Get to the control room, have section A-22 shut down on whatever pretense, text me back, then we're a go."

Muffled talk.

"Yes, sir, good luck and Godspeed to you as well, Mr. President."

Reeder clicked off.

She said, "We're really going to do this. Invade Camp fucking David."

"Yes. But it's all right."

"Is it?"

"Sure. We have the President's permission."

"There's no bigger task than protecting the homeland of our country."

George W. Bush, forty-third President of the United States of America. Served 2001–2009.

NINETEEN

All four were in the Buick now, Reeder riding up front, Rogers behind the wheel, the other two in back. They were driving through Catoctin Mountain Park, not far from their destination in the Maryland woods, when Hardesy leaned forward like a kid wanting to know how many more miles and asked, "Sure we shouldn't wait for dark?"

Reeder said, "That would give away what little advantage we have. They have the tactical night-vision gear, goggles, binoculars, rifle scopes, every toy we don't have. We'd still have surprise, but we have that now."

The vehicle continued threading through the thick poplar forest, sun cutting through to dapple the shade with gold until clouds rolled in to mute the effect. They encountered a few other drivers, tourists, families. Not many. Reeder pointed to a dirt road off to the right and Rogers veered in that direction, the way proving to be more a trampled path. The car bounced and lurched, jostling them but good, until finally Rogers found a place to park between a chestnut oak and a beech, the latter large enough to all but hide the vehicle behind.

All four wore hooded hunting attire, purchased at a Hanover, Maryland, Walmart, where Reeder had also bought various goodies, including one hundred rounds for the various nine mils the quartet was packing (the two AR-15s had come with plenty of .223 Remington ammo). They had stopped at a gas station to get into the camo gear, as well as the four Kevlar vests that Reeder, anticipating a need, had risked purchasing at a Navy Yard area army surplus store back when they were guests of DeMarcus.

As leaves and sticks crunched beneath their camo-colored boots, and trees rustled and birds sang and cawed, Hardesy procured the two AR-15s from the Buick's trunk, kept one and handed the other off to Wade. Reeder had decided to use the rifles to protect the flanks, while he and Rogers came up the middle. Without sound-suppressed weapons, the first time any of them fired, the element of surprise would be over and the firefight would be on.

Before they started out, Reeder gathered them into a kind of commando huddle, and said, "The strategy here requires one part stealth and two parts luck."

Everyone nodded at that.

Reeder went on: "Start by setting your phones to vibrate."

Hardesy, a little edgy, said, "I think I could have figured that out."

Reeder ignored that, saying, "Texting is the only secure communication system we have. A text can be used for specific intelligence, or just a few letters of gibberish . . . because the vibration itself means drop and freeze."

They all had burner phones in hand now.

"After you've hit the dirt," Reeder said, "check for shared intelligence, when you can do so safely. If it's just a few scrambled letters meant to alert you to danger, wait it out, then go when you feel you can."

Wade and Hardesy nodded.

Rogers held up her cell. "I've made a group. You should all have a text from me soon. I'm including Miggie, too."

Reeder felt his phone vibrate, as around him the hum of other cells sang the same song.

He gave Rogers a nod of thanks. With no makeup, under that camo hood, she might have been an adolescent boy. Of course, that would be an adolescent boy with two nine millimeter automatics, one in her hip holster, the other in her right hand.

Like the pines around them, Wade towered over the little group. "How far out are we?" he asked.

Reeder pointed. "Maybe two clicks from the security boundary."

Craning around, taking in the surroundings, Hardesy said, "Some scenery, huh? Breathtaking, really. You know, if I live through this, I could see taking a week out here with the family."

Everybody managed a smile, and Rogers said, "Or if we're caught, when you get out of the federal pen? You can bring your great-grandkids out here."

"Oh, he won't be out that soon," Reeder said.

And now they laughed. Somewhere a bird joined in, somewhat tauntingly.

"All right," Reeder said in a sigh. "Let's get moving—stay quiet, and alert. Nothing riding on this except the line of succession and maybe a shooting war with Russia."

AR-15 in his hands, Hardesy said, "No pressure."

"Well, at least I left out the Armageddon part."

Wade, the other guy with an AR-15, said, "Man, as pep talks go, that comes in *way* behind win-one-for-the-Gipper."

That got a few chuckles, likely the last levity these four would enjoy for a while.

They moved out, all their attention on the mission. They started slowly, single file, till they got to their real starting position. The afternoon was cool, but the heavy camo clothing with the bulletproof vests was warm. Reeder wiped his brow with the back of a hand, knowing some of it was nerves.

The little group spread out at first, the better to know what they were dealing with. For half an hour or more they walked, every step deliberate and yet the leaves and twigs seemed to scream their approach. But not a phone vibrated, and nothing unexpected emerged.

Then they had closed ranks enough to see each other crouching in the underbrush, just outside what Reeder knew to be the security perimeter of Camp David. Shadows thrown by the canopy of trees on a cloudy day combined to give them some semblance of darkness.

Reeder went from face to face, his eyes saying, *Point of no return.* What he got back were expressions as blank as the one he so frequently showed the world.

Then he got out the presidential phone and texted: *In position*

He knew, better than anyone, that it would take time for President Harrison to deal with his end, which included an extra responsibility before making his way down the tunnel from Aspen Lodge to the command center. Settling in for the wait, staying alert, keeping calm, might be the hardest part.

Ten minutes dragged by. Twenty. Wade and Hardesy were getting restless, stretching, cracking their backs, their necks. They were FBI field agents, after all, not Navy SEALs.

He shot them a look: *Patience.*

Another ten minutes. Afternoon was easing into dusk. Everyone's eyes would go to Reeder and Reeder would seem not to see them, then shake his head.

Finally Rogers crept over to him. "Something's wrong."

"We don't know that," Reeder said.

Wade, AR-15 in one hand, clambered over. Whispered, "Man's had time enough."

Hardesy came over, too, hugging his rifle. "Maybe we should abort. Maybe there's another way."

Reeder said calmly, "He couldn't just get up and walk away. Bound to be in the middle of a meeting with everything going on."

"Unless," Rogers said, "the Alliance has already struck and we're too late. We could be waiting for a dead man's signal."

She had just voiced his greatest fear.

Reeder got to his feet and said, "Or he may not be dead yet. Which means we better get our asses in there."

Wade yanked him back down into the weeds. "Man, without the security down, that's *crazy!*"

Hardesy got hold of Reeder's other sleeve and said, "I signed on for the duration, Joe, but I don't do kamikaze."

"Then I go without you," he said, and yanked himself away.

"Joe," Rogers began. "We have to be *smart* about this . . ."

"*You* be smart," he snapped. "The life of the President is on the line, and I'm going in. That's what I was trained to do, and I'm not about to stop now. Screw the security system. If nothing else, it'll get the place locked down, and I have to believe the majority of those on guard are *not* compromised."

They all looked at him with wide eyes filled with alarm and maybe something else, maybe respect or admiration or some damn thing, but if they thought reasoning with him would work, they didn't know him well at all, not even Patti, and then his phone vibrated.

The text message said: *GO*

Reeder said, "Harrison made it. Still want to bail?"

They all shook their heads, maybe a little ashamed.

He texted back: *OK*

Bitching was forgotten and everyone got ready to move out. Hardesy went right, Wade left, while he and Rogers drove straight ahead. Each of the flanks had rifles, he had two pistols, his SIG Sauer and an anonymous nine, while Rogers had her Glock and another nine from DeMarcus's stock. And they had plenty of ammo, thanks to Walmart.

They moved as low and fast as the underbrush would allow, needing to cover almost a mile before they got to their first goal, the edge of the golf course. Between here and there was thick brushwood, dense forest, and roving armed patrols. They were maybe halfway there when Reeder sensed movement to his right: *Hardesy dropping to the ground, swallowed in the greenery.*

Reeder reached over for Rogers and tugged her sleeve and they both fell into leafy cover as well. A two-man patrol was headed their way, uniformed Marines. Wanting to warn Wade, he dug carefully for his phone when it vibrated. A half-second later, Wade disappeared from view. Without checking, Reeder knew the text alert had come from Hardesy.

They watched silently through riffling leaves as the two-man patrol crossed their paths barely ten yards away. *No dogs, at least,* Reeder thought.

Armed with AR-15s of their own, the Marines moved on, oblivious to Reeder and the others at their feet. He gave them a full minute before he poked his head up.

"Gone," he whispered.

They rose slowly, cautiously, like strange plants growing in this piney jungle, then moved on, slower now, fanning out again. Before long they were at the edge of the tree line.

Ahead was the second fairway.

Sixty yards of well-tended open ground yawned before them, beyond which were more sheltering trees. It was as if in the midst of a primordial world a country club had dropped from the sky. If they cut at a diagonal, to make up time and get to Aspen Lodge quicker, they'd have even farther to go out in the open.

The course appeared deserted on this cloudy late afternoon, but the foot patrols could be anywhere. Reeder and Rogers were between Wade (twenty yards from the tee) and Hardesy (twenty yards closer to the hole). In the planning stages, they'd decided that going one at a time across the fairway would be safer, even if moving all at once might be faster.

Reeder signaled Wade with a wave.

Looking like a guerilla in his camos, the former ball player, long legs pumping, crossed the rough on this side, then the fairway, and finally the rough opposite before disappearing into the trees.

They waited.

No sign that anyone had seen Wade.

Hardesy went next, angling slightly up the fairway before disappearing into the woods as well, heading toward his next position.

Looking back toward the tee, Reeder could just barely make out Wade moving through the trees.

"We should go together," Rogers told him, looking so very young.

"Riskier."

"Faster," she said. "Clock's running."

He was about to agree when she jerked him down by his sleeve into the undergrowth again as another two-person Marine patrol, male and female this time, strolled right down the middle of the fairway toward the tee box.

He hadn't seen them coming, and the way they sauntered right past where he and Rogers were belly down, the pair hadn't seen either of them either.

As soon as the patrol was out of sight, Reeder and Rogers sprinted across the fairway and into the trees.

Wade was right there.

"Jesus," he whispered. "Where the hell did those two come from?"

Rogers said, "No idea—they weren't there, then they were. What, were they wearing slippers?"

Reeder said, "Did they see us?"

Wade said, "If they had, we probably wouldn't be talkin' about it right now."

Within five minutes, Reeder, Rogers, and Wade were standing at the edge of the woods with Aspen Lodge perched atop a hill before them, an impressive yet unpretentious structure of three rambling green-clapboard wings with low-riding flagstone walls, an expansive yard between the intruders and the rear of the place.

Two guards patrolled the patio known as the upper and lower terraces, one on each level; two or more guards would be out front. Hardesy, having peeled off back at the golf course, was at the edge of the next sector, ready to provide the diversion they would need to cross the vastness of that backyard.

Reeder's burner vibrated, stopped, vibrated, stopped. A glance at Rogers told him hers had done the same—*Hardesy's signal.* Seconds later, he heard three quick shots from an AR-15. Both guards' heads snapped in that direction.

"*What the hell?*" the lower-terrace guard said, his voice just barely carrying.

"*Check it out!*" the other one called, easier to hear, and both men moved around toward the front.

As soon as the guards skirted the corner, the three invaders sprinted across the sloping yard, staying low, then pressed themselves against the stone wall of the lower terrace. Carefully, a nine mil leading the way, Reeder climbed the few steps to the lower terrace. The patio with its furniture was unpopulated, and he kept going; the only entrance to the lodge on this side was back here on the upper terrace. Behind him came Wade with his AR-15 and Rogers with her Glock.

Six stairs from the lower to the upper terrace were navigated easily by Reeder, fanning his pistol to the left into a small garden, also unpopulated. He kept moving, past the windows of the sunroom, also empty (a nice break), as he made his way to a door he hoped would be unlocked—with those two guards stationed out here, that seemed possible. If not, Rogers had her lock picks, and she was damn good with them.

Their heads all swiveled toward the northeast when they heard more shots. Hardesy was definitely on the move, and they didn't have a second to waste. The camp would be shutting down and locking up any moment now, if it hadn't already.

Reeder tried the door, found it unlocked (another small break), then all three were inside, Wade closing them in. The cedar sunroom and the casual, open-beamed living room beyond were empty. Surely a silent alarm had to be going off right now. The alarm, Reeder knew, sounded in the command center and orders went out from there.

They checked the main floor and, surprisingly, found Aspen Lodge entirely deserted.

Wade asked, "Where the hell is everybody?"

Reeder said, "Likely a conference room in one of the other lodges. Digging in on the Azbekistani situation. That's why they're here."

The sunroom door banged open and all three of them spun, weapons up.

Hardesy tramped in. "Christ, tumbleweed's blowing through this place. What's going on?"

They all lowered their weapons and Reeder asked, "I hope you aren't leading a battalion of Marines our way."

Hardesy shook his head. "I lost their asses in the woods. These young pups can't compete with an old joe like me. Where the hell is everybody?"

Reeder said, "There's a dozen or more buildings between here and Laurel Lodge to the north. The cabinet members, the President and VP could be in any of them. There's conference rooms all over, as well as more informal areas where they can sit around working."

"You ask me," Hardesy said, "we got in way too easy."

"Bullshit," Wade said, jerking a thumb at Reeder. "We just got ourselves a tour guide who knows his way around."

But Reeder said, "I don't know whether we had crazy luck or somebody's opening doors for us. Either way, we have a job—protecting the President and his cabinet. And that won't be easy."

"So we move to the next stage of the plan," Rogers said, "and head down the tunnel to the command center, secure it and make sure the President is unharmed."

"You and I will do that," Reeder said to her. "Lucas and Reggie will stay here and make sure we're not caught in a pincer movement."

Hardesy was frowning. "You really think we should be splitting up? With the grounds and buildings crawling with Secret Service and Marines?"

"You're the one that said this was too easy—if you're right, Patti and I'll need cover on this end. Lucas, watch the door we came in. Reg, take a position with an angle on the living room."

Hardesy and Wade did that, then Reeder led Rogers back to the President's bedroom. Larger than the otherwise similar cedar-walled guest quarters, the unpretentious space had a king bed with a folksy quilt, several comfy chairs, and a big flat-screen over a fieldstone fireplace. Next to a wooden-sliding-doors closet was the sleek non sequitur of a metal door.

Rogers asked, "Gun closet?"

Reeder shook his head. "Private elevator to the command-center tunnel."

He flipped back the notched wooden cover of a round red button, which his right forefinger was poised to push, when her hand caught his wrist.

His eyes met hers as she said, "If you're right about that pincer movement, the other half could be waiting in there. Or at least a gunman or two of it."

They both had weapons in hand and were angled at either side of the metal door when he pressed the button. The door whispered open onto an empty elevator.

"Lucas said it," she sighed. "Too easy."

He said nothing.

"So we ride down," she said, "and the door opens and a welcome committee is waiting with a who-knows-how-many-gun salute. Suggestions?"

"We take the ride," he said, leaning in and pointing to the panel in the roof, "but from the observation deck."

Her eyes opened momentarily wide. "Who doesn't like to travel first class."

They didn't bother disabling the security camera—if they were expected, there was no point . . . not unless their action was caught on a monitor in time for any hosts below to be alerted.

The two-hundred-foot descent happened fast and it was all Reeder could do to haul Rogers up through the escape hatch and get it back in place before their descent slowed, then stopped.

The doors slid open, and bullets sprayed the car.

When the metallic hailstorm stopped, Reeder gazed down through the gridwork of the hatch where two men leaned in, one with a linebacker build, the other wiry, both with short dark hair, immaculate business suits, and AR-15s. Feds, probably Secret Service.

The wiry one said, "Where the hell . . . ?"

When the linebacker stepped inside the car, Reeder kicked down on the hatch, swinging it to catch the man in the forehead and stagger him. Rogers dropped through the hatch, landing in a combat crouch. The wiry one was squeezing in, that AR-15 ready to spit, so she boot-heeled him in the face, knocking him back out and onto the concrete floor of the tunnel, spitting bloody teeth, not bullets. Reeder swung down right behind her, holding onto the edge of the roof, and kicking his already staggered opponent in the face as well, with the flats of both boots. The linebacker went backward and landed hard enough to knock himself cold, if he hadn't already been.

Reeder and Rogers emerged from the elevator, nostrils twitching with cordite, ears ringing from all those rounds expended in the enclosed space. But footsteps in the tunnel were pounding their way, and that they could hear just fine.

They tucked back in the elevator as four more agents—summoned by the barrage of gunfire—rushed toward them, two with automatics, two with tactical machine pistols. Reeder and Rogers had their backs to either side of the inner doors. Nine mils in hand, angled up, they made eye contact.

Reeder lifted his head.

Rogers nodded.

He went high and she went low as they swung their guns through the open door, each picking the nearer machine-pistol agent, aiming center mass. The simultaneous squeezing of triggers doubled the thunder of the nine mils and both feds took a center hit and seemed to bow in thanks before going down in awkward sprawls, their weapons spinning and sliding out of reach.

The other two, faced with a lack of cover, retreated down the tunnel. Reeder and Rogers holstered their nine millimeters and acquired the AR-15s of the first two fallen agents and ammo as well. Moving quickly, they used zip ties to bind the hands behind the backs of all four agents.

They stood for a moment appraising their situation. The tunnel was an oversized hallway cutting through rough rock with a concrete floor and sporadic overhead lighting.

"They know we're here now," she said.

"You think?"

"You figure they'll rush us?"

"Why bother? They know we'll go to them, unless we want to take the elevator back up and devise a new plan that doesn't include getting us killed. Of course, they can send more guns down that elevator and outflank us."

She turned an eye toward the elevator. "You really think that elevator will still work after all those fireworks?"

"Why not? They shot the shit out of the car itself, but wouldn't have hit the motor or any of the cables. Why, you want to go back up?"

". . . No."

They stayed close to the rugged rock walls, one on either side, as they moved down the tunnel, lugging the AR-15s, their footsteps, despite their care, echoing. Both knew that somewhere up ahead, guns waited. A lot of them. But short of sitting down in the tunnel, leaning back against the rock walls, and waiting for death to find them, they had no other real option.

A hissing turned Rogers around, staring at the way they came. "What was that?"

"Elevator doors closing. Thing must be functional. I'd say company's coming."

"Great."

Reeder figured they were about halfway to the command center when a sound from way, way behind them might have been the elevator doors opening. He picked up the pace and Rogers did, too.

Finally they reached the entrance to the command center, an off-white wall blocking the way, decorated with the presidential seal and another seal labeled **JOINT STAFF SUPPORT CENTER, RAVEN ROCK MOUNTAIN COMPLEX**, surrounding a raven perched on a cliff at night. In addition a bold sign said **WARNING, RESTRICTED AREA**. A pair of central metal doors had a guard booth next to it.

Empty.

"Another welcoming committee," he said, "on the other side, you think?"

Rogers grunted a laugh. "Maybe we're the millionth visitor, and they have something special for us."

"Maybe those doors are locked and this is a dead end."

"Don't sound so hopeful," she said.

He tried a door.

Unlocked.

And when they entered into a good-size alcove facing a glass wall with metal-and-glass twin doors, they found no one waiting. Only an eerie silence greeted them.

Pistol noses up, they edged into the brightly lit room, computer terminals and monitor screens lining the walls; off to the left, a massive screen with an overhead map of Camp David, lighted here and there in red, dominated a circular command area. As impressive as all this was, the tableau before them was even more.

Nine men in black suits stood facing them in a row that was just faintly semicircular. Each had a handgun aimed at their just-arrived guests—well, eight did. The center man had his handgun in the neck of President Harrison, who was on his knees, his face bloodied, his tailored charcoal suit rumpled.

"Guess I chose the wrong man to trust, Joe," Harrison said with a weak, puffy smile. "Head of the detail—who'd have thought it?"

That earned the President a whack along the side of the head by his captor. Reeder fought back the anger and disgust at the sight, the very thought, of those privileged to protect the President betraying their oath.

The current head of the presidential detail was not anyone Reeder recognized from Secret Service days, no—too young, too new, for that. But he did recognize the man, having gone tooth and nail with the son of a bitch in an alley near the townhouse, the night this excuse for a man had dropped his flag-lapel camera. Now Reeder got a better look—short-clipped brown hair, relaxed, emotionless face . . . just another anonymous Secret Service agent . . .

. . . *in the sway of the Alliance.*

"Welcome," the presidential detail head said through a slash of smile. "We've been waiting for you. Can't have a political assassination until the assassins get here."

"Heroes may not be braver than anyone else. They're just braver five minutes longer."

Ronald Reagan, fortieth President of the United States of America. Served 1981–1989. Formerly the thirty-third governor of California following a successful acting career.

TWENTY

Reeder—his AR-15 still at the ready, Rogers the same—said, "Why, are we here to kill the President? Or maybe the entire cabinet as well?"

Their smug host nodded toward the kneeling President. "Your target is Harrison here. The cabinet will be taken out by your Russian collaborators, of course."

Almost casually, Reeder said, "Rocket launcher? Take the conference room out and everyone in it? What, Laurel Lodge?"

The leader chuckled, shook his head in admiration. "Well reasoned, Mr. Reeder. You were ahead of us for much of the way, you know. Have to hand you that. But at the end of the day, you and Agent Rogers and her people . . . you'll all just be a rogue element in our government, intent on staging a failed historic coup. Of course, history will not record that you performed this task for the American Patriots Alliance, since of course that group does not, and never has, existed."

Rogers, the AR-15 raised into shooting position, edged away from Reeder, putting a little distance between them—no need to help these traitors out by presenting a unified target.

"*Ms. Rogers!*" the detail head said, his smile like a skull's. "Any further movement will initiate a firefight, and I don't think any of us want that."

Well, the nine-man firing squad facing them surely didn't—the only reason she and Reeder hadn't been cut down yet were the AR-15s in their grasps. Short of taking head shots themselves, they could take out every one of these sons of bitches before dying.

"Put down your weapons," the leader said. "A general melee will surely take the President out early on. And I don't think you want that."

Harrison blurted, "I'm dead *already*, Joe!"

That got the kneeling prisoner another cuff alongside the head with the handgun.

Reeder took this in as casually as if someone were passing him the salt. But she knew he was roiling inside.

"I suppose," the leader said, just a hint of tension in his voice, "I should be grateful to you for identifying yourselves as assassins making an incursion."

"How did you track us?" Reeder asked. Still as casual as dinner-table conversation.

Tiny shrug. "We didn't have to. Your actions stayed off our radar, and you certainly weren't betrayed, except by your own character. You see, we *knew* you'd be coming, Mr. Reeder. Your vanity demanded it. Turns out the great People Reader isn't tough to read at all."

That got a wisp of smile out of Reeder, whose AR-15 remained leveled directly at the leader of the insurrection, or anyway this cell of it.

Rogers—with her weapon aimed to the leader's left, figuring Reeder would handle everyone to the man's right—said, "You can't hope to get away with this. It's madness."

"If so," the leader said cheerfully, the snout of his gun in the bloodied President's neck, "there's method in it. The story is already written and ready for the media, how traitors from within conspired with Russian agents in a vain attempt to wipe out the US government. You will be the chief villains of the piece, even as the nation salutes *this* weakling . . ."—he dug that snout deeper into Harrison's flesh—". . . that we'll have turned into a hero, while the fallen cabinet will become martyrs as the nation says, 'Thank God for Nicholas Blount, our new president.'"

"What," Reeder said calmly over the rifle, "did they promise you and these other disgraces to the Service?"

That made the leader's eyes narrow, his upper lip twitching. "We're patriots, Mr. Reeder, one and all. We want a return to the roots and values of this great nation and its founders. Those of us in the Service are every day witness to the compromises and surrenders of political leaders with no moral compass."

What complete utter, empty bullshit, Rogers thought.

"I'm guessing," Reeder said placidly, "that you're after the director-ship of the Service. And I'm probably looking at the new White House presidential detail, which will really know its stuff having betrayed a president themselves."

The faces above those pointing handguns no longer seemed so impassive—frowns, however subtle, could be discerned.

"Mr. Reeder," the leader said, "you are no one to talk. After all, twenty million dollars from Ukraine sources have been deposited in a Swiss bank account in your name, and another ten million each into similar accounts for Ms. Rogers and her FBI team. You are traitors, headed for vilification today, and pages in history rivaling Benedict Arnold tomorrow . . . so spare us your judgmental condescension."

"Sorry." Reeder shrugged over the aimed AR-15. "I should be thanking you, anyway."

"Thanking us?"

"For identifying yourselves as the cell operating within Camp David. Or are there more of you?"

The skull smile again. "There are patriots everywhere, Mr. Reeder."

"I must have skipped civics class the day it was explained how kill-ing the cabinet, the President, and Vice President, was patriotic."

Another tiny shrug. "What could be more patriotic than the revo-lutionary rebirth of America? In twenty-four hours, the public will be mourning the loss of their leaders, rallying around their new president, and readying to retaliate against the Russians for what will become known as the Camp David Attack."

"Which began," reminded Reeder, "with the murders of four CIA agents in Azbekistan. Who set that in motion, by the way?"

Slight head shake. "Not a name you'd recognize, Mr. Reeder. A CIA official, fairly high up as you'd imagine, who is since deceased. Heart failure. Tragic."

Reeder grinned over the weapon, still trained on the leader. "Hear that, fellas? That's how the Alliance treats its loyal followers. If I were you, and had bought this bill of goods, I'd be reconsidering. If the President will grant me the privilege, I will offer full amnesty to any of you who put down their weapons, or come over to our side. Mr. President?"

"Done," he said.

Their leader was frowning, irritation finally cutting through. "That's enough, Mr. Reeder. We're all quite prepared to die for what we believe in."

"What was that again? To further empower a cabal of corrupt industrialists who are loyal to no one or nothing but their own self-interests? They aren't left, they aren't right, they're just wrong."

The man's eyes and nostrils flared. "If that's your choice, Mr. Reeder, then it's time this Mexican standoff, if you'll forgive the political incorrectness, comes to an end . . . no matter the cost."

Rifle ever steady, Reeder said, "You'll go first, friend. But before you do . . . and your men give their lives out of a misguided sense of patriotism . . . you should know that when your rocket launcher takes out that conference room in the Laurel Lodge, it will be as empty as Senator Wilson Blount's sense of morality."

The frown was almost a scowl now. "Don't bother with lies. They're all gathered around their big table with no sense of what's coming. It will almost be merciful."

"Sorry to disappoint, but I directed the President earlier to move the cabinet members to the location known by code name Cactus—as head of the Secret Service presidential detail, you'll *know* what that is . . ."

"Don't bother bluffing."

"I thought you said I was easy to read? *I don't bluff.* Patti, just so you know, 'Cactus' is the nuclear bunker here at Camp David. And the cabinet has been instructed to stay put within, till the President himself gives them the word."

The cell phone in her pocket vibrated and she and Reeder in a microsecond confirmed that his phone too had vibrated and, as agreed, they dropped. On the floor now, in sniper position, Reeder took out the detail leader with a burst of shots that turned the man's head to bloody mush, while the President hit the deck, staying under the exchange of gunfire.

Taking Reeder's act as permission, Rogers began to take one head shot after another, while behind them Wade and Hardesy came on the run, firing their own AR-15s from the hip, like Audie Murphy charging a tank. The thunder of the semiautomatic weapons fire bounced off the high walls and swallowed the smaller, occasional pops of the handgun fire from the lineup of agents, as orange tracers made a deadly light show. One of the agents managed to hit Hardesy in the chest, and he stumbled, went down on one knee but was firing again, almost immediately.

The air filled with red mist as men in oh so proper suits flew back onto the cement with their skulls cracked open and seeping, their eyes—those that had not been shot out of their heads—staring up at nothing.

The carnage was terrible and complete.

The echo of gunfire faded to a silence broken only by the ringing of the survivors' ears. Thirty seconds had been all it took. The same was true at the O.K. Corral.

Only Hardesy had been hit, and he was hobbling along with a grin and an assist from Wade, basically only winded from the blow to his vest. Reeder abandoned his weapon to run to the President. There was blood all over Harrison's back.

"*Mr. President!*" Reeder shouted, and knelt by the leader of the free world . . .

. . . who pushed himself up with one hand, like he was doing a show-off push-up, and half-smiled at Reeder.

"I guess that's another president you saved," he said. "You'd do anything for a Medal of Freedom, wouldn't you?"

Rogers was right there, too, still carrying the AR-15 in both hands. "Is he all right?"

"Fine," Reeder said, helping Harrison to his feet. "It's not *his* blood."

Hardesy leaned against a wall while Wade went around checking what proved to be corpses.

"Poor misguided bastards," Wade said.

The coppery smell of blood mingled with the stench of bodies evacuating themselves at death. Victory had been complete, but the victors were all sick to their stomachs.

"Was that a bluff, Joe?" she asked him. "About the cabinet being sequestered in the bunker?"

"I said I didn't bluff," he said. "No, that was part of the plan all along. They're quite safe. No offense, Patti, but no one needed that knowledge but me . . . *Lucas, Wade!* Guard the entrance. There may be more of these insurgent pricks around."

The President moved with incredible confidence, dignity, and fluidity to the control desk where he sounded an alarm, and then got on the hotline phone and ordered up Marines to come to Raven Rock.

Reeder went to him and said, "We need to stay alert, sir—those Marines you summoned could include Alliance infiltrators."

The President's puffy smile had melancholy in it. "My guess is that, considering the way things have gone, any traitors will fade back into the woodwork and behave themselves, for now at least. When we get back to DC, I'll be starting an investigation into every agency of government. Some will call it a witch hunt, I'm sure . . . but this time we have actual witches, don't we?"

"We do. And the head warlock is Senator Wilson Blount."

Harrison sighed. "That's my impression, as well. But do we have any proof that links him to this attempted coup? He's a powerful man, Joe, with powerful friends."

"And at least one very powerful enemy, sir. Yourself. As you know, I never did come up with the name of the man who betrayed our four agents. If our late friend over there can be believed, that person is already dead, and we should be able to determine his identity. But I'd like your blessing, your mandate, to go after Blount as best I can."

"Done."

Reeder glanced around at the now bustling chamber. "And I believe, until we have done the most thorough security and background checks possible on the Secret Service here at Camp David, you should allow Agent Rogers, her two agents, and myself to serve as an ad hoc presidential detail."

"Also done."

"We can't leave here, by helicopter anyway, until the threat of a rocket launcher is dealt with. Can you put together a team of Marines that you trust, to comb the surrounding woods—inside and outside of the compound—to deal with that threat?"

The President's half-smile was self-deprecating. "I didn't do so well choosing a Secret Service agent to count on."

"I know. But take your best shot. We'll be here at your side. In the meantime, I would like your permission to have two DC cops I trust, Carl Bishop and Pete Woods, to come out and give you and the Vice President rides. Won't be a limo, though."

Harrison grinned, full on. "I'll survive."

"That's the idea."

A presidential hand settled on Reeder's shoulder. "And, Joe—as soon as you and your friends can get me back to the White House, I'll be letting the Russian premier know that he and his people can get their collective ass out of Azbekistan or this attempted coup will be linked to them big-time in the media. And, boy, would that fire up the American people."

"Kind of would."

Rogers, overhearing all this, said to Reeder, "When we first get a chance, I'd like to drop by and see AD Fisk."

His expression was typically unreadable, but his words weren't: "Thought you might."

"You can fool all the people some of the time, and some of the people all the time, but you cannot fool all the people all the time."

Abraham Lincoln, sixteenth President of the United States of America. Served 1861–1865. President during the Civil War.

TWENTY-ONE

Within minutes of the firefight and rescue of the President, Reeder reported in to Miggie Altuve.

"You and Patti are miracle workers," Mig's voice said.

"Same back at ya. How are the supplies in the cabin?"

"Enough for several months. Cupboard of canned goods, freezer fully stocked. Why?"

"You need to stay put. When I'm able, I'll send reinforcements, but for now, remember—you have precious damn cargo."

"Our house guest you mean? The charming Lawrence Morris?"

"The very guy. A lot's riding on him—he's our most direct evidence against Wilson Blount."

"We'll need more."

"There'll be plenty more, but we need Morris to build on. You and Anne sit on him—but gently. He's our new best friend."

Miggie didn't sound so sure: "He says under no circumstances will he testify. That he's given you all the help he ever will, and that you and he have a deal that you need to honor."

"Let him know the presidential coup has been exposed and violently quashed. Let him think about which side of that he wants to come down on."

"Okay. I assume we're talking immunity and WitSec."

"Oh yeah. Tell him we're going to buy him contact lenses and, when his hair grows out, get him dyed and styled."

Miggie laughed. "He's already got some five o'clock shadow going on that noggin."

"Hang in. I'll be in touch."

The Marines quickly had the compound under control, and if any of them were Alliance, they faded back and fell into line as predicted. Two Soviet rocket launchers, in the forest just outside the security net, were taken out by more Marines; neither of the two mercenaries manning them survived, which was both a pity and just fine with Reeder.

The cabinet gladly vacated the nuclear bunker at the President's command and the members were helicoptered out two at a time, an effort that took several hours.

By ten p.m., Pete Woods in a fresh Ford and Carl Bishop in his black Chevy had whisked away the President and Vice President, with Hardesy and Wade riding along respectively. Not your usual presidential motorcade, but with the Secret Service and God-knew-who-else compromised, protocol be damned.

Before the President left the compound, however, he made a call to the Director of the FBI and instructed him to rescind immediately the arrest warrants on Reeder, Rogers, and the surviving members of her unit.

For now, a media blackout had descended and even intra-government reports were kept at a minimum. What would be told to the public would be discussed and controlled beforehand, and—with various agencies infiltrated by the Alliance—much of it would be marked classified and all of it strictly managed.

Still in commando camo, Reeder and Rogers arrived in Washington, DC, finding its quiet almost unsettling, as if the town had slept through its own near demise . . . and hadn't it? He drove her to her apartment, where she picked up a change of clothes, and then to his townhouse, where she took the spare bedroom. This was over, the coup if not the greater threat, but they wanted to be near each other tonight—each other, and their guns. As with an earthquake, Reeder was prepared to deal with aftershocks.

Before finally giving in to their exhaustion, they sat at his kitchen table in robes, like an old married couple, and had some chamomile tea. Morning now, technically at least, but still dark out there.

"I should call Kevin," she said.

"Not just now. I'm not fetching Amy and Melanie yet, either, or their two undeserving males. There could be some immediate retaliation, and anyway, I don't think I'll sleep soundly till that bastard Blount is in custody."

"Meaning the Senator, not the son."

"The son will be our ally, I think. He may even testify, given what happened today. Right now we have only Lawrence Morris as a witness. But we need another."

"Who?"

"Your boss and mentor, Margery Fisk, Assistant Director of the Federal Bureau of Investigation."

She'd started frowning and shaking her head halfway through that. "No, no, *no* . . . not a witness. A suspect. No, not a suspect, a *perp!*"

"You blame her for Jerry Bohannon's murder, I take it."

"And Trevor Ivanek's, and Anne's kidnapping, and—"

"We don't know that. She is almost certainly compromised, but to what degree, we can't be sure. Do you think she's capable of fingering two of her own people for death?"

Her smirk bore no humor at all. "Who the hell knows what *anybody* is capable of in this thing?"

"Good point. You know what I think?"

"What do you think?"

"We should talk to her."

The next morning, eight a.m. Sunday, as arranged, they found Margery Fisk waiting for them at a table in the Starbucks on Wisconsin Avenue NW. Most of the business seemed to be grab-and-go, the tables on either side of Fisk vacant.

She looked small and not at all the executive in navy-blue sweats and white running shoes; her hair was freshly washed and back in a ponytail, making her look young unless you really looked.

The table was at the side window, with just three chairs. They went through the line—dark roast for Reeder, medium for Rogers, cream for both—then he took the chair across from Fisk, Rogers the one next to her.

"Public place, as requested," Reeder said.

Fisk's smile was small and bitter. "I thought it might keep me from getting shot."

"Then maybe you shouldn't sit by the window." He shrugged. "But you're not mob and this isn't a pasta joint. Should be fine. Or are you thinking of how Patti here may be feeling about you now?"

The AD's eyes stayed on Reeder. "How did you get my home number, anyway?"

"We have our ways." Miggie Altuve being most of them. "So here's the basic program. You tell us everything you know and perhaps you don't face treason charges, which by the way would almost certainly mean execution . . . Can I get you another coffee? I see your cup is empty."

Bleak amusement touched her lips. "I'm fine. Thanks for your thoughtfulness, though."

Rogers, coldly but with a tremor in her voice, asked, "How long have you been Alliance?"

Fisk shook her head. "I'm not Alliance and I never have been."

Reeder said, "We're getting off to a bad start."

Fisk said, "I don't deny complicity in this thing. But the American Patriots Alliance . . . isn't that what they call themselves? . . . I thought was just *National Enquirer* nonsense."

Eyes hooded, Rogers said, "I saw Lawrence Morris leaving your office."

"By the way," Reeder said pleasantly, "Lawrence is in our custody. So we have a kind of baseline for comparison, here."

Fisk said, "I think I will take another coffee."

Reeder got it for her.

Then, settling across from her again, he said, "You were saying?"

"Morris has probably already told you this. He came around and said if I cooperated with 'certain people' in government, who were not fans of President Harrison, I would be next in line for the Director's chair."

"The next president would appoint you."

She nodded.

"What did they want from you?"

Tiny shrug. "What they had in store for me over the long haul, I couldn't say. First order of business was to assign the Yellich death to the Special Situations Task Force."

Reeder and Rogers exchanged glances.

Reeder said, "To keep tabs on the unit."

Fisk nodded again, sipped her coffee; it was too hot.

Reeder said, "What did you tell Morris?"

"I told him no."

"Bullshit," Rogers said.

"I *did* tell him no." Fisk sighed. "That was before Senator Blount called me."

Reeder straightened; Rogers, too.

He asked, "When was this?"

"Right there with Morris in the office, sitting across from me. How he signaled that old bastard I have no idea. But suddenly there was that buttermilk Southern drawl in my ear."

Reeder frowned. "Threatening you?"

"Not exactly. Not directly. It was as if he was an old friend checking in with me. Understand, I had met with the Senator on occasion and dealt with him on some matters—a powerful man like that gets around, and gets his way. But suddenly we were old friends."

"How so?"

Her eyes closed. Tight. "He talked to me about my husband and the work he does at his company, and how distressing it was that accidents occurred sometimes in the plant. He mentioned my son in college at Georgetown and my daughter at NYU and congratulated me on how fine they were, what outstanding young people, but wondered how I could bear having them live in such dangerous cities where 'any terrible thing' might happen."

"A Southern-fried threat."

Her eyes opened and she trained their near blackness on Reeder. "You have a daughter, Mr. Reeder. How would you have reacted?"

"I'd have tracked him down and beaten him to death. But that's just me."

Fisk stared at the table. "It was a phone call that—had it been recorded, and perhaps it was—might seem innocuous as a Christmas card. But the meaning was clear. I could rise to the directorship, or I could wonder every damn day about the safety of those I love. That's what they call a Hobson's choice, isn't it?"

Rogers said, "And when they murdered Jerry Bohannon, you made a choice, too, didn't you? To betray everything your office stands for! And what's a little kidnapping of one of your people? Or a sniper taking Trevor Ivanek out?"

Fisk was immobile, not trembling at all. But tears began to trickle down her cheeks.

"I had no idea," she said, "things would go so far."

Reeder said, "Why not? They'd already killed Amanda Yellich."

"In . . . in retrospect, I realized I'd . . . enabled Agent Bohannon's murder. But I had no contact person—Morris dropped out of sight, no more phone calls came from Senator Blount, and I was sidelined in this awful game. When I put out the apprehend order on the two of you, and everyone else on your team, my thought was to pull you in where I might protect you."

"The operative word," Rogers said, "being 'might.'"

Fisk's shoulders went slowly up and down. "If you don't believe that, there's nothing I can say or do."

"You're wrong," Reeder said. "There *is* something."

Her eyes lifted to his. "I'm listening."

"You cooperate. Fully."

Fisk nodded.

"For now, you retain your office as Assistant Director. You report back to me, or someone else designated by the President, any contact you have with Alliance conspirators. They'll be running scared now, so they may reveal themselves either directly or inadvertently."

Fisk nodded.

"Despite the innocuous surface of Blount's words, they constitute a threat. We may be able to track the way Morris signaled the Senator to make that call—hell, Morris will probably tell us himself. Eventually, both of you will be called upon to testify. In the context of everything else that's gone down, two witnesses should be enough. The Senator will go down, and the Alliance exposed."

Fisk nodded.

"As for your future," Reeder said, "I think your full cooperation will mean you'll see no federal time. I'll ask the President to instruct the Justice Department that you be granted immunity, or he'll give you a pardon if necessary."

"He'd do that?"

Reeder gave her half a smile. "He kind of owes me one."

Fisk shrugged, her expression stoic. "Of course, I'm onboard with this. If my husband is willing to leave his company in the hands of others, would relocation and new identities be a possibility?"

He nodded, once. "I'd recommend it. Highly probable."

She turned to Rogers. "I know you're disappointed in me."

Rogers said nothing, though her glare was eloquent.

"But I do have a kind of peace offering," Fisk said. "From the blood DNA at the scene of the Wooten slaying we identified the shooter—one Jadyn Sims. At first blush, Sims seems to be a mercenary but I believe what we have is a compromised CIA asset. He was brought in yesterday by my Domestic Terrorism unit, and a ballistics matchup links a weapon in his possession to both the Wooten and Ivanek shootings. And a handgun links him to the Bohannon killing."

Reeder said, "That makes him a potentially key witness."

The AD nodded. "I believe he can be turned, now that the conspiracy will inevitably be exposed. He'll be facing treason charges, as well as murder, and we'll give him a chance to bargain for his life by cooperating."

Rogers' eyes flared. "Are you seriously suggesting that the murderer of Trevor Ivanek and Jerry Bohannon should receive immunity?"

Fisk didn't flinch from Rogers' gaze. "Not immunity. Just the avoidance of the death penalty. But know this . . . I'll have to live with the deaths of those two agents for the rest of my life."

"If I had my way," Rogers said, "the rest of your life would be about thirty seconds."

Fisk swallowed. Nodded. "I know there's no making it up to you."

Reeder smiled pleasantly. "Actually, Margery, you already have. And maybe Patti will come around, too, someday. After all, you've done us a big favor."

Fisk's eyebrows went up. "What favor is that?"

He reached out and held his partner's hand, tight. "Now we can go out and arrest that son of a bitch Wilson Blount."

Sunday afternoon, after an Army transport had taken them to Nashville International Airport, Reeder and Rogers rented a Chevy Tahoe from National. They were about to call on a United States Senator in Franklin, Tennessee, twenty minutes south of Nashville—one of the safest and least-taxed cities in America.

This enclave of top CEOs of multinational corporations, with scores of golf courses and dozens of museums in a historic Civil War city, included the Brandon Park Downs gated community, just outside the center of town. Here Senator Wilson Blount lived on a beautiful lakefront estate in a magnificent country manor house in the antebellum manner.

With Rogers at the wheel, they pulled through a high front gate in a stone wall onto a cement drive that wound through an expansive, perfectly maintained, tree-flung front lawn. No other FBI or police accompanied them—no major security force would be awaiting them, according to Miggie, so no SWAT would be necessary. Still, they had little doubt that Blount would know they, or at least someone, would be coming today, so caution was the watchword.

The antebellum mansion had been the Blount family home since the early 1800s, very Tara-like with its stately white columns and neoclassical style. As they'd driven up, however, Reeder noted at the rear a massive array of antennas and satellite dishes—the old home-stead was twenty-first-century–connected.

They left the Tahoe near the front and went up four steps to a white door where Reeder used a traditional brass knocker, Rogers at his side. Both wore dark suits cut to conceal their shoulder-holstered weapons.

Almost immediately a rather distinguished-looking, fifty-ish African American butler, in traditional livery, responded. His hair was peppery and his features were as blank as Reeder at his most guarded.

"Joe Reeder to see the Senator," Reeder said.

Rogers held up her FBI ID and said, "Special Agent Patti Rogers here to see Senator Blount."

The butler nodded with formal disdain. He seemed to taste the words and didn't enjoy the flavor as he said, "You are expected, sir. Madam."

Reeder and Rogers shared a glance. *What century was this again?*

They were led into the grand foyer—marble floor, marble stair-way, pocket doors at right and left, with more down a corridor beside the stairs, a two-story ceiling wearing a crystal chandelier like one ostentatious earring.

The butler knocked at the pocket doors to the left. "Your guests have arrived, Senator."

"Thank you, Mathers," a muffled voice drawled, smooth as honey. "Show them in, please."

The butler slid open a door, gestured with an upturned palm, bow-ing slightly, a human lawn jockey. Reeder and Rogers went in and the butler stepped in after them.

They were in a library as high-ceilinged as the foyer, and library was the appropriate term, because three of the walls were filled with volumes whose mostly leather bindings gave the room a scent of age and scholarship, several sliding ladders allowing access to upper shelves. The wall to the right had a connecting door and an array of framed, vintage oil paintings of Jefferson Davis, Robert E. Lee, Stonewall Jackson, and a few others that Reeder didn't recognize, though he felt sure they were Civil War–era figures. Sprinkled among the Confederates were portraits of Washington, Jefferson, Franklin, and John Adams. Somehow he was not surprised by Lincoln's absence.

The room included an ancient massive desk inserted into the left-side wall of shelves, and some tables with antique lamps, but center stage was an Oriental rug where two overstuffed brown-leather sofas faced each other across a glass-topped coffee table. Senator Blount was sitting on the sofa at right. He stood and smiled in welcome, gesturing to the seating opposite.

The Senator wore a gray suit with a white shirt and a black string tie. He looked immaculate, every hair of his silver-blond mane in place, his eyes blue and rather twinkling behind his wire-frame bifocals. Only his creped neck gave away his age.

"Please join me, Mr. Reeder, Agent Rogers. I expected someone, of course, but I rather hoped it might be you."

Something about the way Blount handled words reminded Reeder of a cat lapping up cream.

"Mathers, would you kindly fetch us a mint julep?" As Reeder and Rogers took their places, Blount settled back on his sofa and added, "I hope you will forgive your host for so predictable and even stereotypical a drink of choice. But my man Mathers makes a wicked julep. Would you please join me?"

"No thank you," Reeder said.

Rogers shook her head.

"Sure?"

They nodded.

"Pity," Blount said, with your favorite uncle's smile, then leaned back, tenting his fingers at his chest. "You don't know what you're missin'."

Reeder said, "Your hospitality embarrasses us, Senator. You see, we're here to arrest you."

Blount smiled as if that were a mildly amusing joke. "Is that right? And what charge would that be?"

"Well, for now, conspiracy to commit murder."

The smile twitched. "Did I help murder anyone in particular?"

Rogers said, "The initial charge will be for the murders of Jerome Bohannon and Trevor Ivanek, both FBI agents. Law enforcement rather frowns upon the killing of their own."

"Don't believe either name is familiar to me."

She said, "That doesn't exactly make it better."

Reeder said, "To that list will be added the names of Amanda Yellich, Leonard Chamberlain, Anthony J. Wooten, oh, and uh . . . four CIA agents killed in Azbekistan, Jake McMann, William Meeks, Vitor Gorianov, and Elizabeth Gillis."

"That's quite an impressive list, Mr. Reeder."

The butler arrived with the mint julep on a tray, transferred it to a coaster on the glass-topped coffee table, nodded to his employer, and left, shutting them back in. Reeder noted that the glass case contained what were most likely first editions of *The Red Badge of Courage*, *Uncle Tom's Cabin*, and *Gone with the Wind*.

"Well, Senator," Reeder said, "conspiracy to commit murder is probably the best you can hope for. You'll more likely be facing treason charges, and the President considers you an enemy combatant, like that rogue's gallery on the wall over there."

Blount's smile disappeared. His face was a cold clay bust that hadn't hardened yet, but was on its way.

He said, "You would consider the likes of those great men to be 'rogues,' I take it. Do you include Washington, Jefferson, and the other foundin' fathers in that way?"

"What do you think?"

"Well, I don't really know. They believed in liberty. They believed men should be free to pursue happiness. And that men are created equal, although people like you get that wrong."

"We do?"

Blount sat forward; the eyes were not twinkling now. "Men are created with equal rights, but they are *anythin'* but equal. Their intelligence varies, their gender, their races, their station. A country so widely varied needs a firm hand, it requires leadership. We have a weak, pampered populace that doesn't even bother to vote, most of 'em. We can't afford to wait for the rabble to wake up, or—if a miracle happened and they did rouse from their collective stupor—trust that they'd do the right thing."

Rogers asked, "What do you consider the right thing?"

His hands were on his knees. "Well, for one, to reinstate the ideals that made this country great—rebuild our military, stand up to our enemies, protect this nation from within and without. And, meanin' no offense, it takes more fuckin' finesse than the kind of civil service mentality the two of *you* represent."

Reeder said, "You mean the kind of finesse that sends four brave Americans to die on foreign soil?"

The Senator leaned back and shook his head sadly. "A pawn can never understand a king . . . but I'll try to make you understand, son, because I know at heart you're a patriot, too. That malleable Senkstone stuff that you and Agent Rogers got messed up with last year? I guess you know that the stabalizin' element in that compound is called portillium. Well, cornerin' the market on that vital mineral would give the United States an upper hand in defending freedom. Pity about those four CIA folks. But we needed a reason to go in and *stop* those

Russians—who, frankly, we encouraged a mite—so we could seize and control the portillium supply."

Reeder was sitting forward. "'Cornering the market' . . . so one of your companies or cronies could makes *millions* off portillium? Or is it billions?"

Blount waved that off. "Well, of course such a thing necessitates private-sector control. Can't leave somethin' *that* important to the government!"

Rogers, aghast, said, "And you'd risk a nuclear war with the Russians over *mineral rights*?"

His smile got so wide, it seemed to have too many teeth in it. "Little lady, the Russians understand that nukes fly in both directions. We'd just have ourselves a little shootin' war, and then negotiate a truce, once we had that portillium source secured, that is."

"And that would be more easily managed," Reeder said, "with President Nicholas Blount, I guess?"

Even more teeth. "Might at that."

Reeder sat back. "Unfortunately for you, Senator, your son does *not* share your enthusiasm. In fact, he helped us on the path that led us here."

Blount's chin went up, as if promoting a poke. "If you think you can convince me that my own *boy* would betray me, you are—"

"He didn't betray you. Not exactly. He feared what you and your Alliance might have in *mind* for him, even though he didn't want to testify against you . . . too bad, considering what he's privy to would make his testimony valuable. Of course, after Camp David, and the exposure of all the treason and murder that led up to it? Perhaps he'll have a change of mind, patriot that he is. Because he's a good man, Senator. You raised a decent son. Much better than you deserve."

Blount said nothing. He was staring between Reeder and Rogers at nothing. Lazily he reached for the mint julep and took a sip, and another. Then he returned the drink to its coaster and reached into his suit coat pocket, for a smoke Reeder assumed, but instead produced a small steel object that resembled a thumb drive. His hand made a small movement.

His eyes closed.

He slumped back.

"Senator," Reeder said, getting up fast.

Blount was still staring, but now it was at the ceiling.

Rogers went around, put fingers to the man's throat. "I don't get a pulse."

Reeder nodded to the mint julep. "Son of a bitch. Hemlock!"

An explosion rocked the rear of the house—the antenna array, Reeder guessed. He glanced at the thumb drive–like object in Blount's limp fingers: *a switch with a red button.*

"We have to get out of here," he told her, "now."

They moved.

Another explosion rocked the rear of the house. The place had been wired in sections, it seemed, perhaps to allow exit from the front.

He hoped.

At least the pocket doors weren't locked. They were able to get out of the library and into the foyer in seconds, then out the front door. They were to the car and inside, motor going, when another section of the place went up, and Rogers hit the gas and, by the time the rest of the house exploded, the two were far enough away for the rain of dust and debris to be something you could drive through and out of, though burning rubble bounced off the vehicle like heavy hail.

The Tahoe was outside the front gate before she braked and they hopped out and looked at what remained of the historic home, which now was nothing but a scorched shell and sizzling timber and crackling flames and billows of dark smoke. The only recognizable remnant was a marble staircase that was not worth walking up.

Reeder slipped an arm around Rogers' shoulder as they watched, their ears ringing, their eyes burning, and soon sirens cried out distantly and built into screams.

Rogers said, "Afraid they won't find much left of Senator Wilson Blount."

Reeder coughed up some dust and said, "Just matching dental work, maybe even DNA, but he was a sly old bastard. I'd rather have a corpse."

"He's dead enough for me," she said.

"I do know one thing," Reeder said.

"Oh?"

"I'm glad we weren't in the mood for mint juleps."

THANKS IN ORDER

This novel is the third of a trilogy based around the three branches of government: *Supreme Justice* (Judicial), *Fate of the Union* (Legislative), and *Executive Order* (Executive).

The following were of help: *The Definitive Book of Body Language* (2006), Allan and Barbara Pease; *Images of America: Arlington National Cemetery* (2006), George W. Dodge; and *Reading People: How to Understand People and Predict Their Behavior—Anytime, Anyplace* (1998), Jo-Ellan Dimitrius and Mark Mazzarella.

Thanks to Eleanor Cawood Jones and Aimee and Eric Hix for Washington, DC, research. And to Chris Kauffman (ret.), Van Buren County Sheriff's Office, and Paul Van Steenhuyse for their expertise with weapons and computers, respectively.

Thank you also to agent Dominick Abel; and everyone at Thomas & Mercer, especially editor Jacque Ben-Zekry.

ABOUT THE AUTHORS

MAX ALLAN COLLINS received the Mystery Writers of America Grand Master Award in 2017, considered the pinnacle of achievement in mystery writing. He has earned an unprecedented twenty-three Private Eye Writers of America "Shamus" nominations, winning twice for best novel and once for best short story. In 2007 he received the Eye, the PWA life achievement award, and in 2012 his Nathan Heller saga was honored with the PWA "Hammer" award for its major contribution to the private eye genre.

His graphic novel *Road to Perdition* (1998), illustrated by Richard Piers Rayner, became the Academy Award–winning Tom Hanks film, and his innovative "Quarry" novels are the basis of a current Cinemax

TV series. He has completed a number of "Mike Hammer" novels begun by the late Mickey Spillane, most recently *A Will to Kill*, and his full-cast Hammer audio novel, *The Little Death* (with Stacy Keach), won a 2011 Audie.

Collins has written and directed four feature films, including the Lifetime movie *Mommy* (1996), as well as two documentaries, including *Mike Hammer's Mickey Spillane* (1998), which appears on the Criterion Collection's *Kiss Me Deadly*. His many comics credits include the syndicated strip *Dick Tracy, Batman*, and *Ms. Tree* and *Wild Dog*, co-created with artist Terry Beatty. His movie novels include *Saving Private Ryan*, *Air Force One*, and *American Gangster* (IAMTW Best Novel "Scribe" Award, 2008).

Collins lives in Muscatine, Iowa, with his wife, writer Barbara Collins; as "Barbara Allan," they have collaborated on thirteen novels, notably the successful "Trash 'n' Treasures" mysteries, including *Antiques Flee Market* (2008) winner of the *Romantic Times* Best Humorous Mystery Novel award in 2009. Their son Nathan is a Japanese-to-English translator, working on video games, manga, and novels.

MATTHEW V. CLEMENS is a longtime co-conspirator with Max Allan Collins, the pair having collaborated on over twenty novels, fifteen short stories, several comic books, four graphic novels, a computer game, and a dozen mystery jigsaw puzzles, for such famous TV properties as *CSI, Bones, Dark Angel, NCIS, Buffy the Vampire Slayer*, and *Criminal Minds*. Matt also worked with Max on the bestselling "Reeder and Rogers" debut thriller, *Supreme Justice*, published by Thomas & Mercer in 2014, and its 2015 sequel, *Fate of the Union*. He has published a number of solo short stories and worked on numerous book projects with other authors, both nonfiction and fiction, collaborating with Karl Largent on several of the late author's bestselling techno-thrillers.

Matt lives in Davenport, Iowa, with his wife, Pam, a retired teacher.